*"It's still   *
*the righ   *
looking for had a headful of
hot red hair, a make-you-hard
smile and a voice…"

Mick made a sound that was halfway between regret and arousal, then walked in a slow circle around her. Grasping her hips, he yanked her hard against his body. Her hands went to his chest to stop herself from falling.

"You're about the right height…the right age…your breasts and hips are right…. But there's only one way to be sure…."

He pushed her back on the bed and followed her down. "Oh, yeah. I remember this. You're the one," he murmured. For a moment he closed his eyes, and a familiar look—arousal, hunger, almost-there satisfaction—came across his face. Then he looked at her, and instead of arousal, there was contempt. "Oh, yeah, you're the one. And you're going to help clear my name."

Dear Reader,

Everyone loves Linda Turner, and it's easy to see why, when she writes books like this month's lead title. *The Proposal* is the latest in her fabulous miniseries, THE LONE STAR SOCIAL CLUB. Things take a turn for the sexy when a straitlaced lady judge finds herself on the receiving end of an irresistible lawyer's charms as he tries to argue her into his bed. The verdict? Guilty—of love in the first degree.

We've got another miniseries, too: Carla Cassidy's duet called SISTERS. You'll enjoy *Reluctant Wife,* and you'll be eagerly awaiting its sequel, *Reluctant Dad,* coming next month. Reader favorite Marilyn Pappano is back with *The Overnight Alibi,* a suspenseful tale of a man framed for murder. Only one person can save him: the flame-haired beauty who spent the night in question in his bed. But where is she? And once he finds her, what is she hiding? Brittany Young joins us after writing twenty-six books for Silhouette Romance and Special Edition. *The Ice Man,* her debut for the line, will leave you eager for her next appearance. Nancy Gideon is back with *Let Me Call You Sweetheart,* a tale of small-town scandals and hot-running passion. And finally, welcome first-time author Monica McLean. *Cinderella Bride* is a fabulous marriage-of-convenience story, a wonderful showcase for this fine new author's talents.

And after you read all six books, be sure to come back next month, because it's celebration time! Intimate Moments will bring you three months' worth of extra-special books with an extra-special look in honor of our fifteenth anniversary. Don't miss the excitement.

Leslie J. Wainger

Leslie J. Wainger
Senior Editor and Editorial Coordinator

Please address questions and book requests to:
Silhouette Reader Service
U.S.: 3010 Walden Ave., P.O. Box 1325, Buffalo, NY 14269
Canadian: P.O. Box 609, Fort Erie, Ont. L2A 5X3

Marilyn Pappano

THE OVERNIGHT ALIBI

Silhouette®
INTIMATE™ MOMENTS®

Published by Silhouette Books

America's Publisher of Contemporary Romance

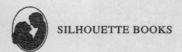 SILHOUETTE BOOKS

ISBN 0-373-07848-X

THE OVERNIGHT ALIBI

MARILYN PAPPANO

After following her career navy husband around the country for sixteen years, Marilyn Pappano now makes her home high on a hill overlooking her hometown. With acreage, an orchard and the best view in the state, she's not planning on pulling out the moving boxes ever again. When not writing, she makes apple butter from their own apples (when the thieves don't get to them first), putts around the pond in the boat and tends a yard that she thinks would look better as a wildflower field, if the darn things would just grow there.

You can write to Marilyn via snail mail at P.O. Box 643, Sapulpa, OK 74067-0643.

Chapter 1

The interrogation room at the Yates County Sheriff's Department was shabby, like the rest of the building, and offered little in the way of comfort. The table was crooked, the wood scarred and marked with water rings. The chairs were straight-backed and uncushioned, and made a body ache in little time.

Mick Reilly had spent two hours in this straight-backed uncushioned chair today—as uncomfortable, numbing and frustrating as the hour he'd spent here yesterday. He'd answered the same questions, first for one deputy, then for another, finally for the sheriff himself. He'd given the same answers so many times that he was saying them by rote. As if he'd planned ahead, the sheriff had mused out loud. As if he'd memorized his story.

Not a story. The truth. Every word he'd said was God's honest truth.

He hadn't been anywhere near the resort Saturday night.

Yes, he'd had an argument with Sandra Saturday afternoon.

Yes, he'd threatened to get rid of her.

No, he hadn't made good on his threat.

No, he couldn't explain why no one remembered seeing him in the bar that night.

No, he sure as hell couldn't explain how the pretty, sexy redhead he'd left with had missed their notice.

No, he did not kill his wife.

He did not kill his wife.

Not surprisingly the deputies didn't seem to believe him.

Wearily he dragged his fingers through his hair. "Look, Sheriff, why don't you send your people out to find Elizabeth? She can verify where I was, and you can start looking for Sandra's killer, instead of wasting time with me."

"Elizabeth. Pretty redhead on the prowl. Pretty enough to tempt a married man into forgetting he's married." The sheriff looked at the deputy on his left. "Sound like anyone you know, Billy?"

"No, sir."

"What about you, Keith?"

The deputy on his right shook his head.

The sheriff looked at Mick again. "Billy and Keith are my only unmarried deputies. They know every single woman in the county. If they don't know this Elizabeth of yours, then she's not from around here."

Mick's fingers folded slowly into a fist. "I never said she was single. In fact, I thought..."

"You thought what, Mr. Reilly?"

He'd thought she was exactly what he'd needed to end eleven years of a lousy marriage and eighteen months of sleeping alone. She was beautiful, hot, wild, her blue eyes full of promise, her husky voice wicked and tempting. He'd thought he had nothing to lose by succumbing to temptation just once in his sorry life. He'd thought he deserved a night of pleasure after so many hundreds of nights without. "I thought she was probably married and looking for a little fun while her husband was otherwise occupied."

"What made you think that? Maybe because you were married and looking for a little fun while your wife was otherwise occupied? Does a married man who fools around learn to recognize married women who fool around?"

Mick made an effort not to grind his teeth. "I didn't 'fool around.' This was the first time. The only time."

"Uh-huh." Two short syllables filled with disbelief. "So what made you think this Elizabeth of yours was married?"

"She didn't give a last name. She didn't want to know my name. She didn't want to talk about herself at all." All she'd wanted was a couple of drinks and sex. The alcohol had been necessary for courage, leading him to believe that she didn't make a habit of picking up strange men. The way she'd hesitated at her motel room had made him wonder if she'd caught her husband in an affair and *he* was her way of getting back at him. Then she'd kissed him—an oddly sweet, hungry, desperate sort of kiss—and he hadn't cared why she was there. He'd just been glad she was.

"Why didn't you take her to your room? Seems a lot more convenient, it being right across the parking lot."

"She wanted to go to hers."

"Which was where?"

Mick forced his fingers to relax, forced himself to breathe deeply and answer the question for the third or fourth or tenth time. "I don't know. Some motel down the road from mine. Maybe...I don't know, ten miles. Maybe fifteen."

"Did you drive?"

"Yes."

"And did she ride with you or take her own car?"

"She went with me." She'd sat in the middle of the seat, pressed right up against him, her breasts rubbing his arm, her fingers rubbing his...

His face flushing, he cut off that line of recall. She'd given him directions between seductive kisses, had pointed out the dingy place on the side of the road between caresses, had unpeeled herself from his body long enough to take him inside room 17, where she had suddenly turned shy. Elizabeth bold and brash had turned him on. Elizabeth sweet and shy had damn near finished him off. He'd found the combination of sweet, shy and sexual incredibly erotic.

"So you drove to this motel, but you don't know the name of it. You can't tell us how to get there."

"You start at my motel and you drive down the highway until you reach it. There aren't that many motels in the area."

"And as of Saturday night, we have one less."

Mick sighed heavily. About the time Sandra had been dying on the floor at the Eagle's Haven Resort, he had been sliding inside Elizabeth for the third time. About the time the flames had engulfed Blue Water Construction's fifteen-million-dollar mistake, he had been experiencing the third best climax in his life. He would surely have to pay for that in the hereafter.

"If you don't mind my saying so, Mr. Reilly, for an innocent man, you don't seem particularly sorry about your wife's death."

Mick locked gazes with him. "I *am* sorry, sorrier than you can imagine."

"But?"

He felt guilty for what he was about to say. "We haven't lived together for more than a year. We were in the middle of a divorce that was no more amicable than the marriage. I'm sorry she's dead. I'm sorry for the way she died. But if you expect a show of grief, I can't give it to you." There would surely be special punishment in the hereafter for that, too.

"You know, whenever there's a murder, the first thing we ask ourselves is who would benefit. You were in the middle of an ugly divorce. Your wife wanted every last dollar you have. She was threatening your lifestyle, your reputation, even the future of your company. So when I ask myself who would benefit from Sandra Reilly's death, the first person who comes to mind is you.''

"But I didn't kill her." Mick spoke each word carefully, quietly, tired of saying them, frustrated because they were true and no one believed them.

"Uh-huh." The sheriff leaned back in his chair, hooked his thumbs in his gun belt and studied Mick. "I'm going to have Billy here type up your statement, and after you sign it, you'll be free to go—for the time being. Before I send him out, is there anything you want to change?''

"Everything I've told you is the truth."

"You know, once you sign what he types, if you change your story later, you could be facing further charges."

Mick stubbornly held his gaze and didn't say a word.

With a nod from the sheriff, the two deputies left the room. Their boss followed, closing the door behind him.

Further charges, the sheriff had said. He'd already decided that Mick was guilty. In his mind he'd already charged him with Sandra's murder and was ready to charge him again for lying. Hell, when you were facing murder charges in a state with capital punishment, what worry could making a false statement to police hold?

Mick dropped his head into his hands and rubbed his eyes. He was sorry Sandra was dead, sorrier than he would have believed, but not sorry enough. He had lived with her, made love with her, planned a future and a family with her. He had loved her the best he was able, and he should feel great grief and sorrow.

But all he felt was regret. Anger that he had managed to be implicated in her death. Fear that, in death, she might have achieved what she'd longed for in life: his destruction. If the sheriff didn't soon turn his attention in some other direction, whoever had killed her was going to get away with it and leave Mick to pay for his crime.

So if the sheriff wasn't interested in looking elsewhere, Mick would. As soon as he got out of here, he would find

Elizabeth himself, somehow, some way, and he would convince her that his freedom—maybe even his life—was more important than her husband finding out where she'd spent Saturday night.

Right. What woman was going to put her marriage on the line for the sake of a stranger? An intimate stranger, granted, but still a stranger.

Rising from the chair, he paced to the end of the room, where a window with rusted bars looked out on a parking lot with sheriff's cars and his own pickup. It was a dry, dusty day without a cloud in the sky, and it made him itch to be out on the lake someplace with a fishing pole and a handful of lures. Hell, he itched to be anywhere besides here, doing anything besides declaring himself innocent of murder.

How had things gone so wrong? People made bad marriages all the time, but they didn't become the prime suspect in a murder case because of them. Companies made bad decisions on a regular basis, but they didn't come under investigation for arson for them. And married men picked up beautiful women in bars all the time with no worries beyond getting caught and safe sex. How did it all go so wrong for him?

Turning his back on the scene outside, he stretched tight muscles, then leaned against the wall. If he had any luck left in the world, the sheriff would come back in and say, "Sorry for the inconvenience, but your wife's killer just confessed. You're free to go." Mick would even settle for something along the lines of "Thanks for the cooperation. We'll let you know when we've made an arrest."

But when the door opened, it wasn't the sheriff but his deputies. Billy handed him a statement and a pen, told him uninterestedly to read the statement carefully before signing it, then cracked his knuckles while he waited.

Mick scrawled his signature on the last page, tossed the pen on the table and straightened. "Can I go now?"

"Sure. We don't have enough evidence to hold you. But the sheriff said to suggest that you not leave the county."

He was halfway around the table when the deputy spoke again. "He also said to tell you that you might want to get yourself a lawyer."

Mick stared at him, his mouth going dry, his muscles tensing again. They had advised him of his rights yesterday before they'd started questioning him, and he had passed on the opportunity to call a lawyer. He hadn't done anything wrong—other than breaking his vows in a marriage about to end—and he'd seen no need to bring in an attorney. Besides, the only ones he knew personally were the company's lawyer—great with contracts, never handled a criminal case in his life—and his divorce lawyer. He had little enough faith in the man's competence regarding divorce law. He certainly wouldn't put his life in his hands in a murder case.

Before he started looking for sweet Elizabeth, maybe he should find a lawyer first. It shouldn't be too difficult. The phone books were full of them.

He acknowledged the deputies with a grim nod as he walked out. When he reached the sidewalk out front, an inordinate sense of relief swept over him, as if he'd been lucky to escape the building a free man.

The next time the sheriff requested his presence, he might not walk out again.

He climbed into his truck, slammed the door and sat motionless, ignoring the heat. For one long helpless moment, he didn't know what to do or where to go. Back to the motel where he'd lived during the construction of Eagle's Haven? Out to the resort where his office was located, where his wife had died? Looking for the motel where his alibi had taken him?

Part of him wanted to go home, back to Oklahoma City. But when he'd just been told not to leave the county, traveling 130 miles away didn't seem the wisest move.

He headed for his own motel four blocks down the street. It wasn't anything fancy, but it was a world better than the place Elizabeth had taken him to Saturday night. Even with a buzz from the booze and in a state of incredible arousal, he'd still noticed that the gravel parking lot was deeply rutted, the building was in need of paint, the ceiling in room 17 was water-stained, and the faucet dripped loudly enough to echo in his sleep. He'd noticed that, other than two cars at the opposite end, his was the only vehicle in the lot, and room 17 was the only room showing lights.

Beyond that, all he'd noticed was Elizabeth. In his long-time-without-sex, soul-weary-and-lonely midnight fantasies, he couldn't have conjured up a more perfect partner. She'd lost her shyness once he'd started kissing and touching her, and she had become as eager, as willing and as desperate as he'd been. If he had been her revenge against a straying husband, for him, at least, revenge had been sweet.

He let himself into his room, recently cleaned and smelling of disinfectant and lemon polish. He'd been living here for the better part of eighteen months, but he still hadn't gotten used to the smells.

He could have rented a house for the duration of the project, as his partner had, but in the beginning he had foolishly believed there was something left of his marriage to save. He'd worked on-site five or six days a week and made the two-hour drive back to Oklahoma City about half those nights. He'd been perpetually exhausted, and Sandra had been utterly disinterested. She hadn't let him touch her, hadn't let him make love to her, hadn't even managed to be home a good number of those nights to see him. Finally, as problems at the site grew, he'd given up and moved into the motel for the duration. He'd accepted that the marriage was over. He'd just been hoping to unload the resort before he had to deal with the divorce.

Naturally Sandra hadn't let that happen.

Sitting at the desk, he opened the Tulsa phone book to the listings for attorneys. There were pages of unfamiliar names and firms. He had just as much chance of finding a good lawyer by closing his eyes and pointing blindly as he did by making a conscious selection. Maybe he should ask Brad for advice.

Brad Daniels was his partner in Blue Water Construction and Eagle's Haven. They were a mismatched team—Brad, born with the proverbial silver spoon, his own stock portfolio and more money than a reasonable person could ever need, and Mick, son of a West Texas dirt farmer and a carpenter by trade. Mick had worked his way up through the construction business until he'd finally formed a small company of his own. In his lucky fifth year, he'd built a house for Brad, who had liked his work and proposed a partnership focusing on high-dollar homes. Mick would build them and Brad would sell them.

It had been a good partnership until Brad had come up with the idea of building a luxury resort on the shores of Lake Eufala. That was when the trouble had begun. But they were still partners, still friends. Brad would help him find the best criminal attorney money could buy.

He dialed Brad's local number, then his cellular, then his home phone in Oklahoma City and finally his pager, then paced the floor for a half hour without a call back. Unable to bear the wait any longer, he grabbed his keys and left the room. Brad had his cellular number. He could reach Mick in the truck while he looked for Elizabeth's shabby motel.

It was an easy search. Ten or fifteen miles straight out of town, as he'd told the sheriff—thirteen and a quarter, to be exact—in a little drib of a town called Sunshine, there it was: Last Resort Motel.

It lived up to its name. No one in his right mind would stay there unless it was a last resort. Its heyday, if it had ever had one, had ended at least twenty years ago. Now it

was just waiting to fall in on itself, at which time the own-
ers would probably give a great sigh of relief and walk
away free.

Why had Elizabeth chosen such a place? Ignorance of
the area? She hadn't known there was a better motel thirteen miles down the road? He hoped that wasn't the case,
because that would surely indicate she wasn't from around
here, and then how the hell would he ever find her?

Maybe she'd chosen it precisely because it was so run-
down. Because there would be few, if any, other guests.
Because the chances that she would run into anyone she
knew there—the chances that she would run into anyone
at all there—were virtually nonexistent.

He waited for an eighteen-wheeler to pass, then turned
into the lot. His truck bumped over ruts that more accu-
rately could be called ditches as he pulled to a stop in front
of the office. Through dirty plate-glass windows, he saw
no sign of activity inside. He would scare up a clerk, a
manager or an owner from somewhere, though.

The double doors led into a combination lobby-
restaurant. The vinyl chairs and stools were patched with
silver duct tape. More than a few of the tables were off-
kilter. Half the fluorescent lights overhead were burned out,
and half of those that did work flickered and buzzed an-
noyingly. But the floor was scrupulously clean, the counter
above the stools gleamed, and appetizing aromas filtered
from the kitchen out back.

Finding no bell at the registration desk, Mick took a few
steps toward the kitchen door. "Hello?"

A moment later the swinging door opened, and a middle-
aged woman with arms full of ketchup bottles came
through. Talking softly to herself, she walked past him,
circled the desk, looked around blankly, then deposited the
bottles in a cabinet. Smiling happily, she closed the cabinet
door, then disappeared through a nearby door.

"Merrilee?" The kitchen door opened again. This time

an elderly woman came through—four foot nothing, maybe eighty pounds, with steel-gray hair curled atop her head and sharp blue eyes that swept over him, then dismissed him. "Where did she go?"

"Through that door."

"Did she take the ketchup with her?"

"It's in that cabinet."

Shaking her head, the old woman retrieved the bottles and placed one on each table. When she was done, she faced him. "What can I do for you?"

"I need some information."

"About what?"

"A guest at the motel Saturday."

Her gaze narrowed. "Are you a reporter?"

"Do I look like a reporter?"

"Lord, these days a reporter can look like anything. Don't you watch TV, boy?"

"Too much." That was all he'd had to fill his nights for the past year—television Sunday through Friday, and a couple of hours of solitary drinking at the bar next door on Saturdays. Except for this most recent Saturday. "No, I'm not a reporter."

She made her way around the tables to the registration desk. "I already told the sheriff yesterday that I didn't rent a room to anyone fitting that girl's description."

So that was why the sheriff had been so skeptical about Elizabeth's very existence. That was why he'd stressed that if Mick wanted to change his story, he'd better do it before he signed his statement. "So maybe someone rented the room for her," he suggested stubbornly. "Room 17."

The narrowed blue gaze settled on him again. "You're not with the sheriff's department 'cause I know everybody over there. You say you're not a reporter. Are you a lawyer?"

He shook his head.

For a time she studied him, then quietly said, "So you

must be the man Sheriff Mills believes killed his wife and set that fire to destroy the evidence.''

His body would have given him away if he'd tried to deny it. Heat flushed his face, and his throat tightened, making his voice hoarse. "I didn't kill my wife. I was here that night. In room 17. With a red-haired woman named Elizabeth.''

She shook her head slowly. "We didn't rent any room to a redhead Saturday, and we didn't rent number 17 to anyone. We only rent that room out when the rest of the place is full because there's family living in 18 that doesn't like to be disturbed. Number 17's been empty longer than I can recall.''

A chill crept through Mick, cooling the heat that reddened his face. "That's not possible. I was there. I spent the night there. We got here about ten o'clock and I didn't leave until almost twelve hours later. I slept in that bed. I took a shower in that bathroom.''

The old woman shook her head again, then turned the register around for him to see. No computers here. Just a big green ledger with the date written at the top of the page and registration information on each guest written in a neat spidery hand underneath. There had been a man from Texas in room 1 and a man from Tulsa in room 3. That accounted for the two cars he'd seen.

His hand trembled when he pushed the ledger back toward her. So did his voice. "I'm not crazy. I'm not lying. I was in room 17 Saturday night. The…the carpet is brown and…and there are water stains on the ceiling and the sink drips and the toilet runs and—''

She shook her head once again. "Son, anyone can look at this place from the outside and guess those things. I'll prove you wrong. I'll show you the room, just like I showed the sheriff.'' She gestured, and he followed her out the door and down the cracked sidewalk to the third-from-the-last door. With a key from the ring fastened around her wrist, she unlocked the door, pushed it open, then stood back for him to enter.

The carpet *was* brown, and even from the doorway he could hear the sink dripping. The water stain was in the corner, just as he'd remembered.

Little else was. The bed was unmade, a bare mattress on top of a box spring. The chair where Elizabeth had laid her clothes was gone, as was the lamp she had insisted on turning off before they made love. Worse, there was no sign that a lamp had ever stood on the bedside table. The dust that spread across the top was thick and even; nothing had been brought to the table or taken away since it had settled. The other table, where the phone sat, was the same. The wastebasket under the sink where he'd disposed of condoms and wrappers was upside down and left an impression in the carpet when he moved it, as if it had stood there a long time.

Mick stood stiffly in the middle of the room. If he didn't know better, he would believe the room hadn't been occupied for at least six months. Hell, there was even a thin coat of dust across the carpet and cobwebs in every corner. But, damn it, he did know better. He had been here.

Hadn't he? Was it possible that he'd made a mistake? That this wasn't the motel Elizabeth had taken him to?

He stared at the bed and remembered white sheets, coarse against his skin, smelling of laundry soap and fabric softener, as if they'd been recently washed. He remembered flat pillows and a popped spring that had scraped his back when she'd rolled on top and he'd gripped her thighs, thrusting into her hard. Resting one knee on the bed, he felt around and found the spring and the small hole it'd torn in the ticking.

This *was* the room.

But someone had gone to a lot of trouble to make it appear otherwise. The old woman? She stood in the doorway, gazing absently at the dirty carpet. If she'd given the room its long-unoccupied look, she was the best actress he'd ever seen, because she looked as guileless as a new-born babe.

The crazy woman who'd walked right past him without seeing him while on her way to store ten ketchup bottles in a cabinet full of office supplies?

Maybe Elizabeth herself?

"What about your housekeeping staff?"

The old woman laughed. "Son, what cleaning gets done around here, we do ourselves. We don't have any house-keeping staff."

"Who is 'we'?"

"Myself, my daughter-in-law and my granddaughter."

The daughter-in-law would be the crazy lady. And the granddaughter... "Does your—"

"No. My granddaughter isn't a redhead. Her name's not Elizabeth and she doesn't pick up men in bars. Besides, you're not exactly her type. You're a fine-looking man and all, but Hannah likes men a little less rough around the edges and a whole lot more single."

So Hannah had something in common with Sandra: he hadn't been her type, either. But Sandra hadn't cared about rough-around-the-edges or single. She had cared about pleasure, about self-satisfaction, about having everything she ever wanted while depriving him of anything he'd ever wanted.

"Maybe Hannah has a friend..."

The woman shook her head again. "Not a redhead. Not the sort of woman the sheriff described."

"Can I talk to her?"

"She's out of town—has been since Saturday morning. You're barking up the wrong tree, mister. You weren't here Saturday."

But he was. He *knew* it. Now if he could just prove it.

"I'd help you if I could, son, but I can't. Now I've got

to get back to the office before Merrilee does something foolish.''

Reluctantly he walked out the door and watched as she locked up again. This was definitely the right place, and Hannah, he suspected, was the key. Maybe Elizabeth was a friend of hers whom Granny knew nothing about. Maybe Hannah had slipped this friend a key to room 17 and kept quiet about it because Granny didn't like giving out rooms for free. Or maybe Granny's morals didn't allow married women to use her motel for one-night stands with married men. Maybe there were any number of reasons for Hannah and Elizabeth to lead the old woman wrong.

''When will Hannah be back?''

The old woman fixed her sharp gaze on him. ''I reckon that's between Hannah and me. I'll tell her about the room and Elizabeth, and if she has anything to say—which she won't—she'll say it to the sheriff.''

''The sheriff isn't particularly interested in anything that might prove I'm telling the truth.''

She didn't say anything to that, just shrugged and walked away.

As he returned to his truck, Mick sighed wearily. He'd like to crawl into bed, sleep twenty-four hours and wake up to find that it was all a bad dream. Instead, what he was going to do was find a place where he could watch the Last Resort Motel without the old lady watching him, and he was going to wait for Hannah to come home. Maybe her grandmother was right and she couldn't add anything to what they already knew.

Or maybe she could.

Across the street there was an abandoned gas station, built probably fifty years ago. The windows were boarded up, the old rounded pumps rusted, and weaving lines of weeds grew two feet high through cracks in the pavement. Vines covered a pile of junk on one side and stretched halfway up the nearest telephone pole. It wouldn't hide his truck completely, but it should give enough cover that no one would notice him.

Seeing the old woman's gaze on him, he backed out and pulled onto the road as if heading back to Yates. Two blocks down, he turned left, came back and eased his truck over bumpy ground right up to the canopy of vines. He rolled down the windows, shut off the engine and settled in to wait.

As lunchtime rolled around, people came and went. Sunshine was a small town, and the Last Resort seemed to be the only restaurant. No one stayed long, though, and no one was young enough to be the old woman's granddaughter.

There were better ways he could be spending his time than waiting for someone who most likely couldn't help him to return home. He needed to track down Brad and to find a lawyer. And there were funeral arrangements to make. Sandra had family, but she'd worked hard at distancing herself from them. She'd been ashamed of her upbringing—not dirt-poor, but close—and ashamed of her parents. At eighteen she'd left their home out in the Oklahoma panhandle, and she'd never been back. She hadn't invited her family to their wedding for fear they would embarrass her, had never spent a holiday with them or acknowledged them in any way. After eleven years of marriage, Mick's introduction to his in-laws would come at their daughter's funeral. How was that for bizarre?

The abrupt ring of his cell phone startled him. He snatched up the handset with a curt greeting.

It was Brad. "Hey, Mick, sorry it took me so long to get back to you. I've been in meetings all day with our lawyers and the insurance people. How are you?"

"My wife was murdered, our hotel was burned down, and I'm the sheriff's prime suspect in both crimes—oh, and my alibi has disappeared off the face of the earth. How the hell do you think I am?"

A moment of silence was followed by Brad's cautious

voice. "I'm sorry about Sandra, man. Jeez, I'm so sorry. I just can't believe—"

"Did you see her after she left the site Saturday? Did you talk to her? Do you have any idea why she went back out there that night?"

"No. The sheriff thinks...he thinks you lured her out there."

"Why would I do that?"

"To take care of two problems at the same time. I told him he's way off base. I mean, yeah, you threatened to get rid of her, but we all knew you were talking about the divorce, not about *getting rid* of her. And, yeah, you did say we should burn the damn resort down, but you didn't mean it. It was just talk. I mean, you're not stupid. If you'd really planned to kill her and set fire to the hotel, you never would have said so, and I told the sheriff that."

With his free hand, Mick rubbed his eyes. He had made both statements, but under the circumstances, their meanings changed drastically. When he'd said he would get rid of Sandra once and for all, he had intended to put a stop to all the haggling and foot-dragging, had intended to call his lawyer first thing Monday morning and order him to get the damn divorce settled immediately so she would be out of his life.

And, yes, he had suggested—sarcastically, ironically, never, ever seriously—burning down the resort. The place had been eating them alive. Construction had gone way over schedule. Cost overruns had been out of control. Labor had been a problem, and the buyers Brad had promised from the beginning hadn't materialized. Instead, they'd been stuck with a big beautiful luxurious white elephant that was costing them tens of thousands of dollars in interest payments. When yet another prospective sale had fallen through and bankruptcy had begun to look more and more likely, Mick had suggested they burn the damn place down, collect the insurance money and get out from under the debt.

But he *hadn't* been serious.

"Mick, are you there?"

"Yeah, I'm here."

"Where are you? I tried the motel and the trailer out at the site, and there was no answer."

"I'm just driving around." He wasn't sure why he lied. Brad was his best friend. He had a lot at stake here, too—not his freedom or his life, like Mick, but a lot. He would be reassured to know that Mick was trying to locate his alibi and clear his and the company's names.

But the last thing he wanted was for anyone to know he was watching the Last Resort. The old woman wouldn't like it, and the sheriff damn sure wouldn't approve.

"I need a lawyer, Brad. You have any suggestions?"

"You think it's that bad?"

"The sheriff believes I'm guilty and he isn't open to any other ideas. Yeah, I think it's that bad."

"I know some people in Tulsa. I'll talk to them and get back to you. Is there anything else I can do?"

Yeah, Mick wanted to say. Quit standing up for me to the sheriff. Discussing the threats he'd made in anger with no intention of carrying them out wasn't helping any.

But he didn't say anything of the kind. "Nothing I can think of."

"I'll look into the lawyers and give you a call as soon as I have something."

Mick hung up, reclined the seat a few inches and stretched as much as he was able. He should have gotten some lunch, even just a candy bar and a Pepsi, before pulling in here. He hadn't eaten much since the deputies had knocked on his door Sunday morning with the news of Sandra's death.

His response, in his own mind and surely in the deputies', had left much to be desired. He had been shocked, in the same way he would have been shocked if his secretary or his neighbor back in Oklahoma City had been killed, less than if it had been Brad or a member of his own family. There had been a brief sense of loss for what he and Sandra should have had and a shameful sense of relief that what they *had* had was over. There would be no more fighting, no more rages, no more battles over every aspect of their lives together and apart. No more daily sorrows, no more hatred, no more contemptuous exchanges.

His wife had been brutally murdered, and he couldn't feel anything more than a general sadness. What kind of man did that make him?

A sorry one.

Damned sorry.

It was another hot dry day, a prelude to the hotter drier days of July and August. Hannah Clark regretted leaving the isolated cabin the moment she stepped outside and the heat wrapped around her. If the air-conditioning in her car worked, she wouldn't mind so much, but it'd gone belly-up last summer and she hadn't yet found the money to fix it. Even if she had any money to spare, there were so many other things that needed fixing more—the dishwasher in the restaurant kitchen, the computer gathering dust in her of-fice, the leaky roof, the half-dozen room air conditioners that had quit working, eighteen leaky faucets, twenty-four mattress sets that had seen better days, thirty-six sheet-and-towel sets that were approaching threadbare… The list went on.

She didn't mind living on a budget. It was a fact of life when you earned your livelihood from a motel located as far off the beaten path as the Last Resort. Her parents had budgeted every penny, and her grandparents before them. But her parents and grandparents had at least kept up with the outgo. They'd kept the place in reasonably good repair.

Since her father's death ten years ago, she'd been struggling to keep her head above water.

Lately she'd felt as if she'd lost the struggle. She was drowning, one slow painful breath at a time. This weekend, though, she'd at least broken the surface and was treading water. She'd bought herself a ten-thousand-dollar reprieve, and it hadn't cost her so much, had it?

Just her pride. Her dignity. Her self-respect. Her decency.

Her smile was thin and unforgiving. She'd always said she would do anything to save the Last Resort. Now she'd proved it.

She tossed her overnight bag in the passenger seat, spread a towel over the driver's seat to protect her legs from the hot vinyl and climbed inside. She hadn't wanted to come to the cabin two days ago. Now she didn't want to leave. With no radio, television or telephone, it was quiet and peaceful here. She'd passed her days doing nothing. When she'd gotten antsy Saturday afternoon, she'd walked down to the lake and swum until she was exhausted. When she'd remained antsy Sunday, she'd done it again, and then she had slept the afternoon away.

As soon as she walked back into the motel, there would be so much to do that she wouldn't sleep away another afternoon for, oh, ten years or so.

It was a ten-minute drive on a winding lane back to the paved road and another fifteen minutes from there to Sunshine. She didn't look at the shabby buildings and homes she passed on her way to the motel. Looking just reminded her of the life she'd wanted for herself away from Sunshine, working at a job of her choosing, living comfortably, worrying about nothing but the narrow details and problems of her own life. She'd even made a start at fulfilling her dream when she'd earned enough scholarships to go away to Tahlequah to college.

Then her father had died, and her mother's always fragile health had taken a turn for the worse. Her grandmother—

Mom to the family, Mrs. Clark to everyone else and Sylvie to her granddaughter—had hated calling Hannah home from school, but she'd had no other choice, and Hannah had had no choice but to go. She'd never regretted being available when her family needed her, but she'd always regretted giving up her dreams.

She had learned to hate the motel even as she had devoted herself one hundred percent to it. She had humbled and demeaned herself to save it, but she would burn it to the ground herself if she could get away with it. She hated it and needed it and would sell her soul to the devil to hang on to it.

She'd already sold her body. What would it hurt to put a price on her soul?

She parked in front of the two rooms that served as her quarters, took her bag inside, then went to the office. Her timing wasn't the greatest. The lunch crowd had come and gone, and the dinner crowd wouldn't show for another two hours. She would have too much time to deal with her mother, too much time to try to hide secrets from Sylvie.

Picking up the mail from the desk, she sorted through it quickly—nothing but bills—then returned it to the counter. This time of afternoon, she could find her mother in the two-bedroom apartment the two women shared right next door, and Sylvie would be in the kitchen, baking pies while their cook, Earlene, took a break to pick up her grandkids from their mother. No use putting off the inevitable.

Sylvie was up to her elbows in flour. Her rhubarb and strawberry pies were popular in the restaurant, but Hannah's summer favorite was dewberry cobbler. One was cooling on the counter near the sink.

"Cut yourself a piece and have a seat," Sylvie invited. "I'll tell you about the excitement in Sunshine this weekend."

Hannah obeyed her, topping a big piece of warm cobbler with vanilla ice cream before sliding into a chair at the table where she and Sylvie shared most of their meals. Excitement and Sunshine were words a person rarely heard in the same sentence. The last exciting thing she could recall happening here was back in high school when the postmistress had chased her husband buck naked down the street with a cast-iron skillet after finding him in bed with the divorcée next door.

"Wouldn't you know, I leave town for two days, and something finally happens," she said dryly, then turned her attention to the ice cream melting over succulent berries and thick flaky crust. "What was it? Did Mr. Tyler's pigs get into Miz Coffman's garden again?"

"It was murder. Late Saturday night."

Wide-eyed, Hannah stared at her grandmother. They hadn't had a murder in Sunshine since...well, ever. Everyone around here was too nice, too well mannered, too boring. "Who was murdered? Someone we know?"

"No, she was from Oklahoma City. One of those resort people. They think her husband did it. Odd thing is, he insists he was right here when it happened. In room 17. With a woman."

Turning cold inside, Hannah continued to stare. Dear God, this couldn't be true. There must be a mistake. Sylvie must have misunderstood. But Sylvie *never* misunderstood. Something had gone wrong, terribly, horribly wrong, and God help her, *she* was involved. She, Hannah Clark, a major failure at life in general, was involved in *murder*. Sweet heavens, what had she done?

"What did the sheriff say her name was?" Sylvie went on. "Sheryl? Susan? No, Sandra. That was it. Sandra Reilly. They found her body in the ruins of the resort—"

"Ruins?" Hannah's voice sounded choked, as if she couldn't quite catch her breath. As if all her muscles and nerves were knotted up tight inside her with fear, alarm and pure panic.

Sylvie turned from the pie crusts. "Whoever killed her

burned the place down around her. Guess we won't have to be worrying about the competition anymore.''

Hannah was going to be sick. The few bites of ice cream and cobbler she'd swallowed threatened to come right back up. Oh, God, this was none of her business, none of her fault. It was a mistake—lousy luck, bad police work, no more. It had nothing to do with her or her weekend, oh, please, God, *nothing*.

Halfway across the kitchen, Sylvie was giving her a strange look. She was still talking, but Hannah couldn't make sense of the words over the roaring in her ears, and after a moment she stopped trying. She closed her eyes and concentrated on keeping the food in her stomach, on slowing the painful thud of her heart, on controlling the rapid tenor of her breathing and the trembling that exploded through her.

When Sylvie laid her hand against Hannah's cheek, she jumped. Her eyes flew open and heat flooded her face. ''I—I'm sorry. Wh-what…''

''You don't look so good. You did a little too much partying up there in Tulsa this weekend, didn't you? I haven't seen you looking so washed-out since you came dragging in sicker than a dog with a hangover after your high-school graduation. Don't you know you can't go years without drinking, then get drunk without getting sick?''

''I didn't…'' She let her denial trail off, let her grandmother believe what she would. It was far better than the truth, which she wouldn't offer if she could.

''Why don't you go on to your room and lie down? I don't need any help here until suppertime.''

Scooping up the cobbler dish, Hannah took it with her. She'd lost her appetite—she might never eat again—but if she left it behind, Sylvie would know there was something far more wrong than a few too many drinks, and Hannah would get no peace until her questions were answered.

She walked outside, her stride measured, her movements

controlled, until she was out of sight of the plate-glass windows. Then she raced to her room, fumbled the door open and slammed it behind her. She tried Brad's local number first, got his machine, then dialed his office in Oklahoma City. The secretary politely informed her that he was in a meeting. Near hysterics, she demanded to speak to him, anyway.

He sounded cool, placating, when he came on the line. "Hello, Hannah. I see you've heard the news."

"What's going on, Brad? You told me this would be so simple, just a little favor to help Sandra out of a bad marriage, to help her get her fair share of her husband's assets. You said she would get some money, you would get control of the company and no one would get hurt. Well, she's *dead,* Brad, and the sheriff is saying he killed her!"

"Yes, the sheriff is saying that, isn't he? He thinks he's got an open-and-shut case. He isn't even looking for another suspect." Brad's tone chilled a few degrees. "Don't leave yourself off the list of people who got something out of the deal. Remember that ten-thousand-dollar note I wrote off for you? You profited, too, sweetheart."

She began trembling again, and for one frightening moment she couldn't breathe, couldn't think, couldn't speak. Finally, with a great ragged sob of air, she said, "We both know where Mick Reilly was Saturday night and Sunday morning. We both know he didn't kill his wife. When I tell the sheriff—"

"The sheriff knows all about the nonexistent Elizabeth. He's already questioned your grandmother and examined the room. Everything was taken care of before he got there."

Stretching the phone cord, Hannah unlocked the connecting doors between her room, number 18, and the next and stepped into the doorway. Shafts of light came through gaps where the curtains weren't properly closed and highlighted the dust heavy in the air. The last time she'd been in this room, it had smelled of sex, heat and passion. This afternoon it smelled of must and dust and looked as if it had stood empty forever.

"How did you do that?" Her voice was little more than a whisper, and it was heavy with fear.

"That's none of your concern, darlin'. It discredits Mick's alibi, and that's all that matters. Do you understand that? His alibi will remain discredited."

"But, Brad, if I don't talk to the sheriff, they'll charge him. He could go to prison for the rest of his life. He could get the death penalty!"

"So could his accomplice. I have a carbon of a check here, Hannah, drawn three days ago on Mick's personal account, for ten thousand dollars. It's made out to you and apparently signed by him. If you go to the sheriff with this outrageous story that *you're* the mysterious Elizabeth, it would be my duty as a law-abiding citizen to pass this on to him. The fact that the check hasn't yet been cashed would be inconsequential. Of course, Mills would want to know why Mick was giving you that kind of money. For sex? No woman's that good. For work? Everyone knows you haven't worked for him. What could possibly be worth that much money?"

An alibi, Hannah thought numbly. And in one move Brad would destroy Mick's alibi *and* implicate her in Sandra's death. Dear God, she *was* implicated. She had lured Mick to the room next door while ten miles away Sandra had been lured to her death. She had helped cast suspicion and blame on an innocent man while the real killer...

She sank to the floor and let her head fall forward. She had helped frame an innocent man while the real killer— while Brad—murdered his wife. Oh, Lord, she was in such trouble.

"I assume by your silence that you understand what I'm saying. Our original agreement was that you would keep your mouth shut about everything until I gave you permis-

sion to talk. That agreement still stands. If you break it, if
you talk to the sheriff, your grandmother or anyone else,
I'll make you sorry, Hannah. I'll see that you become a
suspect right alongside Mick. I'll see to it that you lose
your precious motel and that your crazy mother and the old
woman wind up on the streets. Do you understand?''

"I understand.'' Her words had no voice, though. Clearing her throat, tightening her grip on the phone, she repeated them in a frightened whisper.

"Write this down.'' He gave her a name, address and
phone number. She scribbled them on the first piece of
paper she found. "That's a friend of mine in Tulsa. If anyone asks, she'll swear you were there with her from ten
o'clock Saturday morning until one o'clock this afternoon.
Got it?''

"Yes.''

"Don't betray me, Hannah. Don't make me destroy your
sorry little family.'' He didn't wait to hear her response,
but hung up, leaving her listening to the faint hum of a line
that had gone dead.

Chapter 2

Mick rolled his head from side to side, then checked his watch. He'd spent ten hours in the truck watching the motel, except for the fifteen minutes it'd taken to drive to the Texaco down the street for snacks. The dinner crowd had come and gone, and four guests had checked in for the evening, filling rooms 1, 3, 5 and 7. The wandering granddaughter had returned, too, driving a junk heap that looked perfectly suited to the motel.

In his heart he'd harbored the hope that Hannah was Elizabeth, but the moment he'd seen her, that hope had been lost. Hannah looked as wholesome and innocent as Elizabeth had looked sexy and sultry. Her hair was blond, while Elizabeth's was fiery red. Her clothes were loose and shapeless while Elizabeth's had been chosen to seduce. Hannah was rather plain, as if she belonged at the Last Resort, while Elizabeth had stood out like a diamond among stones.

So he'd moved on to his next best hope. Elizabeth must be a friend of Hannah's. There was no other reasonable explanation, and he'd been trying for hours to think of one. All he had to do was catch Hannah alone and convince her that it was in everyone's best interests if she came up with the information he needed.

Catching her alone hadn't yet proved possible. After spending more than an hour alone in room 18 this afternoon, she'd spent the rest of the time in and out of the guest rooms, the dining room, the kitchen and the office. Practically every time he'd seen her through the big windows, she'd been accompanied by either the crazy woman or her grandmother. She'd waited tables, checked in guests, carried extra towels to room 3, delivered pillows to room 5 and made multiple trips to room 7. It wasn't beyond believing that there were multiple problems with the room, or it was entirely possible that the man who'd checked into the room just liked having the young woman wait on him.

Tired from sitting and doing nothing, Mick got out of the truck and walked a few yards to stretch his legs. The night was still, the air heavy with the promise of rain. A mosquito buzzed his ear before settling on his neck, and he slapped it away, then walked to the telephone pole and leaned against it. With no street lamps in the entire town of Sunshine and no more than a quarter moon in the sky, he could have been invisible.

Hannah stood behind the counter, ledgers open in front of her. She emptied the cash register, counted the money a couple of times, then zipped it into a slim deposit bag. Periodically she stopped what she was doing, ducked her head and covered her face with her hands. Did she know about Sandra's death? Did she suspect that her friend Elizabeth had something to do with it? He hoped so—hoped she was shocked, stunned and willing to do something about it.

But what if she wasn't willing? What if she would protect her friend no matter what the cost to him?

If he could get inside her room he could look for some

proof of Elizabeth's existence himself. Surely Hannah kept an address book. Surely he could find *something*—an address, a phone number, even just a full name. Then he could ask for her cooperation, and when she lied—if she lied—and insisted she knew no Elizabeth, he could confront her with the proof.

It wasn't a great plan, he acknowledged as he started toward the shoulder of the road, but at least it was something. He had a tremendous urge to do *something*.

When he was about even with the last two rooms, he crossed the highway and walked right up to the door she'd used earlier. Her quarters appeared to encompass two rooms, one marked 18, the number removed from the second door. He assumed she lived alone—Granny and the crazy woman hadn't gone near the rooms all day—and there were no lights on inside.

Quickly he twisted the knob on 18. It was securely locked. Without breaking stride he crossed the few yards to the unmarked door. Also locked. Not quite ready to break down doors, he circled behind the building and hit pay dirt. There was nothing in back of the end room, not even a tiny grimy window, but in an effort to make the rooms a little homier, a portion of the wall of number 18 had been knocked out and replaced with a sliding glass door that opened onto a small secluded patio.

He'd never liked sliding doors. Most people failed to secure them properly. Without some type of bar, they were notoriously easy to open from the outside, even when locked. Hannah's was no exception. He opened the door just wide enough to slip inside, closed it again, then listened. There was the quiet hum of a refrigerator somewhere to his right and the expected steady drip from a sink nearby. Other than that, there was no other sound.

He felt for and found a light switch, and a single bulb lit up, illuminating a tiny kitchenette and another light switch. That light showed the living room, a long narrow rectangle better suited for two beds and a night table than a sofa, chairs and television.

A green banker's lamp sat on the desk near the connecting door. He turned it on, then rifled through the drawers and found nothing of interest. No address book. No letters. No photographs of beautiful sexy Elizabeth arm in arm with plain blond Hannah.

There was nothing in the drawers of the two end tables. Nothing in the purse on the sofa or the overnight bag she'd left on the coffee table. The drawers of her nightstand. Her dresser drawers. Her bathroom drawers.

Muttering a curse, he turned to leave the bathroom when his gaze fell on the contents of the wastebasket under the sink. For a long blank moment, he stared, so stunned that he almost didn't grasp the significance of what he was looking at. Numbly he picked it up, turned it over in his hands, then abruptly spun around and headed for the closet.

His slow smile started with relief, but turned bitter before it formed. Surely plain blond Hannah would return to her room soon, and when she did, he would be waiting. He had plenty of questions.

By God, she would give him answers.

A station wagon with mismatched panels pulled into the parking lot, its headlights making Hannah blink before they went dark. She watched as an elderly woman with an enormous bag climbed out and came inside. Brightly colored yarns spilled across the registration counter when she laid the bag down. Hannah brushed one away from the books she'd been trying for the past hour to balance and smiled halfheartedly. "Hi, Ruby."

"Hannah. Did you enjoy your little getaway?"

"It was fine." She'd given the same response to the last fifteen people who'd asked. Not a soul in Sunshine hadn't heard that she'd spent a couple of days in Tulsa, and not a soul who'd come in for dinner had missed asking about it.

Ordinarily such lack of privacy made her feel smothered. Tonight she felt guilty.

"You look a little peaked. Are you coming down with something?"

"Maybe. I thought I'd go to bed as soon as I get these books balanced. I'm having a little trouble concentrating." How could she care whether she had eighty dollars in the drawer or eight hundred when she'd helped get a woman killed?

"I'll take care of that. Just let me get a cup of coffee, and then you can go on."

On a normal night Hannah would have turned down her offer, gotten the coffee herself and stood right there until everything balanced. Tonight she nodded, waited until Ruby was coming back through the swinging door with a coffee mug in hand and left with a listless good-night.

She walked past a row of empty rooms to her own, let herself in and automatically locked the door behind her. Without turning on a light she tossed her keys in the direction of the couch and made her way around shadowy lumps of furniture, through the closed door and into the bedroom.

She was four steps into the room before she realized something was wrong. She never closed the bedroom door except on the rare occasions she had company, and when she'd left this afternoon, she'd left the two rooms in darkness. Now the lamp beside her bed was turned on, and its shade was tilted to direct the light onto her bed and the items lined up there: a skinny white tank top, a curling iron and an empty box retrieved from the trash that had held one application of temporary rinse in Burnished Copper Sunset.

Her heart thudded so hard that she pressed one hand to it. Her throat tightened, squeezing off all but the slightest whisper of air, and her legs became paralyzed, unable to obey her brain's command to run. All she could do was stand in the middle of the room, a picture-perfect case of terror, and stare at the bed in horrified fascination.

The voice came out of the shadows somewhere behind her, startling her even though she expected it, making her tremble. "You're good. I've been watching you all afternoon, and I never even suspected... Even now I can't say for sure." Cool and smooth disappeared with his abrupt icy command. "Take off your shirt and put on the tank top."

She raised her hands to her T-shirt hem, but couldn't obey his demand, couldn't make her fingers curl around the fabric and pull it up.

"What's the problem, darlin'? You want my help, like Saturday?" Cool steady hands touched her from behind, inching the shirt above her waist, fingers brushing her skin. When he tugged higher, she shrugged away and yanked the shirt over her head. The air-conditioning, comfortable only a moment ago, was cold on her bare breasts, raising goose bumps all the way down to the waist of her jeans.

Forcing herself to move, she pulled the tank top on. It covered her but was sadly lacking in modesty. The fit was snug, the fabric nearly sheer, the overall effect just the other side of decent. Those were the reasons she'd bought it Saturday morning. Exactly the reasons she'd worn it Saturday night.

"Turn around."

She did slowly, her eyes working to adjust from the bright light of the lamp to the shadows that filled the rest of the room. After a moment she could see work boots and faded jeans, but from midthigh up, her visitor was in darkness. There was no denying it was Mick Reilly, though. She knew the voice. She knew the fear.

"Still hard to tell if you're the right woman. The one I'm looking for had a headful of hot red hair and a make-you-hard smile and a voice..." He made a sound that was halfway between regret and arousal, then walked in a slow circle around her. "What's with these jeans, darlin'?

There's room for you and me both in there.'' Grasping a handful of denim, he yanked her hard against his body. Her hands went to his chest to stop herself from falling. ''You're about the right height...the right age...your breasts and hips are right. But there's really only one way to be sure....''

He shoved her back on the bed and followed her down. Panic rising in her chest, she struggled, pushing against him, but he easily subdued her, easily pinned her hands above her head and forced her thighs apart, so he could grind his hips hard against hers. ''Oh, yeah. I remember this. You're the one,'' he murmured, rubbing suggestively. For a moment he closed his eyes, and a familiar look— arousal, hunger, almost-there satisfaction—came across his face, and a familiar feel—long, solid, hard—came in contact with her body. Then he looked at her, and instead of arousal, there was contempt. Instead of desire, there was hostility. Clasping both her wrists in one hand, he slid the other into her hair and knotted his fingers, bringing tears to her eyes. ''Oh, yeah, you're the one. You're the lying bitch who's trying to screw up my life.''

''Please,'' she whispered. ''Don't hurt me.''

He leaned closer until his body covered hers, until his mouth brushed hers, until his coldly furious gaze locked with hers. ''Hurt you?'' He whispered, too, a soft deadly sound. ''Oh, darlin', I ought to kill you. But I need you.'' He stood up from the bed in one swift move, adjusted the lamp shade, turned on every other light in the room.

By the time she struggled into a sitting position, he was leaning against the edge of the dresser, watching her with his intense brown gaze. His palms were braced at his sides, his boots crossed at the ankle. His stare was bold, his manner cold. He wasn't the least bit embarrassed by the erection that stretched his jeans taut, wasn't the least bit disturbed that intimidating her had turned him on.

Well, *she* was embarrassed. And afraid. Sick. Distraught. Guilty. Ashamed.

She retrieved her T-shirt from the floor and pulled it on over the tank top, then removed the band that had secured her ponytail and shook her hair loose. That done, she sat motionless, waiting for some action from him. One long moment slid into another, and his stare never wavered. His anger never lessened.

When he finally spoke, he asked exactly what she expected. "Why did you do it?"

Her shrug was jerky and as far from casual as possible. "I like pretending to be someone I'm not. I like picking up strange men."

"Bullshit. You weren't any good at it."

"I got you here, didn't I?"

"Only because I'd gone without for a long time. I would have left with any woman in the place that night. My only requirement was that she be warm and breathing."

It was foolish even to think about ego at a time like this, but her feminine vanity was pricked by his claim. She had demeaned herself, sold off her principles along with her body, and now the unwitting partner in her prostitution was telling her that she'd been nothing special; any woman would have done.

Dear God, she wished she'd never heard of Blue Water Construction, Eagle's Haven Resort, Brad Daniels or Mick Reilly.

"Who sent you after me?"

"No one. I picked you out in the bar."

"Then why the disguise? I would have taken you like this, given the right incentive. Why the fake name? Why all the effort to make it look like we were never in that room? What's your game, Hannah?"

The only answers she had were the truth, and Brad had made clear what would happen if she told Reilly that. Rather than the lame excuses that were all she could offer, she dropped her gaze to the floor and simply, stubbornly, shook her head.

Before her mind could register that he'd moved, he was standing directly in front of her. He jerked her to her feet, gave her a shake and got right in her face again. "Who are you afraid of?"

"You." That was the truth. But she was infinitely more afraid of Brad.

His grip gentled on her arms, and he took a step back. "Who are you covering for? Who sent you to pick me up?"

Once again she said nothing.

He released her completely and took one more step away. "You know whoever it was killed my wife. You're protecting a murderer."

"I'm protecting myself."

"He threatened you?"

She looked away, rather than meet his speculative gaze. "Look, I'm sorry for what happened. I didn't know…" She drew a deep breath, then sighed. "I didn't know." Had she been incredibly gullible, incredibly stupid or just incredibly desperate? Brad's story had made sense to her. She'd known women whose divorce settlements had miraculously become more equitable when proof of their husbands' infidelity had become a matter of record. She'd known too many women whose husbands had amused themselves with outside diversions to doubt for one moment Brad's claim that Sandra Reilly's had. She had believed the scheme was basically harmless: Sandra got what she wanted, Brad got what he wanted, and Hannah got out from under a ten-thousand-dollar debt she couldn't pay—more than adequate compensation for a night's sex with a stranger. The only person who would lose was the philandering husband, who deserved to lose.

Only it had been Sandra Reilly who paid, and the price had been dear beyond belief. Now Mick would pay, too, and Hannah, and Merrilee and Sylvie, while Brad…Brad would get what he wanted. The only guilty one in this mess, and he would walk away free.

"The police can protect you. If you talk to them, if you tell them—"

Hannah cut him off. "I can protect myself. I can keep my mouth shut, and everything will be all right."

"Not for me, it won't!"

His shout made her cringe, but it didn't sway her. "I'm sorry about that, but I've got to look out for myself. There are people depending on me, and I can't help them if I'm in prison or dead."

He turned away, but she could see his reflection in the dresser mirror as he made an obvious effort—deep breathing, clenched muscles—to control his temper. When he turned back, he wasn't noticeably calmer. "You're going to talk to the sheriff. We're leaving here together, and we're going to his office, and you're going to tell him the truth."

The courage to stand up to him came from pure terror. She stood straighter, folded her arms across her chest and regarded him with a flat, even stare. "The only truth I know is that I was out of town this weekend. I went to Tulsa Saturday morning, and I didn't come back until this afternoon. The truth is, I don't know you from Adam. I didn't see you Saturday night. I didn't spend the night with you. I can't provide you with an alibi for the time your wife was killed." She swallowed hard over the disgust and revulsion building inside her. "I'm sorry. But that's what I'll tell the sheriff and anyone else who asks."

I'm sorry. The deceitful little bitch said it as if she meant it. Mick scowled. Hell, maybe she did. Maybe she really was sorry that she had royally screwed him over, that his one lousy night with her might cost him his life. But *sorry* wasn't going to change her mind. It wasn't going to clear his name.

Shoving his hands in his pockets, he walked to the door

and stared at the shabby furniture. One lousy night. One lousy, incredibly sexy, steamy, wild night. If things had turned out differently, he still would have gone looking for her. Once the divorce was taken care of and he was legally free again, he would have tried to find the elusive Elizabeth, would have seen if that night was a fluke or if there really was something between them.

But things hadn't turned out differently, and there was something between them, all right—starting with her lies. Her stubborn refusal to talk. The information she knew he needed.

How to get it from her when she was obviously scared? He could think of only two options: coax it out of her, or scare her more. He disliked the first idea and hated the last. He wasn't in the habit of terrorizing women. Besides, how could he say or do anything that might compete with the threats her accomplice had already made? After all, her accomplice had already murdered one woman. If the success of his—or her—whole elaborate scheme was at stake, would he hesitate to kill another?

He glanced over his shoulder. She still stood beside the bed, arms folded, posture rigid. She thought she looked tough, but in truth, she just looked small and very afraid. "Get an old broomstick or a dowel cut the width of the stationary patio door and keep it in the track. It'll stop someone from getting in as easily as I did."

He was halfway across the living room before the overhead light flickered on and she appeared in the doorway. "That's it? You're leaving?"

"Are you going to the sheriff with me?"

"I can't."

"Then I'm leaving." He opened the front door, then looked at her once more. "Right now, Hannah, you're probably the only person in the world who knows who killed Sandra. All he has to do to keep his secret forever is kill you." He watched with satisfaction as the color drained from her face. "Keep that in mind, darlin'."

He stepped out into the night's heat and closed the door behind him. For a time he just stood there, half hoping she would come after him, all too sure she wouldn't. When five minutes had passed with no sound from inside, he strode across the parking lot and the highway to his truck.

It took fifteen minutes to get to his motel in Yates, a half hour to pack up a year's worth of accumulated belongings and another fifteen to return to Sunshine. Once again he parked in front of the office, went inside and waited for the elderly woman behind the counter to put down her crocheting and pull her girth from the seat.

"Can I help you?"

"I need a room."

"No credit cards. Cash only." She slid the register to him. "For one night?"

"Indefinitely." He scrawled his name and Oklahoma City address in the book, then pulled out his wallet. Luckily he'd gone to the bank Friday. He should have more than enough to get what he wanted tonight.

"I'll put you in room 9—"

"I want 17."

She shook her head, and her thick glasses slid down her nose. "Sorry. We only book that room when—"

"—the rest of the place is full." He'd heard that line before.

"Which you can see for yourself it's not. Nine's exactly the same room."

"I want 17." His smile was the best he could manage, the best he'd managed since Sunday morning. "It's my lucky number."

"I'm sorry, sir. I can't let you have that room. It's not made up, and it needs cleaning. There's not even sheets on the bed."

"I can make the bed myself. I've done it before." He

drew a thin stack of bills from his wallet and fanned them out on the counter. ''The first week's rent in cash for room 17.''

Her eyes widened, then she let out a great laugh. ''Oh, honey, that would buy you a whole month in any of our other rooms.''

''But I'm not interested in the others.'' Except 18. ''Forget your policy, take the money and give me the key. Your boss won't mind. A place like this can always use the cash.''

The old woman's look turned indecisive. She would have to be a fool to turn down the money he was offering, regardless of Hannah's preference for privacy. At last, with a great sigh, she returned the key she held to the Peg-Board and picked up the one he wanted, instead. ''I don't know about this,'' she grumbled. ''Policy is policy…but that is a lot of money. You can have the room tonight, but you just might have to take it up with the owner tomorrow.''

''I'll do that.'' He could deal with Granny. If necessary, he could offer her so damn much cash she would invite him right into Hannah's bed—a place he had been and thoroughly enjoyed. A place he wished he'd never known existed.

''I can't do up the room tonight, but I can come down and make the bed.''

He brushed off the offer. ''Just give me the bedding and towels. I'll do it.''

''A guest doing his own housekeeping. Sylvie's not gonna like this.'' She went through the door behind her, then returned a moment later with bedding, towels, pillows and two tiny bars of soap. ''Let me get your receipt.''

''I'll pick it up in the morning.''

The lights were still on in Hannah's rooms when he approached the end of the building. He left everything on the bed, then returned to the truck for the bags he would need tonight. He would move the rest of his things in tomorrow. Tonight he was tired.

As he finished making the bed, the pager on his belt went off, its annoying beep loud in the stillness. The number was Brad's Oklahoma City house. Using his calling card, Mick dialed it, then sank onto the bed.

"Where the hell are you? I've been calling your truck with no answer, and the clerk at the motel said you checked out tonight. Where are you?"

Mick chose to ignore the question. "Have you found a lawyer for me?"

"Yeah. You're supposed to call him first thing tomorrow. What's going on, Mick? You're not planning to skip town, are you?"

"Why would I do that?"

"Gee, I don't know. Maybe because you're a suspect in an arson and a murder?"

"I'm going to find Elizabeth. I'm going to prove I haven't lied."

"And how are you going to do that? You don't have a last name. You have no idea where she's from. You don't even know if her name is Elizabeth. How the hell are you planning to find her?"

Mick slid down until the pillow was beneath his head. There was a reason he wasn't telling his partner and best friend where he was or that Elizabeth, better known as Hannah, was right next door. Later he would figure out what it was. "I'll find her."

"Oh, yeah, you've got so much to go on. You know she's a redhead, she's got nice boobs, she's hot and easy and hell in bed. Yeah, that's gonna make the search a whole lot easier."

"What's the lawyer's name?" Mick made a mental note of the name Brad gave him and thought he might pick his own attorney, after all.

"So where are you?"

"I'll let you know when I settle someplace."

"Come on, Mick, don't be—"

He hung up, but remained where he was. Using the remote, he turned the television on and got nothing but audio. He left it on, using the noise as he had for the past year to disguise the fact that he was so alone.

Letting his eyes drift shut, he shifted on the bed. The mattress was about twenty years past its prime, but he'd gotten a good night's sleep here Saturday. Of course, that had been after Eliza—Hannah had exhausted him. Once she'd gotten over her shyness, she had made love to him—snidely he substituted another word for the quaint phrase—with a greedy, needy passion that had matched his own. He had thought in one brief, lucid moment that she must be lonely, like him, and eager for intimate contact that didn't involve fighting, pain or hostility. She had seduced him as if not just her body but also her soul had been starved for a personal touch.

And the whole time she'd been helping someone frame him for Sandra's murder.

I didn't know, she'd said, leaving the words hanging as if there were more to follow. *I didn't know he was going to kill her.* Had that been the rest of it? He hoped so. He hoped she wasn't so cold, so heartless, that she could lose herself in pure sexual pleasure while another woman's skull was crushed and the building set on fire around her. He prayed he couldn't possibly be attracted to a psychopath like that.

Who was the someone she'd been helping? Sandra had had her share of enemies. There were the men she'd slept with and callously dumped. The wives who'd watched her threaten their marriages all for her own brief amusement. The people she'd used and abandoned, the ones she'd treated as beneath her notice. And, of course, Mick had nursed his own animosity toward her for a long time.

When he'd married her, he had loved her more than he'd

thought possible. They had met when she'd come to his office to interview for a secretary's job. He'd taken one look at her, listened for one moment to her sweet, lazy voice, and hired her on the spot. He hadn't known or cared whether she could handle the job. He'd only wanted to see her every day. After a year they'd gotten married. He thought she had fallen in love with him. He suspected now that her decision had more to do with the impressive growth his company had shown that first year. She had finally been convinced that he could keep her in the style she wanted to become accustomed to.

She had been a beautiful woman, a good office manager, a perfect hostess. She might have grown up poor, but no one ever would have guessed it. Her style had been impeccable, her taste expensive and elegant. There'd been times, when she was dressed for some formal event, when she had intimidated the hell out of him, when he'd felt so lower-class average—and so damned lucky.

When had he stopped feeling lucky? When had she started treating him as if he were inferior? When had the love started to fade?

It had been a gradual change. Once he'd hooked up with Brad and Reilly Homes had become Blue Water Construction, he'd worked longer and harder than ever before, often at jobs that sent him away from home overnight or for a week at a time. The free time he could give Sandra had shrunk, but she hadn't seemed to mind. At the time he'd thought that she was being supportive, that she understood how much the company demanded of him, that she was willing to wait until they were better established and he could spend more time with her. Now he knew that she simply hadn't cared. She'd had his money—no small amount the way business had tripled and tripled again—and she'd had her men.

He had never been unfaithful to her—not when he'd found out about her first affair, not when she'd stopped making love with him, not when he'd acknowledged that their marriage was beyond saving. Until Saturday night, he had slept with his wife or he'd slept alone.

He'd picked a hell of a time to forget his morals. But he'd had little enough say in the matter. If he hadn't been willing—eager, even—to leave the bar with Hannah, she would have convinced him. Seducing him—keeping him occupied and leaving him without an alibi—had been her job, and she'd been determined to do it right.

Hell, yes, she'd done it right. Just thinking about those long dark hours in this bed was enough to make him hard. Knowing that she was right next door was enough to make him want her again. Even knowing that she'd lied. That she'd set him up. That she was helping ruin him. He would take her to bed again in a heartbeat.

And then he would ruin *her*.

Hannah gave up her night-long efforts to sleep, got ready to face the day and went to the office to relieve Ruby. The night clerk was comfortably tucked into the padded swivel chair, watching the television on the corner of the desk. It was tuned to an early-morning exercise program led by a woman cheerful enough to drive any sane person to commit murd—

Swallowing hard, Hannah cut off the thought. "Morning, Ruby."

"You're up early."

"I couldn't sleep."

"Hope your neighbor didn't disturb you."

Hannah rested her arms on the counter. "My neighbor?"

"He insisted on room 17. Said it was his lucky number." Rising from the chair, Ruby pulled open the cash drawer and furtively displayed a stack of money. "He paid five hundred dollars for one week in that particular room. Can you believe it, Hannah? Of course, I told him he'd have to take it up with you this morning. I know you like your privacy, but how could I turn down five hundred dollars?''

Hannah stared at the money as a chill raced through her. She grabbed the register, praying it would disprove her fears, but it didn't. Of course not. Nothing else was going her way. Why should this?

Why was Mick Reilly staying at her motel? Obviously he wanted information from her. He wanted to make her nervous, wanted her to know she was being watched. Well, he simply couldn't stay. If Brad found out—and he would—he would suspect Hannah of betraying him, and he would carry out his threat to destroy her family. She couldn't let that happen.

Even if it meant letting him destroy Mick.

''Is something wrong, Hannah? You look feverish. Maybe you should take some aspirin and go back to bed.''

She felt feverish—cold with fear and hot with anger— but she brushed off Ruby's concern. ''I'm all right. I'll take care of this. If you could stay at the desk until I get back…?''

''Heavens, honey, I'm not scheduled to leave for another hour. Take your time. But I doubt that fellow's awake yet.''

''Then I'll wake him,'' Hannah said through gritted teeth. She left the office, blinking at the sun that had just cleared the hills to the east before her gaze settled on the midnight blue pickup parked in front. She hadn't even noticed it earlier. Her gaze had been down, like her mood, and she'd walked right past it. Of course, it was Reilly's.

At room 17, she didn't settle for a polite knock. She pounded her fist on the door, releasing every bit of fear and anxiety into the action. Then, without giving him a chance to respond, she used her master key, flung the door back and stalked inside. The television was on, the air conditioner ran at a low hum, and the bare bulb over the sink gave off a dim light. A shaft of sunlight illuminated Reilly stretched out on the bed, on top of the covers and wearing nothing but unbuttoned jeans. The remote was loosely clasped in one hand, and the other was raised to protect his eyes from the sun.

With his long lean body, dark skin, dark hair and day's growth of beard, he was quite possibly the handsomest and sexiest man she'd ever seen.

Oh, God, she was in trouble.

"Why don't you come on over here and crawl into bed with me like you did the other night?" His voice was thick with sleep and desire. It made her remember the sweet things he'd whispered to her Saturday night—promises, encouragement, endearments. It also made her remember the sharp contrast of his contempt last night.

When she said nothing, he shifted to lean on one arm. His face was in shadow now, his body still gleaming deep golden brown in the sun. The sight made her hot, trembly, and scared her to death.

He shut off the television and tossed the remote aside, then sat up, stuffing pillows behind his back. "I take it that banging on the door was your way of saying welcome to the Last Resort."

"You can't stay here."

"I *am* here, darlin', and I don't intend to leave. Of course, if you want to do a little persuading, feel free. My body is yours. Do what you will." His grin was wicked and teasing, but there was real danger underneath it. She could feel it. "Do what you did Saturday night."

Moving farther into the room, she picked up the shirt, shoes and socks he'd discarded last night and laid them at the foot of the bed before turning her attention to the neatly folded clothes on the table and toiletries around the sink. "Ruby was wrong to rent you a room. You're not welcome here. You can't stay. I'll pack your things, and you'll go to the office and get your money back—all of it. There's no charge for last night. You just have to go. *Now.*"

She was concentrating so fiercely on returning everything

on the counter to the nylon duffel that she wasn't aware he'd left the bed until he stopped too close behind her. Reaching around, he pulled the bag away, then stilled her hands by gripping both wrists. "I'm not leaving."

"You *have* to! You can't stay here!"

"Then tell me what I want to know. Tell me who killed Sandra…and then tell the sheriff and make him believe it."

She met his gaze in the mirror. His eyes were dark, almost black, and his expression was ruthless. In contrast, she looked pale and frightened. "If I tell you, he'll destroy me. He'll—" She bit off the words, clamped her mouth shut.

"Who?" When she didn't answer, Reilly leaned closer. "If you don't tell the sheriff everything, *I'll* destroy you."

She believed him. She just believed Brad more. Still, she tried in a quavery voice to reason with him. "If I help you, he'll implicate me. He'll make us both look guilty. He'll put me in jail and my mother and grandmother out on the street. I'm the only family they've got. There's no place for them to go. Sylvie would have to go to a nursing home, and my mother…she's not well. She doesn't cope well here, but she can't function at all away from here. She's—"

"—crazy," he supplied. "She probably wouldn't mind Vinita at all."

She shrank away as far as the counter would let her. The small town of Vinita in northeastern Oklahoma was home to Eastern State Hospital, a state-run psychiatric hospital. Merrilee had gone there for treatment soon after Hannah's father's death and had come back in worse shape than before. It was one of her greatest fears that she would someday have to go back there. Leaving Sunshine and the Last Resort was her greatest fear of all.

"Frankly, darlin', I don't give a damn about your crazy mother or your grandmother or you. I don't care whether you stay here until this place falls down around you or if they rot in a nursing home and a mental ward while you rot in jail. All I care about is the truth and saving myself. Now who are you working with? Who set me up? Who told you to entertain me while he killed my wife?''

She twisted to face him and wished she hadn't. It was easier meeting his gaze in the mirror than face-to-face. Some small measure of the malice and threat got lost in the mirror. ''If I tell you, will you leave?''

''When you tell me *and* the sheriff.''

''I can't do that. You can get the sheriff to help you prove it, but I can't be your alibi.''

He stared at her a long time, then made a frustrated gesture. ''All right. Who was it?''

''You'll leave? And never come back? And never mention my name to the sheriff or anyone else?''

''Yes. Who was it?''

''Think about it. Who stood to profit?''

''According to the sheriff, me.''

''Not from Sandra's death. Who stood to profit from getting rid of *you?*''

He shook his head slowly. ''Only Sandra. She wasn't satisfied with the property settlement our attorneys had worked out. She wanted everything. But no one tried to kill me. Sandra wasn't mistakenly killed in my place.''

''How much is Blue Water Construction worth?''

He named a figure that made her blink. Her shabby little business venture here wasn't worth even one-hundredth of that. In her entire lifetime she would never see a fraction as much money come through here. No wonder Brad wanted it all for himself.

''But this had nothing to do with—'' He caught his breath. His eyes narrowed, and he backed away. He paced to the bed, his movements tightly controlled, then came back. ''The sheriff assumed the fire was set to cover up the murder. But the resort was heavily insured, and it was about to bankrupt Blue Water. So maybe the fire served to get the company out from under that debt and to cast suspicion on me, because I'd said before that since we couldn't sell the place, we should burn it down. And it made it look as if the fire was connected to the murder. Although Brad might have a motive for arson, there's no reason he'd want to kill Sandra. I, on the other hand, had reasons for both.''

For a long time he remained silent, then abruptly he shook his head. ''Brad had nothing against Sandra. They hardly ever saw each other, except on the rare occasions we had dinners with clients. He and I have been partners and friends for *years*. And you expect me to believe that he sacrificed her life—that he killed a woman he barely knew—just to get me out of the company?''

''I don't care whether you believe me. I just want you out of here. If he knows that you've found me, if he even suspects that you've connected me with Elizabeth, he'll make me pay. He'll take everything I have and frame me right alongside you.''

Mick gave her a long hard look, then went to the phone, punching in numbers for a long-distance call. Hannah's heart sank when, after a moment's wait, he said, ''Hey, Brad, it's Mick. I told you I'd let you know when I found a place to stay. I'm at the Last Resort Motel, room 17.'' His gaze locked with hers. ''I think I'll find something here that will lead me to Elizabeth.''

She sank against the counter, her legs too weak to support her. That was it. Brad had promised her punishment, and he would deliver where it would hurt most. He would foreclose on that ten-thousand-dollar note, which she'd paid in full with her body and the loss of her self-respect, which he'd promised to write off legally upon her return from the cabin. He would evict them, and her mother... Oh, God, her mother wouldn't be able to handle that.

The distant sound of a ringing phone drew her attention back to Reilly. He'd hung up and was watching her now. ''Your phone's ringing.''

Brad, no doubt. She was afraid to talk to him, afraid of

his anger and his threats. But when Reilly opened the connecting door, then swung hers open—left unlocked in the shock of yesterday's phone call with Brad—she numbly walked through and answered midring.

There was no ranting, no loud fury, no screaming accusations. Just a quiet, deadly voice. "I warned you once, Hannah. Now I'm promising you. If Mick makes the connection between you and Elizabeth, if he finds out one damn thing that will help him, you'll live to regret it. Merrilee won't like being locked up with all those crazy people, miles from Sunshine, knowing she'll never be able to go home again, will she? What do you think that will do to her, Hannah? Probably cause her mind to snap completely. She would never recover. And what about Sylvie? It'll break her heart to see her daughter-in-law in Vinita and her granddaughter in Mabel Bassett."

Hannah's fingers tightened around the receiver until they were numb. She'd heard of the Mabel Bassett Correctional Center for women, heard it was a hellish place even by prison standards. It *would* break Sylvie's heart to see her there, even if—especially if—she knew Hannah was innocent.

"You know, for a woman Sylvie's age, all that heartache and disruption and loss just might be more than she could bear. It just might put her in an early grave. And it would all be your fault, Hannah."

"I won't tell him anything," she whispered stiffly. "I swear, Brad. But I can't stop him from figuring out things on his own."

Tired of waiting in the doorway, Mick crossed to Hannah in two strides and placed his hand over hers, pulling the receiver far enough away from her ear so he could hear, too. What he heard made him sick. It stirred a helpless, furious anger deep inside.

"You'd better stop him," Brad said, his voice easily recognizable to Mick after so many years of working side

by side. ''You're too young and pretty a woman to spend
the rest of your life in prison, and you're much too young
to die.''

The line went dead. Mick pulled the receiver from her
numb fingers and hung up. He'd had several reasons for
calling Brad. He'd known that, if Hannah's story was true,
Brad would call her—had figured, if the story was true, that
call would include threats. He'd wanted to frighten her, to
convince her that her best chance was working with *him*.
He'd succeeded at one. She was scared. But scared enough
to cooperate?

She sank into the chair and buried her face in her hands.
Her hair—long, silky, pale blond—fell to camouflage her
face. How easy it had been to change her appearance. A
temporary color rinse, a curling iron, makeup and skintight,
nothing-to-hide clothes. Even knowing the truth, he found
it difficult to reconcile sexy, sultry Elizabeth with scrubbed-
clean, straight-haired, baggy-clothed Hannah. But the voice
was the same. The feeling was the same. In the dark he
would know the woman was the same.

Snagging a low stool with his foot, he drew it close and
sat in front of her. ''Let me see if I have this straight.
You're telling me that Brad sent you to the bar—''

She looked up sharply. ''I'm not telling you anything.''

She had promised Brad that. Soon Mick would persuade
her to change her mind, but not now. ''All right. I figured
out that Brad told you to spend Saturday night with me
here while he got Sandra out to the site, where he killed
her. You said last night that you didn't know he was going
to kill her. What did you think he had planned?''

Her sigh rippled through her whole body. ''He said you
were in the middle of a nasty divorce. That Sandra knew
you'd had a number of affairs but had no proof. That if she
could get proof, she could get a better settlement.''

''So you were supposed to spend the night with me, disappear from my bed, then show up in court as the whore

with whom I betrayed my wife.'' His choice of words made her flinch and her cheeks turn pink. ''So Sandra would get at least a portion of my half of the company, and through her Brad would get control of the company, and you would get...?''

''I owe Brad some money. I've missed the last four payments. Sandra was supposed to pay him for my help, and he would cancel the note.''

''How much money?''

Her face turned pinker, and her voice dropped to a murmur. ''Ten thousand dollars.''

He laughed. ''Oh, sweetheart, you were good, but you were nowhere near that good.''

Her only response was to close her eyes. She looked ashamed. Vulnerable. Defenseless. That one simple act made him feel like a bastard for his laughter and the scorn that had accompanied his insult.

''So you believed Brad.''

She nodded miserably.

''When did you find out the truth?''

''When I came back to the motel yesterday afternoon. Sylvie told me about Sandra's death. I called Brad, and he—''

''Admitted it?''

''—said he would frame me, too. He's got plans ready to set in motion to implicate me if I try to clear you.''

''And you believe he'll do it.'' He didn't need her nod. Of course she believed it. After hearing Brad's threat on the phone, *he* believed it. ''Even if you do everything Brad's way, you're still screwed. What happens to you after I'm convicted and sent to prison? Do you think Brad's going to write off your note, go away and let you live here in peace? Do you think he's going to trust that you'll never have a change of heart, that your conscience will never get the better of you? Do you think he's going to take even the slightest chance that a year from now, or five or ten, you could ruin things for him?''

She stared sullenly.

''He's already lied to you once. He told you that all you had to do was spend the night with me, and your note would be paid in full. But he still has the note, doesn't he? You upheld your end of the bargain, but he didn't. He's still holding it over you. And what can you do? Take him to court? Testify that sleeping with me was supposed to relieve you of a ten-thousand-dollar debt? Darlin', you're screwed, and so am I, unless we can prove that Brad's behind this whole mess.''

For a long time she gave his words serious consideration. When she finally responded, though, it was with a shake of her head. ''I can't help you. I know I can't trust Brad to leave me alone if I cooperate, but I *can* trust him to destroy me if I don't.''

The look Mick gave her was pitying. ''You're a fool, Hannah. If he can murder a woman in cold blood, burn down the project that was to be his personal triumph and threaten you and your family, all to get rid of me, then once he's succeeded, he will almost certainly kill again to protect himself.''

Still looking stubborn, she refused to meet his gaze.

''Your cooperating with Brad has already gotten me in a world of trouble. It's going to get you killed. How will your mother and your grandmother deal with that? Who will take care of them then?''

Still no response.

Muttering a curse, he stood up and returned to the open doors. ''You *are* a fool, Hannah,'' he repeated. ''One of these days all too soon, you're going to be a dead fool.''

Chapter 3

The dining room was three-quarters full when Mick walked in an hour later. Hannah was waiting tables. She sent a dark scowl his way as he slid onto a stool, but didn't come to take his order. Instead, her mother, moving as if it were a lazy, slow day and he was the only customer in the place, brought him a menu. "Good morning. What can I start you with this morning?"

"Coffee."

She returned in a moment with a heavy white mug, a spoon and a dish of plastic-packed creamers. "I'll be back in a minute for your order."

While looking over the menu, he reached for the coffee. Though he normally used a free hand with both sugar and cream, this morning he could use a dose of straight black caffeine to jolt his system. Unfortunately the cup was empty, and there was no sign of either Hannah or her mother.

The man two stools down leaned over the counter and picked up the coffeepot, then passed it along. "Sometimes

Merrilee's a little forgetful," he said in explanation. "If Hannah's not too busy—that's her daughter, the blonde— she keeps an eye on her. If she is busy, we sort of take care of ourselves."

Mick filled his cup, then returned the pot to the man. Just as he was taking his first sip, Merrilee returned from the kitchen with a cheery smile and set a plate in front of him. "Here you go. If you need ketchup or anything, just holler."

"But I..."

She was gone again before he could say more. Only a moment later, though, Hannah scooped up the plate. "That's not your breakfast."

"I know. I haven't ordered yet. What do you recommend?"

"That you eat someplace else. Yates has several restaurants. They've got a pretty good motel, too. You would probably be a lot more comfortable over there."

"I'm comfortable here. I'll have the number 3."

That sullen look was back in her eyes. "You know, I don't have to serve you."

"So what are you going to do? Call the sheriff and have him remove me from the premises?"

"He'd do it, no questions asked."

Leaning closer, he lowered his voice so no one else could hear. "You think so? A suspect in a murder case, at the motel where he claims he was at the time of the murder, and a woman who, except for the hair, perfectly matches his description of the woman he was with at the time of the murder. You don't think he'd have a question or two about that?"

Scowling fiercely, she yanked the order pad from her apron pocket. "One number 3. How do you want the eggs?"

"Over easy. With bacon and hash browns. And a Coke."

He grinned as she stalked off, irritation obvious in every stiff line of her body.

''That Hannah's a pretty one, isn't she?''

Mick took a deep drink of coffee before swiveling to face his neighbor. ''Yeah, she is.'' Not like Elizabeth, who was all pure, hot and fluid sexual heat, but not plain, either, as he'd thought yesterday. So she made little effort with her hair, pulling it back in a ponytail or letting it hang straight and silky. So she dressed with the complete opposite intention of Elizabeth, to conceal, instead of reveal. So she didn't bother with one bit of makeup. She was still pretty—a sort of basic natural beauty that was innocent and sweet, even though he knew beyond a doubt that she was neither.

''She's a good girl. She works hard around here. It's a real struggle keeping the place going, but she's managed since it passed to her after her father died. Most girls her age would've refused to give up all their plans for school and a different life, but not Hannah. She's devoted to her family, and with the Clarks, that means being devoted to this place.''

Hannah Clark. He had frightened her, threatened her, insulted her and had sex with her, and that was the first time he'd heard her full name. It fitted her—sort of old-fashioned, sort of plain. Sort of pretty.

The kitchen door swung open, and Hannah, still scowling and balancing four plates, came through. She delivered the other three first, then brought his, setting it down almost hard enough to crack the heavy dish. ''One number 3,'' she said defiantly, and one look at the plate showed why. Instead of over easy, the eggs were fried almost to a crisp. The bacon was sausage, and the hash browns were biscuits and gravy.

He grinned. ''Lucky for you, I'm easy to please. Of course, you already knew that, didn't you?''

Her face flushed. He *had* been easy Saturday night. He'd

been celibate so long that the mere prospect of sex had been painful. The first couple of times had been quick, desperate, needy as hell, but she hadn't minded. She'd been needy, too. The last two times had been lazy, a slow, killing buildup of hunger and heat, a leisurely exploration that had sharpened, intensified, then shattered. The first two had been easy satisfaction. So had the last two.

She set a glass of pop in front of him, then left. He watched her while he ate—clearing dishes from tables, running the cash register, checking out guests, delivering orders from the kitchen. In the forty-five minutes until the dining room was empty, she didn't slow down for a second. Even when he was the only customer left, she didn't stop but swept the floor, washed the counter, restored order to the menus tossed in a basket—anything to avoid dealing with him. That was all right. He was incredibly patient.

Finally the kitchen door opened, and three women emerged—Merrilee, Hannah's grandmother Sylvie, and a round, white-haired woman who would have looked the perfect granny if not for the sour look on her face and the unlit cigarette dangling from the corner of her mouth. Two of them walked on past, but Sylvie stopped short when her gaze settled on him. "What's *he* doing here?"

Hannah, refilling napkin dispensers at the end of the counter, refused to look up. "He's having breakfast."

"Do you know who he is?"

"Yes. He's a guest."

Sylvie's eyes widened. "Huh-uh. Not in my motel."

"Need I remind you that it hasn't been your motel since you and Granddaddy signed it over to Mom and Dad?"

"That murder I was telling you about? This is the man the sheriff believes did it. The man who claims he was right here with some mystery woman while someone was bashing in his poor wife's skull. We don't need his kind here."

As Mick watched, a dozen napkins fluttered from Hannah's trembling hands to the floor. Grabbing them up, she dropped them in the trash, then shoved her hands into her pockets. "His kind, Sylvie? You mean the kind with money to pay? It's pretty obvious looking around here that we haven't been catering to that kind of guest for a good long while."

"Hannah, we don't need trouble."

"For heaven's sake, Sylvie, we're renting him a room. That's all."

That wasn't quite all. Of course, he couldn't blame her for not wanting to go into more detail with her grandmother. Sylvie might be an old woman, but she still exercised a fair amount of influence, and Hannah obviously cared a great deal for her. She was risking her life for her.

Turning her back on Hannah, Sylvie came to stand in front of him. "Why are you here?"

"The sheriff doesn't want me going back to Oklahoma City just yet."

"Why can't you stay at the motel over in Yates?"

"Because I didn't spend the night with Elizabeth at that motel."

Without taking her gaze from him, she directed a question to Hannah. "You know anyone named Elizabeth with red hair and loose morals?"

Hannah looked right at him and lied, plain and simple. "No. No Elizabeths. No redheads. No loose morals."

"There. You've got your answer. Now leave."

Mick picked up the bill Hannah had shoved under his coffee cup a half hour ago, got to his feet and pulled a handful of small bills from his pocket. "Sorry. I'm paid up for a week. Hannah, how about ringing me up?"

She left the napkins and dispensers and crossed the dining room to the registration desk. Her movements were jerky, so different from the easy, graceful way she'd seduced him. Once arousal had overcome nervousness, every small gesture, every action, every move, had been womanly, pure sensuality. If he hadn't already been hard, he would've gotten so just watching her.

She announced the total, took his money and counted out the change on the counter, instead of in his hand. It seemed she would do anything to avoid touching him—and too often, touching her was all he could think of.

He added a couple of ones to the change and slid it toward her. "Keep it."

"No. I deliberately screwed up your order, and the service was nothing to reward."

He picked up the money, rolled the bills around the coins and pressed it into her hand. "Take it. If I'd realized our little interlude Saturday night was a cash deal, I would have tipped you then—though a hell of a lot more than two and a half bucks. But since I was the idiot in the dark…"

She leaned across the counter, practically nose to nose with him. "Would you stop it!" she hissed, then sagged back, looking vulnerable again. "Keep your money. Here, keep *all* your money." Fumbling in the drawer, she pulled out the five one-hundred-dollar bills and threw them on the counter. "Just please stop."

She went into the room behind the desk, then came out with a housekeeping cart and made a quick exit. He watched until she was out of sight, then picked up the hundreds and tapped them together on the countertop. That reference to the money and the sex had been a low blow. He knew she was ashamed of what she'd done, knew she'd been desperate and believed she had no choice. He also knew that, while the money had gotten him into her bed, it hadn't bought her passion. It hadn't made her greedy and hot. She'd been alone a long time, too. She had needed the intimacy, too.

A thin, pale hand darted out and snatched the money from his fingers. He focused his gaze on Sylvie, who was looking at the bills as if they were funny money. "If you're going to stay, you might as well pay.'' She gazed up at him. ''You *are* going to stay?''

''You aren't going to call the sheriff on me, are you?''

''You haven't actually done anything deserving of it.'' Then she clarified, ''That I know of.''

''And I do have five hundred dollars cash. Or, rather, now you do.''

She returned the money to the drawer. ''It's been a long time since this place has seen that much cash at once.''

He bent to lean his arms on the counter. ''Business isn't so great, huh?''

''Nope. It's never been too great, but the last six, seven years have been particularly hard. If that resort of yours had opened up, we'd've been out of business for sure.''

That was probably true. Eagle's Haven had been a luxury resort, but with plans for separate units at budget prices. Brad had even remarked when he'd shown Mick the chosen site that they would most likely put the area motels out of business. At the time Mick had been too consumed with his doubts about the project Brad was pushing so hard that he hadn't spared a thought for what that meant to the people who earned their living from those motels.

Obviously it meant a lot. The effort to hang on to this place had driven Hannah to borrow a tremendous sum from Brad, and it had put her in the mess she was now in. She'd sold her body, and before it was all over and done with, she might pay with her life.

''It was never my intention to put anyone out of business.''

''But it would have happened, anyway. It still might. This place is too much for Hannah to handle on her own, and all she's got for help is poor Merrilee and three old women. She does her best, but she's not too handy with tools, not like her daddy and her granddaddy were.''

He was handy with tools. In fact, there wasn't much that could break that he couldn't fix. He'd learned from his father down in Texas, from his grandfather and the people he'd worked with. If it was part of building a house, he could do it, and do it well.

The old woman's voice turned pensive. "You think Hannah's lying about knowing that Elizabeth person, don't you?"

He wasn't about to answer truthfully. Instead, he turned the question back on her. "Do you?"

She straightened to her full height. "My granddaughter does not lie."

But she was afraid that, maybe this time, Hannah *had* lied. Mick could read it in her face. "No," he agreed. "Hannah doesn't lie." He pretended to mean it.

With a worried nod, Sylvie pretended to believe it.

It took Hannah little enough time to clean the rooms that had been occupied last night. Pushing the cart in front of her, she dragged her feet on her way to the last room. To Mick's room.

She hoped he wasn't there, but his pickup was still parked out front, and she'd seen no sign of him in the lobby or the dining room as she'd passed. She hoped he would leave the room while she cleaned it, but knew she couldn't be so lucky. He would stay, hovering over her, making her uncomfortable with snide remarks about Saturday night or frightening her with reminders of Brad's threats and his own.

She knocked twice at his door. When there was no answer, she unlocked the door and swept the room with a wary gaze. The bathroom door was open, the lights were off, and the bed was unoccupied. Maybe the sheriff had picked him up. More likely he was in the kitchen, sweet-talking Earlene out of a midmorning snack to make up for the breakfast Hannah had served him.

Leaving the door propped open, she opened the drapes, closed the connecting door and locked it, then gathered damp towels and stripped the bed. Housekeeping was a job she'd had since she was ten, one she could do in her sleep. This room required a little extra attention, though. Besides the fact that it'd been used only two nights in the past several hundred, Brad's efforts to reinforce that unused image had been impressive. The dust on the bedside tables looked as authentic as any of the other long-unused rooms.

She dusted, vacuumed, scrubbed and washed, and brought in a chair and a lamp from next door to replace what Brad had removed. Even with her best efforts, she had to admit when she was finished, the final product wasn't much of an improvement. It was still shabby. Everything was still old. It wasn't the sort of place most people would choose to spend the night.

It was the perfect place for her.

When she turned, she was surprised to see Mick standing in the doorway.

"Good, you're finished. Come to Yates with me."

She gave Mick a dry, disbelieving look. "Why in the world would I want to do that?"

"Because you don't want me making your mother or Sylvie suspicious about the exact nature of our…ah, relationship."

"Where do you need to go in Yates?"

"The hardware store. That leak is going to drive me crazy."

She glanced needlessly at the sink. All the faucets leaked, but she couldn't afford a plumber and didn't have a clue how to fix them herself. "You can't fix it."

"Yes, I can. I can fix just about anything."

Except this mess they were in, she thought as she shook her head. "I can't let you."

"Would it make you feel better if I promise to make it leak again before I leave?"

Rather than accept responsibility for the silliness of his question, she changed the subject. "Don't you have better things to do with your time, like finding a lawyer or arranging a—'' As his expression turned grim, she bit off the words and looked away.

"A funeral? I've done that. The medical examiner in Tulsa has released Sandra's body. The funeral home will pick her up later today and the service will be held tomorrow.

She had arranged one funeral—her father's—and that had been one too many for her. She didn't envy Mick the task of burying his wife, especially when he was suspected of killing her. By now the rumors had surely spread through their circle of friends—helped along, no doubt, by Brad. Mick would be the subject of speculation and gossip at what was already a difficult time. "I'm sorry."

After a long moment, he shrugged and let it drop. "I've also found a lawyer—though not the one Brad suggested. He's driving down from Tulsa this afternoon. While I wait, I thought I'd fix the faucet."

She pushed the cart through the door while he followed, then picked up the pile of laundry on the sidewalk and balanced it on one hip. "What if Brad's in town?" Silly question. She sounded as if she was considering Mick's invitation when she didn't have time to waste going off to Yates with him. There was laundry to do, windows to wash, supplies to order and other endless chores. Besides, the last thing in the world she wanted was to spend more time alone with Mick Reilly.

Being seen alone with him by Brad was the very last thing she wanted.

"He's in Oklahoma City, trying to expedite the collection of fifteen million dollars from the insurance company. He's not likely to drop everything to come here."

"And how much insurance are you expecting to collect?"

He looked puzzled. "The insurance on the resort was in

the company's name. It goes to whoever owns the company, not to either of us individually.''

''I meant life insurance.''

''None. We carried insurance only on me. If I died, Sandra would get my insurance and my share of the company. If she died...'' His shrug was awkward. ''I wouldn't be at a financial loss.''

Meaning Sandra hadn't contributed much in the way of money to their marriage. She didn't seem the type who had bothered herself with housekeeping or cooking, so Mick had probably hired someone to do that. She apparently hadn't shared her bed with him for a long time—according to Brad, they hadn't even lived together for more than a year—and she hadn't offered him friendship or wifely support, either. As far as Hannah could see, Sandra's sole contributions to their marriage had been to spend Mick's money and make him unhappy.

''Will the sheriff let you go to the funeral?'' she asked quietly.

''He asked me to stay in the county, but he can't order it unless he arrests me. Though honestly I'd rather be sitting in jail than attend her funeral. Everyone's going to think I'm guilty.''

''Even your friends?''

''Most of the people we socialized with were *her* friends. Other than Brad, my only friends were people on our crews. People beneath Sandra's notice.'' Shoving his hands into his hip pockets, he stared at the abandoned gas station across the road. ''Hell, I feel guilty even though I didn't kill her. If Brad hadn't wanted to get rid of me, maybe she'd still be alive.''

''You can't blame yourself for someone else's warped actions.'' She'd been trying to convince herself of that ever since realizing what Brad had done yesterday. She was luckier than Mick, though. No one had died because of her

actions...yet. If he was charged, convicted and sent to
prison, if he got the death penalty...God help her.

"So will you go?" At her blank look, he explained. "To
Yates."

"To the hardware store and nowhere else?"

He nodded.

"I have laundry to do."

"It'll wait."

"And windows to wash."

"I'll help you."

"And carpets to shampoo."

"Putting it off a little while longer won't hurt."

Looking down the sidewalk, she saw Sylvie standing in
the glassed-in foyer, watching them with hands on her hips.
If Hannah turned down the invitation and remained here,
Sylvie would be on her heels for the rest of the day, wanting to know what was going on between them. She couldn't
tell Sylvie the truth, but couldn't lie to her, either. From
the time she was a small child, she could wrap both parents
and her grandfather around her finger, but not Sylvie. Sylvie had always seen through her lies, no matter how innocent, and this one was far from innocent.

"All right. If Sylvie doesn't mind watching the office..."

"I'll meet you at my truck."

He went into his room, and she started toward the office.
When she reached the glass doors, Sylvie held one open
while she pushed the cart through.

"For someone you just met this morning, you two seem
pretty cozy."

"We were just talking. I talk to guests all the time."

"We don't have guests like him all the time. In fact,
we've never had a guest like him...have we?"

Hannah met Sylvie's gaze and held it, even as her cheeks
began to warm, even as the certainty that she'd been caught
in a lie began to grow in her stomach. "To the best of my
knowledge, last night is the first night Mick Reilly has ever

checked into this motel,'' she said evenly, hoping desperately that Sylvie wouldn't nitpick over her phrasing of the denial.

But Sylvie always nitpicked. ''He doesn't say he checked in the other time. Says he was brought here by a redhead named Elizabeth. Says he was in her room when his wife was being killed.''

''I was in Tulsa Saturday night. How could I know what went on here? Seems you should be asking Ruby these questions, since she was working that night.'' With a smile that felt as false as her words, Hannah pushed the cart around the desk and into the utility room. She wasn't safe, though. Sylvie came through the door as she unloaded the dirty linens.

''You don't have a clue who this redhead might be?''

''You know all my friends, Sylvie. There's not a redhead in the bunch.''

''I don't know this woman you went to Tulsa to visit. What was her name again?''

Hannah dumped a cup of detergent into the washer and tried to remember the name she'd written on the paper in her room. She'd been so shocked by Brad's revelation that she'd finished the call in a haze, making note of her alibi automatically without much of it registering. But the name... ''Rebecca Marsters.''

''And who is she?''

''I knew her from school.''

''Is she a redhead?''

''No.''

''So what about Reilly? Is he lying? Mistaken? Confused?'' Sylvie waited a beat. ''He doesn't strike me as a dishonest man or one easily confused. If he says he was in room 17 with a redhead, I have to give serious thought to the possibility that he *was* in room 17 with a redhead.''

After adding bleach to the hot, sudsy water, Hannah dumped in the sheets and watched the agitator pull them relentlessly down. She'd felt that way ever since agreeing to Brad's scheme—as if she were caught in a whirlpool of lies, regrets and guilt that kept pulling her down, that might spit her out but more likely would suck her under to drown. "I don't have any answers to give you, Sylvie. I guess only Elizabeth can explain that."

"Maybe Elizabeth—" Sylvie gave the name a sarcastic twist "—will take a notion to do so before they send that boy to prison for something he might not have done."

Drawing her self-protective instincts around her, Hannah faced the old woman with a steady expression. "Do you think I'm lying, Sylvie? Is that why you wanted him out of here? Because you think I'm somehow involved in his wife's death?"

Thankfully Sylvie looked aghast. "You would never hurt anyone."

"Do you think I'm protecting Elizabeth?"

She wasn't so quick to answer this time. "I think I don't know what's going on."

Hannah brushed past her. "Well, if you figure it out, let me in on it. Right now, if you don't mind watching the office, I'm going to run an errand."

"With him? I saw you talking to him, and he's waiting outside beside his truck."

Glancing out, Hannah saw that Mick was indeed waiting at the truck. "Yes, with him. We're going to the hardware store."

"He can pick up washers and whatnot without your help."

"You don't want me to go?"

Sylvie hesitated, then waved her hand. "Go on. I've got nothing better to do than hang around here. Why don't you get enough washers and whatnot so he can fix all the leaks?"

"He's a guest, not a handyman."

"He's a guest who happens to be very handy. Here, this

ought to cover it.'' Sylvie pressed a hundred-dollar bill into
Hannah's hand, then picked up the clipboard used for in-
ventorying kitchen supplies. ''Be careful.''

Her farewell made Hannah's mouth turn down. She'd
always been careful, and look what it'd gotten her: a shabby
motel with little future and a shabbier life with no future
at all.

Maybe even no life at all.

The hardware store in Yates was small but carried a wide
variety of supplies. Though most of the materials for the
resort had been brought in from Tulsa, Mick had frequently
sent one or another of the crew here for small orders. He
was grateful now that he'd never come himself. The fewer
places he went where someone might recognize him, the
better.

''You have plans to paint your rooms anytime soon?''
he asked as he selected a variety of supplies to repair the
sinks.

''We try to periodically. Why?''

''I'll show you how to patch the cracks and holes.'' He'd
noticed that the last time his room had been painted—a
long time ago—no effort had been made to fix anything,
and it showed. ''All you need is some Spackle, a putty
knife and a few gallons of paint. It'll only take a couple of
hours per room.''

She gave him a long, even look that he figured was leading to a refusal. Instead, when she replied, it was on a
different subject. ''You're getting too much stuff for one
sink.''

''You have more than one sink that leaks.''

''So I'll call a plumber.''

''You can afford me a whole lot easier than you can a
plumber. I'm free.'' He closed his mouth before the dig
that she was the one with a price tag attached could slip
out. He would prefer to think that she'd been foolish, reck-

less or desperate for affection than to know that she'd been paid—or, at least, promised payment—for seducing him. He would *really* rather think that she'd been motivated by desire—like him—and not financial gain. It was going to take him a while to get over the fact that it'd taken money to get him into her bed.

She was shaking her head. "You can't—I can't—"

"How about if I teach you how to fix the leaks yourself? Will that satisfy your pride or propriety or whatever makes you refuse?" At her reluctant nod, he added the last of the O-rings and washers, along with a couple of replacement seats, to the shopping cart. "So, what about Spackle and paint?"

After a long moment of indecision, she shrugged. "I suppose it can't hurt."

He added the necessary supplies to the cart before moving on to the paint. "Why don't you pick a pretty color and do your own rooms first?"

"I have to live in those rooms, and I don't like the smell of paint."

"You have sixteen rooms where you could stay temporarily." He meant to stop there, not to say anything else, but the words escaped in spite of his good intentions. "Seventeen, counting mine."

She stiffened and refused to look at him, and her cheeks turned pink. "White will be fine."

For a moment her words didn't register, but her eyes did—blue, wary, vulnerable. The delicate contrast of her skin did—pale gold brushed with the faint pink of embarrassment. The full curve of her mouth did.

Swallowing hard to clear his throat, he forced his attention to the paint samples in front of them. "Which white? Winter white, off white, bone white, Navajo white, antique white? There are a million different whites." He picked up a sample card and held it against her cheek. "How about this one, instead? Morning Blush. It's an exact match for your cheeks when you're naked and sweaty and you've just—''

She brushed his hand away impatiently, almost fearfully. ''Would you stop it?'' she demanded, barely able to manage a whisper.

He drew the sample back and twisted it in his hands. ''Stop what? Making you blush? Suggesting you could sleep with me? You did it before—at least, you had sex with me. I don't know if you slept at all or if you waited until I was asleep so you could run off.''

''Stop reminding me. Stop talking about it. Stop implying—'' She clamped her mouth shut and stared at the cans of paint.

''Implying what? That I would like to do it again?'' He made his voice cold and hard, spoke his words with great deliberation. ''I was sexually attracted to you before I knew about Brad and his money. I'm still sexually attracted to you now that I know.''

''Well, I'm not—''

He touched her jaw, and her denial died a quick death. ''Lie to your grandmother, to the sheriff, to yourself, but, darlin', don't lie to me. It's still there. Whatever made Saturday night the best damn night in eleven years for me is still between us. Don't make me prove it to you, not unless you're ready to spend another six or eight hours in my bed.''

Looking as if she might cry, she edged away from his touch, then turned her back on him. ''Forget the paint. I'm ready to go. I've got to get back.''

He watched her walk to the door, then moved a five-gallon can of Morning Blush from the shelf to the cart.

Once everything was paid for and loaded in the back of the truck, he started the engine and switched the air conditioner to high. The blast of cold air raised goose bumps on Hannah's arms and made her nipples rise to prominence underneath her thin shirt. She had nice breasts, nice hips, nice everything under those oversize clothes. He could understand not wanting to dress like Elizabeth all the time, but he couldn't understand wanting to dress like this. Her T-shirt was shapeless and, even tucked into her shorts, it swallowed her. The shorts were baggy, hid even a hint of the curve of her hips and reached all the way to her knees. Maybe they were fashionable. He didn't know, since Sandra had never allowed anything so casual as shorts in her wardrobe, but they sure as hell weren't appealing.

On the other hand, because he knew what they hid, they weren't discouraging, either.

"Are you really in a hurry to get back?" he asked as they drove out of town.

Her response was a mute shake of her head.

After a couple of more miles, he turned off the highway onto a wide paved road. At Brad's insistence, it wound through the trees, instead of making a straight shot for the lakeshore. Eventually, if everything had gone according to plan, there would have been a golf course on one side, a jogging trail on the other, with broad borders of well-tended azaleas that would have surpassed the springtime show at Honor Heights Park over in Muskogee.

But if everything had gone according to plan, Sandra wouldn't be dead. He wouldn't be under investigation for murder and arson, and Hannah wouldn't be in fear for her life.

"Have you ever been down here?"

"No."

"Not interested in the competition?" He asked it with a grin, but she wore the same stiff look as she shook her head. "I never wanted to get into the resort-building business. We'd made our reputation on high-dollar homes, and I wanted to keep doing what we did best. Brad insisted that this opportunity was too good to pass up, and I let him talk me into it." Honesty forced him to amend that. "Frankly, once I agreed, I liked the challenge. A million-dollar house was one thing. A fifteen-million-dollar resort was a whole different animal.''

''What went wrong?''

''We had problems on-site—weather, crew, materials. Brad had a couple of interested buyers before we even broke ground, but the deals fell through. So did the next one. The only offers he could get after that were for substantially less money than we'd invested, and he wouldn't consider them. He came up with the idea of running it ourselves, but I refused. The construction business kept us both busy eighty hours a week. We didn't have either the time or the expertise to run a resort. So we fought about it, and he looked for a buyer while this place continued to eat us alive. If it hadn't burned down and we hadn't managed to unload it, we would have lost everything.''

He rounded the last curve, slowed to a stop and stared. A few days ago a beautiful, sprawling four-story hotel had stood in the center of the site. This morning little of the structure remained standing. The floors had collapsed one atop another, and the heavy-duty steel beams that had supported them were grotesquely twisted from the intense heat. Imported Mexican tile, acres of wood flooring, railings and paneling, thousands of square yards of top-dollar carpeting and Palladian windows by the dozen. Two hundred luxurious rooms, two hundred beyond-luxurious baths, meeting rooms, restaurants, bars, offices. All reduced to a few tons of soot-blackened rubble.

And Sandra had been part of it.

The whole place was cordoned off with yellow crime-scene tape, but if he'd wanted to go closer, it wouldn't have stopped him. This was close enough, though. It was bad enough from back here.

After a moment he shut off the engine, climbed out and went to stand at the front of the truck. After another moment, Hannah joined him. In the stillness of the morning, he heard her tiny whisper. ''Poor Sandra.''

Sympathy and pity. He felt it, too, though Sandra would have hated it. "The sheriff said her body was found in what eventually would have been the poolside restaurant. Over there." He pointed to the south side of the ruins. "It was the one part of the hotel that was a single story, all tile, stone and glass, designed to be as much at one with the outdoors as possible."

"Then she... Her body wasn't burned."

He shook his head.

"How does the sheriff explain that? If he believes you set the fire to cover up the murder, why would you leave her body in the one place where it wouldn't be destroyed by either flames or falling debris?"

"I didn't ask. I wasn't thinking very clearly."

"So what happens now?"

"I don't know. The insurance company may pay off, or it may find some loophole, since one of the partners is the only suspect in the arson. Blue Water may or may not declare bankruptcy. Brad may or may not come out of this a very rich man. The only certainty is that I'm screwed."

"Brad can't have planned the perfect frame. It just can't be done."

He gave her a mocking look. "Have you ever met Sheriff Mills and Billy and Keith? The frame doesn't have to be perfect. Just sort of close is good enough to hang me with them."

Shoving away from the truck, he turned his back on the resort and walked toward the water's edge. Lake Eufala was quiet, serene, undisturbed by boat traffic this morning. The lake had been one of the few bright spots in his eighteen months on this project. After yet another disagreement with Brad or Sandra or yet another problem with the job, he'd come here. Sometimes he'd taken out the little boat tied to the dock. Sometimes he'd fished, and sometimes he'd simply sat there and listened to the quiet lap of water against the shore. On or beside the water had been the only place he didn't feel pressured, in over his head or lost.

Hannah's shadow fell over the water as she stopped beside him, a quivery ripple of arms and legs. He looked at it, instead of her. "How long have you known Brad?"

"I met him when he was looking for this place."

"How well do you know him?"

She became as still as the hot June air. She didn't want to answer, and he knew why, knew it as sure as he knew he hadn't killed his wife. Her sigh sounded explosive, her words ugly. "We were involved."

Jealousy streaked through him—irrational, illogical, but no less heated. He knew nothing about her—except that she aroused in him needs he had all but forgotten. That her skin was creamy and soft, her breasts full, her hips just right for cradling his. That her voice was more seductive than any he'd ever heard. That common words and sensual promises took on new meaning in her husky tones. He knew that one certain sultry look could make him hard, and another could finish him off.

He knew that she had helped frame him for murder. He also knew that she could help clear him.

And he knew he hated the idea of her with another man.

Continuing to stare at the water, he asked, "Are you still seeing him?" The question was heavy with hostility.

"No."

"Were you seeing him when he asked you to help destroy me?" He gave the words—*seeing him*—an ugly twist.

"No." Her jaw was clenched so tightly that her mouth barely moved. "Not for months."

He gave her a long, intimate, scornful look, then turned back to the lake. "Right."

"I haven't been involved with him for more than a year. Look at me. I'm not the sort of woman Brad has a long-term relationship with."

He didn't look. He knew she was right. For relationships

Brad preferred elegant, sophisticated women whose background was as privileged as his own. For fun, he chose women like Hannah.

The thought brought to mind a comment Sylvie had made yesterday morning when showing him room 17. *You're a fine-looking man and all, but Hannah likes men a little less rough around the edges...* Ironic. He wanted Hannah, but he wasn't her type. She'd wanted Brad, but she wasn't his type.

"Do you care?"

"I wish I'd never met him." The words were right. So was the tone. She meant what she said, and it eased a bit of the tension that held him rigid.

He glanced at the sun directly overhead. "It's almost noon. Your grandmother will be needing you in the restaurant. We'd better get back."

The last of the lunch customers walked out the door at one-thirty, and Hannah sank onto a stool. A short break for her own lunch, and then she would sweep the dining room, help Sylvie and Earlene with kitchen cleanup, throw a load of towels in the washer, fold sheets and about a dozen other tasks. Then, if she had any energy left—and she knew from ten years of experience that she would find it if she didn't—she would track down Mick to see if he was serious about teaching her how to fix the sinks. She'd never had any aptitude for mechanical repairs, mostly because she'd had no interest, but she was a bright woman. She could learn.

The kitchen door squeaked as it swung open, and Sylvie stuck her head out. "Come back and have a sandwich."

With a nod Hannah slid to the floor. Her feet protested—heavens, her entire body protested. She hadn't done nearly as much work today as she was accustomed to, thanks to her unexpected trip to Yates and the detour to what was left of Eagle's Haven, but she was already more tired than she usually was at the end of the day. Maybe it was because she hadn't slept well last night. Maybe it was Mick's presence or Brad's threats or her guilty conscience. Whatever the reason, she wanted nothing more than to find a cool dark place to hibernate and not come out until life was safe and sane again.

If it would ever be that way again.

She picked up a tub of dirty dishes, then pushed through the door. The temperature in the kitchen was just a few degrees below unbearable, in spite of the best efforts of two window air conditioners and two high-velocity fans. It was a cozy place in the middle of a rare January snow-storm, but in summer, Hannah imagined, hell would be just about as hospitable.

The heat didn't seem to bother anyone but her. Sylvie, in her three-quarter-length sleeves and her gray hair in a neat bun, looked as cool as the proverbial cucumber. Earlene seemed undisturbed, as did Merrilee, and even Mick—

She frowned at the sight of him, sitting at the family table with her mother and grandmother as if he belonged there. She had assumed he was in his room. She had assumed that even if he did venture around Sylvie, her grandmother certainly wouldn't make him feel welcome.

Welcome, hell. As Hannah put the tub of dishes on the counter next to the sink, Sylvie was serving him a big piece of dewberry cobbler, complete with vanilla ice cream and a jumbo glass of fresh-squeezed lemonade.

"Have a seat, Hannah. I'll get your lunch," the traitor offered.

"I'll get it myself." She took the covered plate from the top shelf of the refrigerator, poured her own glass of lemonade and crossed to the table. The only seat left was next to Mick. She put her dishes down, slid into the chair and peeled the foil off the plate. For ten years Sylvie had been fixing her lunch: a sandwich of some sort, usually based on the day's specials, and a salad, always with something for dessert. Today's sandwich was roast beef, the salad a gelatin-carrot mixture, and the dessert would be cobbler. Just before she finished her sandwich and salad, Sylvie would put the cobbler in the microwave, spoon on ice cream and set it in front of her when she removed the empty dishes.

There was comfort in such predictable behavior, especially since most areas of Hannah's life had become incredibly unpredictable. Starting with the man beside her. He scared her half to death. He had deliberately put her life in danger by telling Brad that he'd moved in here just so she would reconsider his demand that she help him. He had every right to despise her, and sometimes, when he looked at her the way he had at the lake or when he reminded her that she'd sold herself to him, she knew he did.

But he was still attracted her—to her body at least, even if he did feel contempt for her actions—and, God help her, she was attracted to him. Even though there was no future for such an attraction. Even though she'd helped jeopardize his reputation, his freedom and maybe even his life.

What she'd done was unforgivable. Refusing to make amends was unconscionable.

He wanted only one thing from her—an alibi. He'd made it clear in the store this morning that he wouldn't object to a little sex along the way. But when it was over, when he walked away—*if*, please, God, he walked away—he would never look back. He would use her, and when he'd gotten all he wanted, he would leave. It was no less than he deserved. No more than *she* deserved. Still, the prospect left her with a sleazy, dirty, used-up-and-thrown-away feeling. It left her with the utter certainty that it would be one of the biggest mistakes she'd ever made, second only to getting involved with Brad.

The conversation, carried on mostly by Sylvie and Earlene, continued around her while she ate. Suddenly, into a moment of silence, Merrilee spoke. "Hannah, why aren't you in school? And look at the way you're dressed. You know Mr. Haverson won't let you in class like that. Heavens, child, your hair needs combing, those clothes are much too big for you, and you haven't got a speck of makeup on. I swear, honey, how in the world do you think you're going to get Rodney Whiteside to look at you if you go out dressed like that?''

Hannah stiffened. They'd had this conversation a hundred times over the years, so she knew where it was leading, and she hated it. There was no diverting Merrilee, though. It always had to be played out. "I'm not in school, Mom.''

"Really? When was the last day?'' In one moment her mother's expression went from surprise to consternation to delight. "That means I'll have to plan the annual end-of-school Clark family outing. Let's see, we can do a day at the lake…but we've done that so many times. Wouldn't it be nice if we could go someplace for the weekend—the Ozarks or Dallas or someplace different. But your father just hates to leave this place overnight. Of course, it is a burden on Sylvie. But just one weekend… I'll talk to him. I'll remind him that you're almost grown and soon you'll be going away to college and we'll only see you on holidays, and we should have one big last hurrah. I'll go find him now.''

She rose from her chair and started across the kitchen. Earlene stared out the window. Sylvie sat with her hands folded tightly on the table. Mick watched curiously, and Hannah stabbed her salad with her fork, silently counting down. Just as she reached one, Merrilee's steps slowed, then stopped. She turned to them, her face screwed up, her blue eyes round and full of sorrow. Hannah hadn't been at the motel the day the sheriff had brought the news of her father's death, but she'd watched her mother relive it time after time. Merrilee's anguish that spring day couldn't possibly have been more potent, more heart-wrenching, than it was right now.

Her tears were almost silent, just soft hurtful sounds. She would cry until the tears were gone, and then she would continue with a quiet keening that could go on for hours. The following depression might last a few days or a few weeks, then in the blink of an eye, she would be smiling, cheery and talking to herself again.

Sylvie went to her, slipped her arm around her waist and guided her from the room, murmuring sympathetic phrases all the way. Earlene left the table, too, picking up her cigarettes and lighter from the counter and leaving through the back door.

It seemed a long time had passed when the fork was pulled from her hand and the plate moved away. She didn't look at Mick but, instead, focused her gaze on his hand—brown, strong, callused from a lifetime of hard work. So different from Brad's hands. So like her father's.

"How long has she been like this?" His voice was quiet, with no scorn or revulsion, with none of the mockery he'd displayed earlier in talking about Merrilee.

"She's always been…fragile." That had been her father's word. Most mothers were normal, some were sickly, and hers had been *fragile*. Like a china doll that might break. "Her problems were manageable until my father died. He was killed in a head-on collision on the way to the lake. She's never been the same since."

"What does her doctor say?"

She wondered if that was a polite way of making sure that Merrilee was under a doctor's care. After all, they were probably the most raggedy bunch he'd seen since leaving his own family in West Texas. Most likely he knew from experience that when money was short, medical care was one of the first things to go, but that wasn't the case here. There was nothing Hannah wouldn't do to keep Merrilee in Dr. Denton's care. "He says she has presenile dementia. It's an organic mental disorder, caused by a physiological or pathological problem. He says be patient with her. Watch her as if she were a child. Consider institutionalizing her.''

"Can't it be treated?"

"She's on several medications. You should see her when she's not. Then she's *really* crazy." She regretted the last comment, a dig at his earlier remarks, as soon as it was out. He didn't dignify it with a response. "Usually she's okay—the way she's been the past few days. But sometimes something sets her off and…" She shrugged. "And the answer to your next question is no."

"And what do you think my next question is?"

"The same question people always ask. Have I considered following the doctor's advice and putting her away."

He looked annoyed that she'd put words in his mouth. "Why would you do that? She's not dangerous to herself or anyone else. She doesn't require constant care. It's not as if she's completely dysfunctional. She's just detached from reality." He pushed his chair back and stood up. As he walked behind her, he bent, bringing his mouth close to her ear. "Let me tell you from personal experience, darlin'. That's not always a bad way to be."

Chapter 4

Mick was rinsing his dishes at the sink when a voice called from the dining room. "Anyone back there? Miz Clark? Merrilee? Hannah?" The voice was familiar, though the tone wasn't. Every time he'd heard it, it had been heavy with suspicion, smug condescension, distrust. This afternoon it sounded downright cheery.

"Do me a favor," Mick said as Hannah pushed away from the table. "Don't volunteer the information that I'm staying here."

"Sheriff Mills isn't a stupid man. He'll see that truck parked out front and know it's yours. If you want to go unnoticed, then you should park around back." She went into the dining room, setting the door a-swing. "Good afternoon, Sheriff. What can I do for you?"

"Hannah, you're just the girl I'm looking for."

The door came to a stop and cut the conversation to a low mumble. Mick shut off the water and went to the door. A narrow gap showed a thin wedge of the counter where the sheriff sat on a stool. Hannah stood opposite him, hands on her hips. She would have looked perfectly casual if her fingertips weren't turning white, if she wasn't constantly shifting her weight from one foot to the other.

Mills ordered a cup of coffee and a piece of Miz Clark's fine banana cream pie, then took the time for a few pleasantries. *How is Miz Clark? How is your mama? How is business? How do you like this weather? How did you enjoy your little vacation?*

From that last question, he worked his way down to business. "You don't get away often, do you? What with your responsibilities here at the motel and your mama."

"No, I don't." Even to Mick, who barely knew her, she sounded stiff and uneasy. How could the sheriff, who'd known her all her life, not hear it, too?

"In fact, that was your first vacation in... How long has it been?"

"Ten years. Since Daddy died."

"Your daddy was a good man." Mills waited for her to murmur agreement, then went on, "I imagine Miz Clark has already filled you in on what happened—that poor woman dying over at the resort and the fire, and her husband claiming he was right here in your motel with a red-headed woman name of Elizabeth. Do you know anyone fits that description?"

"No, Sheriff, I don't. Sorry." She started to walk away, but he called her back again.

"Hold on, Hannah. I'm not done yet. I know you're awful busy around here. I won't keep you too long. You know this Reilly fellow?"

"We've met."

"Did he strike you as the sort of person who would murder his wife?"

"No."

"You sound pretty sure."

"I *am*. I trust my instincts, Sheriff. Like you."

Mills chuckled. "I trust my evidence, and right now my

evidence is pointing directly at the husband. He wanted to get rid of his wife. He wanted to get rid of the resort. Crack her over the head with a pipe, pour eight or ten gallons of gasoline all around the place, and boom. No more nasty divorce, no more threat of financial ruin and, ideally, no evidence to point to you. Just ashes and soot.''

"Except, according to you, there *is* evidence. Sandra's body was left in the one place in the hotel where the fire wouldn't reach it. Why didn't he move it? Why didn't he want it destroyed?''

"Maybe the actual murder wasn't as easy as the planning. Maybe he panicked.''

The screen door creaked as Earlene came in, her cigarette break over. She gave Mick a look, but didn't show any curiosity as to whom he was eavesdropping on or why. Still, he felt embarrassed and more than a little guilty as he directed his gaze back to Hannah.

"And maybe he didn't kill her at all,'' she was saying. "Maybe whoever did kill her wanted it to look as if Mick were responsible.''

"Who besides her husband would want her dead?''

"I don't know.'' She sounded evasive, even a bit guilty. "I don't know that *he* wanted her dead.''

"This divorce was going to eat him alive. According to his partner, the wife had evidence of his infidelity and was going to use it to squeeze every last nickel from him.''

His *infidelity* was blushing now. Mick hoped the sheriff put it down to the heat and wished Hannah could better control her responses. On the other hand, he was relieved to see that she wasn't an accomplished deceiver, grateful that the lies didn't come easily to her.

"Reilly threatened to stop her, to get rid of her once and for all. He also threatened to burn down the resort if Daniels couldn't find a buyer right away. Then surprise, surprise, the resort's burned down and the wife is gone.'' Mills changed the subject with an abruptness that made Mick's nerves tighten. "So...what did you do up there in Tulsa?"

"Nothing special. Went shopping, saw a movie, went out to dinner and talked."

"You stayed with a friend?"

"Yes."

"And what would her name be?" The sheriff's voice became sharper, less genial, and the friendliness didn't disguise the fact that he was talking business again.

"Rebecca. Rebecca Marsters."

"How would I get in touch with Miz Marsters if I wanted to?"

Hannah drew a deep breath and clasped her hands behind her back, her fingers working nervously against each other. "I have her address and phone number in my room. If you'll give me a minute, I'll get them for you."

"Go ahead. Take your time. I'll just have another cup of coffee."

Mick leaned back against the wall beside the door. Rebecca must be a friend of Hannah's, the sort of friend Sandra had surrounded herself with, the sort who would lie to God Himself if their best friend asked. It was only through her friends' willingness to cover for her that Sandra had kept her affairs secret for so long. They had provided her with excuses and alibis until she'd decided that she didn't care anymore. He had learned to hate them almost as much as he'd hated her. For that reason alone, he would find it easy to hate Rebecca, too.

But he didn't hate Hannah. Even though she'd helped Brad frame him. Even though she refused to try to clear him. Even though she was putting her own concerns ahead of his freedom and his life.

No, not her own. That sounded selfish. Hannah hadn't cooperated with Brad—and she wasn't refusing to cooperate with *him*—for personal gain. Everything she'd done was for this place and her family—her fragile mother and

the three old women who depended on her. If she'd had
only herself to look out for, Mick had no doubt circumstances would be different. If she had only herself, she
would have walked away from the motel, the town and her
life here before agreeing to Brad's scheme.

She returned to the dining room and gave the sheriff a
slip of paper. He looked at it, then put it in his pocket as
he slid from the stool. "Tell Miz Clark that was mighty
good pie as usual. And give my best to your mama. And
you take care of yourself, too."

Mick watched Hannah watch him leave. After one long
moment, the tension that held her stiff drained away, and
she leaned on the counter for support, bowing her head. He
pushed through the door and joined her. "Who is Rebecca?"

She didn't lift her head. "I don't know."

"What do you mean, you don't know? You gave her
name to the sheriff as your alibi for this weekend. Who is
she?"

Finally she straightened and faced him. "A friend of
Brad's. I don't know."

He stared at her as a chill shivered down his spine. "You
let Brad provide you with an alibi? *Brad?* The man who
set this whole thing up? The man who's got you up to your
pretty neck in trouble? The man who blackmailed you into
this mess and is still blackmailing you to keep you there?"

"He told me to tell anyone who asked that I stayed with
Rebecca. He said she would swear that I was with her from
ten o'clock Saturday morning until one o'clock Monday
afternoon."

Curling his fingers around her upper arms, Mick gave
her a gentle shake. "Think about it, Hannah. The man
threatened to destroy you, to implicate you as my partner
in Sandra's murder, to take everything you have and put
your mother in Vinita. And you're trusting the alibi he gave
you? What if Rebecca Marsters doesn't even exist? What

if she does exist and the sheriff calls her and she says, 'Why, no, I didn't have a houseguest last weekend. I've never even heard of that woman'? For all you know, he could have copied her name and address out of the phone book.''

"But he told me—" She broke off, apparently—hopefully—realizing the futility of trusting in anything a lying, scheming murderer told her.

"He told you he would implicate you. What better way to do that than to give you an alibi that doesn't stand up?''

Looking frightened, dismayed and weary, she asked, "So what do I do? Call the sheriff and say, 'Sorry, I made a mistake. I wasn't with Rebecca Marsters, after all. I was someplace else, but I can't tell you where'?''

"Where were you? Besides with me?''

"I went shopping Saturday to buy the clothes and the hair-color rinse. After I left the motel Sunday morning, I went to Brad's cabin.''

Mick knew the place. He'd been there once before they broke ground on the resort. It actually belonged to Brad's grandfather and had been used by the men in the family for hunting and fishing trips for the past fifty years. The old man had offered it to Brad for the duration of their work in the area, but, beyond air-conditioning, electricity and running water, the cabin had none of the luxuries Brad was accustomed to. Instead, he had rented a steel-and-glass showplace on a bluff overlooking the lake.

So the cabin wasn't good enough for him, but it was fine for Hannah. Typical of Brad's thinking.

"Had you ever been to the cabin before?''

She shook her head. "He gave me the key and directions.''

"Where's the key?''

"He told me to leave it there. Under the welcome mat.''

"The job on the room here—making it look unoccupied—who was responsible for that?''

"Brad."

"I wonder if he's done the same at the cabin. Want to find out?"

"I've got to work."

"This evening, then. When you're finished." He released her, took a few steps back. "Want your first plumbing lesson?"

Wide-eyed and wary, she nodded. He wished he could tell her that everything would be okay, but he had no reassurances to offer. He might go to trial and face prison for the rest of his life, and she might let him. Brad might leave her alone, bankrupt or kill her. If her conscience got the better of her and she tried to help Mick, Brad would expand his frame to include her, and she would almost certainly face prison herself. Without a miracle, there was no rosy future ahead for either of them.

He retrieved the plumbing supplies and the necessary tools from the back of his truck, then went into his room. The space around the sink was limited, but there was no cabinet underneath to deal with. "First you have to figure out which side is leaking. You do that by turning off one shutoff valve underneath. If you shut off the left valve and the leak stops, then the problem is in that handle. But check both, just to be safe, because both sides could have a leak."

She looked from him to the sink, then back, as if waiting for him to do something. All he did was lean one shoulder against the bathroom door and gesture. "Go ahead."

She knelt, disappeared halfway under the sink, then came back up to check. The spout was still dripping. "When I turn off the water on the other side, do I turn this side back on?"

"You can't find a leak with both valves shut off."

She gave him a narrow-eyed look. "A simple yes will suffice."

Once she'd figured the leak was in the right handle, she got to her feet, and he gave her step-by-step instructions to repair it. She worked in silence, her lower lip caught between her teeth, totally absorbed in the learning. While there were repairs on this old place that required a professional's expertise, there was much that she could fix herself, if she just had someone to teach her—and the time to devote to learning, the money for supplies and tools, the time to make the repairs. She was already in over her head here, and there was no one to help her.

Except him. Temporarily.

Until he got arrested or cleared of suspicion. If he was cleared, he wouldn't care if he never saw Yates, Lake Eufala or this place again.

Though he suspected he might care a great deal if he never saw Hannah again.

"This place has a lot of potential," he remarked even as his gaze settled on a water stain on the ceiling that had crept more than two feet down the wall. "How long has it been around?"

"My grandparents built it in 1950." She looked ruefully at the stem she'd removed using a tape-wrapped wrench. "I think some of this is original equipment."

He showed her how to replace the washer, then returned to the subject. "With some money and a lot of work, it could be turned into a nice little motel. You could cater to the lake crowd in spring and summer, to the hunters in fall and the fishermen year round, and keep a pretty high occupancy rate."

"The only problem is I don't have any money. I can't make repairs or improvements without guests, and guests don't want to stay at a place in disrepair."

"How long have you been in trouble?"

"Since my father died." She reassembled the faucet, then bent to open the valve. When the spout remained drip free, she allowed herself one tiny smile of triumph before picking up the tools. "The motel was never a major success. Granddad and Sylvie did all right, and so did Mom and Daddy. But I never wanted to be in the business. After high school I went away to college intending to never come back for more than a few days at a time. I had all kinds of plans and dreams.'' For a moment there was such wistfulness in her eyes, then it faded and was replaced with grim acceptance. ''Now I just try to keep from going under for the third time.''

Before he could respond to that, she walked away, going through the connecting door into her own rooms. He picked up the bag of washers and O-rings and followed.

All too aware of the man behind her, Hannah went into the bathroom, set the tools on the counter and knelt on the vinyl floor. Years ago, when these quarters had belonged to her grandparents, her grandfather had done a little remodeling—adding the tiny kitchen, the glass doors and enclosed patio, building a closet into the bedroom and moving the sink so it was part of the bathroom and not in a corner of the bedroom. The changes made the rooms a little homier, a little less motel-like.

But it still wasn't a *real* home—not a house, with rooms of different sizes and shapes, hallways, space. At the rate things were going, she might never have a real home. She might go from here directly to jail. *Do not pass Go,* as her favorite childhood board game said. *Do not collect $200.* Or, in her case, ten thousand dollars.

Her mood turned bleaker as she worked. She couldn't handle jail. Oh, maybe if she didn't have Merrilee and Sylvie to worry about. Maybe if she were actually guilty of something other than stupidity and desperation. But she did have family to worry about, and she hadn't done anything illegal. Unethical, maybe. Immoral, definitely. But not illegal.

She had to disassemble the stems in both handles on this sink, replace both washers, then reassemble them. When she was finished, she turned the water on again, then stared at the sink. The spout had dripped for more years than she could recall. In the beginning, it had driven her crazy. Now she had become so accustomed to it that she suspected she would lie awake at night, unable to sleep for the silence.

That silence was broken almost immediately by Mick. "What was the ten thousand dollars for?"

Uncomfortable with the cramped location now that her work was done, she gathered the tools and went into the living room. Mick sat on the arm of the easy chair. She chose to stand at the window, even though she didn't bother to open the drapes. Instead, she stared at pale yellow curtains that covered ugly, rubber-backed drapes. "It was twelve thousand, actually. I've already paid back two thousand. We had a couple of particularly bad years. Our insurance increased substantially. Mom was worse than usual. Sylvie and I had both been sick, and the guests just didn't come. We couldn't make our bills. We were only a couple of weeks away from having our power shut off and the phones disconnected. We'd been turned over to a collection agency for the medical bills, and our restaurant supplier was demanding payment before we could get another shipment. We were about to be put out of business."

She had foolishly thought that was as desperate as she could possibly get. She'd been wrong. "I went to the bank for a loan, but our local bank had gone out of business itself, and the new bank over in Yates didn't think I was a very good credit risk."

"So you asked Brad for the money, and after a particularly satisfying evening, he gave it to you."

The muscles in her jaw tightened so much that her teeth hurt. "No," she said flatly. "I wasn't seeing him by then. I ran into him in Yates one day, and he invited me to lunch. He asked what was wrong, and when I told him, he offered the loan." After a moment's silence, she quietly asked, "Why do you do that?"

He didn't ask for an explanation. He knew she was referring to the sarcastic comment about her, Brad and sex.

For a long time she thought he wasn't going to answer. When he did, his voice was full of self-directed mockery. "Do you want the truth? I don't like the idea of you with him."

She would like to think that what he was describing was jealousy, but it sounded more like a case of revulsion that he and Brad might have been intimate with the same woman.

Still staring at the curtains, she went on, "Brad gave me twelve thousand dollars. It was a straightforward loan—interest, signed papers, regularly scheduled payments of five hundred dollars a month. The money went for bills, supplies, a few critical repairs. It was gone in no time. I set aside enough to cover the first four months' payments, hoping that by the time it ran out, I would be able to manage the payments on my own. But I couldn't."

And her failure had given Brad the perfect ammunition to force her into his scheme. On the bright side—though she had to look really hard to find one in all this bleakness—in becoming Brad's prostitute, she'd met Mick and had one special night to remember, a night she could never forget. On the down side, she'd destroyed his life, her own, her mother's and Sylvie's, and there was nothing she could do to make things right.

"What will you do if you lose this place?"

"I don't know. I'm not exactly overwhelmed with options or talents. I've proved I can't run a motel. I'm not particularly handy. I dropped out of school before completing my second semester, so I have no education to fall back on."

He stood up and started toward the kitchen. "Since you're ill prepared for anything else, we'll just have to see to it that you keep the motel."

"And how will we do that?"

"By proving that Brad killed Sandra."

"And how will we do *that?*"

"I don't know." He grinned over his shoulder as he opened the cabinet under the sink. "We'll have to come up with something. Starting with the cabin tonight."

She didn't want to go back to the cabin, didn't want to see that Brad had worked his magic and erased every sign of her two days there. She didn't want to face the truth of just how much trouble she might be in, didn't want to have to worry about whether the alibi he'd provided her would cause the sheriff to look at her as Mick's accomplice. She didn't want to do anything at all. She just wanted to wake up from this nightmare.

Since the kitchen sink was a different setup, he made the repair himself, then they moved on to the next room. By the time they finished, there wasn't a drip to be heard anywhere in the motel, and Hannah was convinced she could repeat the repairs in her sleep. While Mick put his tools away, she turned her attention to the laundry. She did at least one load a day, and sometimes, when they were lucky enough to fill more than a few rooms, five or more. It was another task she could do in her sleep. In fact, the only challenge around here was paying the bills.

And escaping Brad's trap.

Sylvie came into the utility room as Hannah began folding the sheets she'd washed that morning. The old lady took two corners of the first sheet, and they gave it a sharp snap before starting the folding process. A second followed, then a third, before finally her grandmother spoke. "Merrilee's resting."

"Good."

"What have you been up to?"

"Fixing the sinks."

"You mean helping Mick do it."

"No, doing it myself. He showed me how."

The fifth sheet joined the others on the shelf where they were stored. "He seems like a nice enough young man."

Hannah reached for the next one without answering.

"This place could do with a nice young man who's handy like him. You'd be amazed at how much easier running the motel would be if you had a husband to help. Neither your granddaddy nor I could have done it without the other's help. The same was true for your parents."

"I have help."

Sylvie snorted. "I know you don't mean Merrilee. Seems like we all spend more time undoing what she does than we would doing it right the first time ourselves. And I'm too old to be of much help. Besides, what I don't know about fixing things could fill a book." She nodded toward the door. "I imagine what that boy doesn't know about fixing things wouldn't fill a postage stamp."

"This is a big change of heart. This morning you didn't want 'his kind' staying here. Now you're talking as if I should drag him off to the preacher before he can get away."

Sylvie refused to see the inconsistency. "This morning was before I talked to him this afternoon. Besides, I don't mean him necessarily. There's plenty of nice young men out there who know how to take care of things, and I think it's past time you found one. You're not getting any younger, Hannah. You've got a future to think of, children to have, a home to make."

Not if Brad made good on his threat. By the time she got out of prison, she wouldn't have much of a future left, she would be too old to even think about children, and her home would be someplace like this. Dreary. Shabby.

"If finding a husband was that easy, Sylvie, I would have done it by now."

Her grandmother snorted again. "If you didn't set impossible standards, you'd've found one by now. I can't even remember the last time you dated."

"What about Brad?"

"Doesn't count. It was plain from the beginning that he would never marry you, and even if he would've, you never would've had him. I always figured that relationship was just about sex. Was it?''

In spite of her laughter, Hannah felt her face grow warm. ''You're not supposed to know anything about my sex life. You're my grandmother, for heaven's sake.''

''I know about sex. If I didn't, your daddy never would've come to be, and you wouldn't be here, either.''

After laying the last sheet aside, Hannah turned to the dryer and began folding pillowcases. ''Well, you're wrong about Brad. I liked him. I liked him a lot.''

''Did you ever for a minute believe he was going to get serious about you?''

Knowing all she knew now, Hannah was ashamed to answer. The truth was, she'd known from the start that she wasn't his type. Heavens, he'd told her so on their first date. But there had been some small part of her that had hoped, anyway, that she could be the exception to his rule, that she could be the average, everyday nobody who won the heart of Brad born-to-a-fortune-and-making-a-second-one-now Daniels.

''No. I never believed it.'' It had only been a wish in her heart, and not a very strong one at that.

''So. Mick seems a nice young man. He's got the skills to have this place in tiptop shape in no time.''

''What in the world would he want with a place like this? He's part-owner of a multi-million-dollar construction company,'' Hannah pointed out dryly.

''All the better. He's got the money to do things right.''

''He's also a suspect in his wife's murder.''

''Do you believe he did it?''

''No. But guilt isn't a prerequisite for a conviction.'' Especially when someone as cunning and determined as Brad wanted that conviction. ''Mick Reilly might be spending the rest of his life in prison—'' and she might be there herself ''—so don't go marrying me off to him, okay?''

''He probably wouldn't have you, anyway. You're

cranky and stubborn and convinced that you have to do everything on your own.''

And a liar, Hannah thought. A deceiver. A desperate woman who tried desperate measures with desperate results. ''Sounds like you're describing yourself.''

With a great laugh, Sylvie started toward the door that led to the quarters she shared with Merrilee. ''Even if I had other grandchildren, you'd still be my favorite, Hannah, because you're just like me.''

Once she was gone, Hannah left through the other door, went to the kitchen and filled a bucket with sudsy water, then returned for the weekly chore of washing the plate-glass windows. At least it was supposed to be done weekly. Usually she wound up waiting until the morning sun was merely a hazy glow through coated glass. It was the one job she hated even more than scrubbing toilets, and so she didn't allow herself to think about it. She just went to work, climbing onto a chair to reach the top, using the sponge side of the squeegee to wash away dust and fingerprints, the rubber side to wipe the glass dry.

''Don't you have a ladder around here?''

Bracing one hand on the wall above, she deliberately kept her gaze off Mick as she leaned across to reach the farthest corner. ''Somewhere, but I'm not going to drag it out just to wash windows. I always use a chair.''

''Great. Then you can fall and break something, and who will run things then?''

''I did fall once.'' She pointed with the dripping tool. ''Broke that tile with my knee. Didn't do my knee much good, either.''

He slipped one arm around her waist, and every muscle in her body tightened. He lifted her to the floor and, for a moment, continued to hold her. Not close. They had been much closer than this, intimately close, naked, together, their bodies joined. But still she felt edgy. Nervous, as if in a situation she didn't have a clue how to handle. She felt shy. She, who had stripped off his clothes along with her own, who had seduced, as well as been seduced, who had, in one long night, become as familiar with his body as she was with her own, felt *shy*.

When he raised his free hand, she tried to shrink away, but all he did was tuck a strand of hair behind her ear. His touch was gentle. His fingers were strong. His hands had touched her in ways that other, different hands had, but the sensations had been heightened. Because of the illicit appeal of sex with a stranger, she'd thought. Because what she was doing was so wrong. Because he'd been alone so long, and so had she, and they'd both had enough to drink to loosen their inhibitions.

Or maybe because there was something between them. Sexual attraction. Lust. Pure base need.

And though that was apparently enough for him, it wasn't for her. She didn't want to feel cheap or easy again. Once was more than enough.

He was looking at her in the same intense way he had studied her Saturday night when she'd invited herself to join him. She had walked up to his booth in the bar's dimmest corner and said what she hoped was a sultry come-on in a sultry voice. "You look like you could use a little company, cowboy." He had returned the look, but where hers had been appreciative, his had merely been measuring. After a long minute, he'd turned back to the drink in front of him and replied, "You look like more than I can afford."

The memory brought the same hot flood of shame that she'd felt then, when she had swallowed hard, tried for sultry again and said, "I'm not for sale, darlin'." Only because she'd already been bought and paid for. No, she corrected herself now. Bought. Not yet paid for. Maybe the distinction made a difference to some, but not to her. She'd had sex with a stranger with the expectation of profiting financially from it. The fact that the payment had never been made didn't make her any less guilty.

When he spoke, Mick's voice was soft, thoughtful. "Your mother's wrong. You don't need makeup or different clothes to attract a man. Of course, I have an advantage over most men. I know what that shirt's hiding. I know the shape of your breasts and your hips. I know your skin is this same creamy gold all over." He rubbed his fingertips across her jaw, down her throat, to just above the ribbed neck of her T-shirt. "I know how hot you get, how sensitive you get, how the simple stroke of my fingers across your stomach makes you quiver."

She had trouble opening her mouth, forcing words out when her tongue was thick and her temperature was rising and her mind was focused on remembered sensation, but she managed. "Please...don't do this."

"Do what?"

"Don't touch me. Don't talk... Don't remind me."

"Remind you of what? The way you smiled at me in the bar? The way you touched me in the truck? The way you damn near burned when I kissed you? The way you whimpered when I was inside you? Or how about the way..."

She shoved the chair out of her path and started to walk off, but he caught her wrist and pulled her back, this time right into his arms. Right against his body—his clearly aroused body. She didn't struggle, didn't try to free herself. She'd already learned that he would let her go only when he was ready.

"Feeling a little remorse, Hannah?"

"Far more than a little. I regret ever meeting Brad. I regret borrowing money from him and agreeing to his stupid plan. I regret going to the bar Saturday night, and most of all I regret you." With those last words, she looked right into his steady dark gaze.

"That's too bad," he murmured. "Because I don't regret you at all. The circumstances, definitely, but not you." He leaned closer, as if he might kiss her, as if he might give her a whole new set of regrets—might-have-beens, could-have-beens—then abruptly he released her and moved a dozen feet back, where he leaned against the wall and folded his arms across his chest. The stance pulled his shirt taut. The soft swelling of arousal pulled his jeans taut. He watched. Waited.

She looked at him warily. He looked as innocent as any sinfully handsome man could, as harmless as any wickedly sexy man could, but he was neither. In fact, it was a toss-up as to who was more dangerous to her—him or Brad. Brad could take her home, her freedom, even her life.

Mick could break her heart.

"Excuse me." The interruption came from behind her, from the man who stood just inside the glass doors. Like Mick, he wore jeans and boots, but instead of a T-shirt, his was a polo in emerald green. He was probably in his thirties, not bad-looking at all and definitely a stranger in town. "I'm looking for Michael Reilly."

Hannah looked from the newcomer to Mick. It was his turn now to wear the wary look. "That's me."

"I'm Trey Landry."

The name meant nothing to Hannah, but it increased the wariness in Mick's expression as he pushed away from the wall. He met the man halfway for a handshake. "You're not quite what I expected."

"You expected a three-piece suit, a Jag and the instincts of a shark? I've got the instincts. I also have a few small college and law-school loans to pay off." He pushed his hands into his hip pockets. "Speaking of expectations, what I saw a minute ago wasn't quite what I expected for a man whose wife has just been brutally murdered."

Heat rushed through Hannah as she turned her back, dipped the squeegee in the bucket and returned to work. Parked in front of her and just a few yards down, the only vehicle in the lot besides her car and Mick's truck, was an old Grand Am that looked as if it belonged. How had Landry driven up and parked without their notice? And what kind of lawyer was he? One fresh out of law school, it seemed, without the experience, expertise or wherewithal to handle a case like this. Given ten years, Trey Landry—great name, great face—might be one hell of a lawyer, but that would be too late for Mick.

And once it was too late for him, it would forever be too late for her.

Maybe it already was.

It was a still night. There was no traffic on the road, no loud guests, not even an occasional plane flying overhead. The sky was dark, clouds blocking the moon and stars, and the air was uncomfortably warm and sweet with the promise of rain. An infrequent flash of lightning to the west spread its glow in long fingers to the horizon, but the storm was miles away. Mick wished it were closer. He could use a good storm tonight.

He leaned against the faded siding beside his door and watched Hannah through the glass. She stood behind the counter in the office, head bent over work, shoulders rounded. She'd had a long day and probably wanted nothing more than to go to bed. He felt guilty about imposing his will on her, but he needed to see Brad's cabin.

And he wanted to spend more time with her.

The lawyer had taken up the rest of his afternoon and the first few hours of his evening. He'd asked more questions than the sheriff had ever dreamed of, and he'd accepted Mick's answers with no indication of whether he believed them. He had said his schedule was tight, that he would be back Sunday unless something happened before then. Before he'd left, he'd given Mick a warning. "Your wife was murdered a few nights ago," he'd said, his gaze never wavering from Mick's. "You've already admitted that at the time of the murder, you were in bed with a woman you know only as Elizabeth, and when I arrived this afternoon, you were all wrapped up with another woman. Looking callous, uncaring and promiscuous doesn't do much for your image as a grieving husband.''

"I'm sorry Sandra's dead," Mick had replied, "but I'm not a grieving husband. I won't pretend to be."

"The problem, Mick, is husbands who don't grieve tend to lose sympathy. They look real good as suspects. Have your affairs if you want. Just don't be so public about them."

Mick hadn't reminded him that he'd never been promiscuous or that Elizabeth had been his first and only affair. He sure as hell hadn't told the lawyer that Elizabeth and Hannah were one and the same. What purpose would it serve? If Landry questioned her, she would deny it. Besides, he'd made a promise that if she told him who set him up, he wouldn't name her to the sheriff or anyone else. If telling would benefit him, maybe he would break that promise. Since it wouldn't…

The rumble of a car drew his attention to the parking lot. The night clerk had arrived. She climbed out and made her way inside, limping heavily, carrying her weight with little ease. Hannah, the elderly and the infirm. She claimed she was no good at running a motel, but with the help she'd had, she'd done okay.

The two women talked for a few minutes before Hannah finally came out. Her head down, her hands in her pockets, she made her way along the sidewalk, passing from light into shadow, then into light again. He waited until she was only a few yards away before he stepped in front of her. "Ready?"

She looked up. The weariness that he'd recognized at a distance was more prominent up close, in the droop of her mouth and the shadows underneath her eyes. She didn't try to back out, though. "Sure. You have a flashlight?"

He nodded, then unlocked the passenger door and held

it open for her. Once she was inside, he circled around and joined her. "We'll make it quick. I know you're tired."

"No more so than usual. Head toward Yates."

He followed her directions, eventually turning onto a dirt road that wound through the trees and offered occasional glimpses of the lake, a shadow among other shadows. There were turnoffs along the way, but he followed the road until it ended about fifteen feet in front of the Daniels cabin.

Once he shut off the headlights, it was eerily dark. He sat for a moment, listening to the sounds of the engine settling, then to the sounds of the night—tree frogs, crickets, whippoorwills. The lapping of water against the shore. The soft, uneven whispers of Hannah's breathing.

She sat all the way across the seat, right against the door. She wasn't looking at the cabin or at him, but off into the dark woods.

"Nice place," he commented.

"Uh-huh. But not nice enough for Brad."

"Did you…" He thought of the word he'd been about to say, discarded it and chose another less important. "Did you care about him?"

She was silent a long time. In the darkness he couldn't get even a hint of her feelings from her too-expressive eyes. "I liked him," she admitted. "Yes, I cared about him. But I wasn't heartbroken when it ended."

He wondered if that was true and decided that he wanted it to be, so it was. He didn't leave it at that, though. "Have you ever been heartbroken?"

"When my grandfather died. When my father died. When I realized that I was stuck at that motel for the rest of my mother's life. For the rest of my life."

"You hate it that much?"

"I just wanted something—" she shrugged "—different."

She didn't go into detail, and he didn't ask, because he suspected her *different* was very similar to the *different* he'd been looking for when he'd left the family farm seventeen years ago. A life with less hardship. A town where not everyone knew him. A place with people his own age. A place with choices. His hometown in West Texas had one grocery store, one café, one bank, two gas stations and four churches. Sunshine offered even less.

Living in Monroe had been hard for him, and Sunshine was hard for Hannah. There was no one to date, certainly no one to fall in love with and marry, no one to merely be friends with. There was not much chance of a future different from her immediate past, just a lifetime of hard work, little money and no one but her ill mother and old people who desperately needed her.

Where would she have gone? What would she have done? He doubted that she knew, just so long as it was different. But if she'd been able to live her dreams, he would have missed meeting her. He would have missed the best night of sex he'd ever experienced. *Then* he would have had regrets.

As a trickle of sweat slid down his back, he realized that it had grown uncomfortably warm in the truck. Pulling the flashlight from under the seat, he got out. By the time he reached the end of the flagstone path that led to the steps, Hannah was beside him. She retrieved the key from under the doormat and handed it to him. In spite of the heat, her fingers were cool and clammy.

He opened the door and was reaching for the light switch when she stopped him. "Brad said he can see the place from the house he rented. If he's there and he sees lights over here..."

"He's probably still in Oklahoma City."

"But we don't know that for sure." She left his side and disappeared into the darkness, leaving only a trail of small sounds for him to track her movement. Soon he heard the metallic stirring of venetian blinds, followed by the rustle of drawn curtains. Then she reappeared. "That should help hide the flashlight."

He flashed the powerful beam around the room. This was the living room, dining room and kitchen all in one, and it filled half the house. The other half was bedrooms, three of them, with a single bathroom to share.

Dust floated on the air and collected on every flat surface the light skimmed across, including the wood floor. The room was warm and stuffy, as if it'd been shut up too long. Out of curiosity he went to the kitchen sink and turned a handle. No water came out. He turned a burner on the gas stove. No pilot light, no flame, no smell of gas. He turned the switch on a lamp. No light.

"He's had everything shut off since I was here," Hannah whispered.

"Yeah." He flashed the light on the refrigerator. It was pulled out from the wall and unplugged, with the door propped open. It looked as if it'd been that way for a long long time. The trash can in the kitchen corner was empty and coated with dust. "Which bedroom did you use?"

She led the way to the back room, the one with a view of the lake. The bed was stripped bare, and the dust was heavy. The room looked exactly like the two bedrooms that had gone unused. So did the bathroom.

Without a word, Hannah turned and walked out of the cabin. Mick returned the curtains and blinds to their former positions, locked up and put the key back, then sat down on the steps beside her.

"As long as I cooperate with Brad," she said softly, "his friend in Tulsa will support my alibi. But if he decides he can't trust me, the alibi's blown. And if I try to tell the sheriff the truth, well, that's blown, too. He'll take one look at this place and believe that no one's been here in months. He'll think that I was supposed to be your alibi and you were supposed to be mine, but in fact, we killed Sandra together. And Brad will help him reach that conclusion by telling him that we'd been having an affair, that I was pressuring you to get rid of Sandra without letting her take all your money.''

Mick didn't say anything.

''So what do we do?''

''We find proof that Brad killed her and set the fire.''

''And how do we do that?''

''I don't know. It would help if he had a motive for killing Sandra, other than simply getting rid of me. Look at him. He comes from a powerful, highly respected family. He's charming, intelligent, likable. He's never been in any trouble, never even had a speeding ticket. No one's going to believe that he would cold-bloodedly murder an innocent woman just so he could force her husband out of a business partnership.''

In the silence that followed, lightning split the western sky. This time a low rumble of thunder accompanied it. Maybe they would get that storm, after all. He wished it would come right now, wished he could stand out in it and get washed away with all its force and fury. He wished it would sweep him up like a tornado and take him away to someplace where his problems couldn't follow.

Where Hannah could.

''Why were you getting a divorce?''

He glanced at her. Once again she was staring into the woods at images he couldn't see. ''You mean the fact that she hated the sight of me wasn't enough?''

''Did you hate her?''

''I resented her. I didn't like her. I didn't want to be married to her any longer, but no, I didn't hate her.'' After a long moment, he went on, ''My parents have been married for more than forty years. Both sets of my grandparents have been married over sixty years. I just assumed that when I got married, it would be like that.''

''But?''

''She changed. I don't know, maybe it was my fault. I

worked such long hours. I was never around. Maybe she got lonely or bored. Whatever the reason, she had an affair. And another. And another. It got to the point that the only thing she wanted from me was money—not my companionship, certainly not sex. Just cash, and lots of it.''

"Maybe she had an affair with Brad, only she intended to make it much more. Maybe that was why he killed her. Maybe the fact that he could blame it on you was just icing on the cake."

Mick looked at her. The idea that Brad could have been another of Sandra's men had never occurred to him. Maybe because he'd expected better of her than to seduce his best friend and partner. Maybe because he'd expected better of that friend and partner—though only God knew why he thought either of them would set limits on their betrayals. She'd bedded every other man she'd wanted; why should Brad be off-limits because of their business association? If Brad was willing to frame him for murder and see him in prison or dead, why in hell would he be squeamish about having an affair with his wife?

Feeling foolish, resentful and just a little more betrayed, Mick asked, "Much more in what way?"

"When Brad presented his plan to me, he said that if I slept with you, Sandra would get a better settlement—presumably at least a portion of your half of the company—and he would get control of the company. I assumed they had an agreement in which she would sell whatever percentage of Blue Water she got to him. But maybe she changed her mind. Maybe she intended to use her share to manipulate him into marriage."

"She wasn't his type. She grew up poor, and Brad knew it. He commented a time or two that no one would ever guess it, but he never would have forgotten."

"So she was like me. Not his type for a serious relationship. I could accept that," Hannah said evenly, and he knew by looking at her that she could. She had. "But Sandra doesn't seem the accepting sort."

"No. She had remade herself from a poor, no-account nobody into a beautiful, sophisticated, elegant woman, and she had come to believe the illusion."

Hannah yawned, and he slipped his arm around her waist and pulled her against him as he stood up. "Come on, let's get you home and to bed." The feel of her against him, the faint scent of her and the mere mention of the word "bed" were enough to stir his desire. He forced himself to ignore it, though, lest she sense it and pull away. Right now touching her was enough. Just barely, but enough.

Chapter 5

On Wednesday afternoon Hannah was going over the budget, wondering how much bleaker things could get, when Mick pulled into the parking lot. She watched him climb out of his truck and walk, head down, to his room, and knew that was the answer to her question. He was as bleak a sight as anything she could imagine.

It hadn't been a nice day for a funeral. Last night's storm had brought little rain and left a steam bath in its wake. Though there were chores she could be doing outside, she'd stayed in all day, seeking the slight comfort of the air conditioners, wishing for a break in the weather, in her troubles, in her life. Now she felt guilty for her silent whining, because things could have been worse. They had been for Mick.

She hesitated over the books, her concentration broken, her attention eight doors away. Finally, not stopping to question the wisdom of her actions, she left the desk, made a stop in the kitchen, then knocked at Mick's door.

He swung the door open, then walked away without a

greeting, stopping at the dresser where he'd been pouring himself a drink. When he finished, he faced her, still standing outside the open door. "You can't afford to air-condition all of Sunshine."

Wishing she'd stayed at her desk, she stepped inside and closed the door. Once her eyes adjusted to the dimmer lighting, she took a long look at him. In his charcoal gray suit with plain white shirt and tie in stripes of burgundy, gray and white, for the first time, he looked the part of highly successful businessman. He looked incredibly handsome, incredibly distant and even less her type than Brad.

"Want to keep me company while I drink?"

She looked down at the tall glass of iced tea she held. "I brought this for you."

"Thanks, but I brought my own." He scooped up the liquor bottle, let it dangle by its neck, then set it down again. "You come for all the gory details of the funeral?"

Stung by the mockery in his voice, Hannah turned and opened the door. Before she could walk out, though, he spoke again, this time without the mocking, this time with quiet need. "Please don't go."

She hesitated, then closed the door once more.

He took a long drink, then set the glass down and removed his jacket, hanging it on the back of the chair. His tie came off next, a splash of rich color against the dark gray. In spite of the day's heat, the shirt was long-sleeved. He removed the cuff links, rolled back the sleeves, unfastened the top few buttons, then sprawled in the chair and picked up his drink once again. "I hate funerals."

She set the tea on the dresser, then took the only other seat available—the bed.

"Sandra and I never set foot in a church together—we didn't even get married in a church—so I settled on a graveside service. It was hot, and these mounds and mounds of flowers were wilting, and everyone was staring at me, except her parents, who were too busy crying. Today was the first time I'd met them. I'd been married to their daughter for eleven years, and I'd never met them. And Brad..." Shaking his head, he took another long drink.

"Why hadn't you met her parents before?"

"Because she was ashamed of them. They knew that, but they loved her, anyway, and they mourned her. No one else did. Not the people she'd considered friends, not Brad, not me. Everyone else was there to see the suspected murderer bury his poor murdered bitch of a wife."

Hannah clasped her hands together. "Did you talk to Brad?"

"He sat beside me through the service. He rode with me from the house to the cemetery." He scowled at her. "Of course I talked to him. I treated him just like I always have. If I hadn't, he would have suspected that I knew. He would have suspected that I'd connected you to Elizabeth."

How hard had it been to treat the man who'd murdered his wife and framed him for it as an old friend? And yet he'd done it, in part to protect *her*.

"He asked about you—if I'd met you. He said he knew you."

Hannah's smile was bitter. So Brad admitted to knowing her. Not to being friends with her. Never to being her partner in crime. No, he merely *knew* her.

"He also asked about Elizabeth. I told him that I'd seen you around, that I'd talked to you but you were no help. I said I didn't have a clue who or where Elizabeth is. He said to give you his best." Mick's smile was thin. "Of course he already did that, didn't he?"

She ignored that last sly remark. "Was your family there?"

"No. My parents offered to come, but I told them no. The marriage was already over, and they never liked Sandra, anyway." He fixed his dark, weary gaze on her. "They would like you."

Not if they knew what she'd done to their son. That was enough to make her dislike herself.

He emptied the glass, refilled it and half emptied it again, then blurted out in a sorrowful voice, "She didn't deserve this. Damn it, neither do I."

But *she* deserved everything that had happened, Hannah knew. She had been willing to do almost anything for money—anything, it seemed, except murder. That made her little better than Brad.

Rising from the bed, she turned down the covers, then took the glass from his hand and set it aside. "Drinking isn't going to help anything. Why don't you get some sleep?"

"I don't want to sleep," he protested, but it was obvious that the emotional strain of the morning had worn him out. He reached for the glass again but, when she moved it out of reach, settled for her hand, instead. "Why don't you come to bed with me? I need that a lot more than I need sleep."

That. Sex. She might have felt insulted if she hadn't been suddenly so incredibly sad. "Get some rest. Then you can find someone to give you 'that.'"

"I don't want someone. I want you." He held her hand tighter when she pulled. "I don't understand, Hannah. We've done it before. It was good then, and you know it would be good again. Why are you so resistant?"

"I've already sold myself once, and I didn't like the way it made me feel. I don't want to do it again."

He gave her a charming grin. "I wasn't thinking of offering you money."

She crouched beside the chair, putting herself more on his level. "You weren't thinking of offering anything else, either," she said softly. "Just sex."

"And pleasure. Incredible pleasure." With his free hand, he stroked her cheek. "And passion. And need. And—"

"And that's not enough." She pulled loose, took his

glass and the liquor bottle and left the room. Outside, with the door firmly closed behind her, she lifted the glass and took a gulp, then spit out what she was able to stop herself from swallowing. Drinking wouldn't help anything. It would only make her sick, and she'd been feeling ill for about five days now. She didn't need to add to it.

She stowed both the bottle and the glass in the utility room, then returned to the desk and the books. She had no sooner sat down than the phone rang. At the caller's greeting, an icy chill crept over her.

"Hello, Hannah."

Her fingers tightened painfully around the receiver. "Brad."

"Is Mick back yet?"

Her first impulse was to lie. Before giving in to it, though, she swiveled her chair to look at his truck, then swept her gaze from one end of the road to the other. She wanted to believe that Brad was two hours away in Oklahoma City, but he could easily be somewhere nearby. He could know that Mick was already in his room, that she'd been in there with him. He could be testing her. "Yes, he is."

"Have you spoken to him?"

"I took him a glass of tea."

"The Last Resort doesn't offer room service."

"To a guest who pays double our rates, we do."

"Of course, you've already serviced him, haven't you?"

Her fingers clenched harder. "What do you want, Brad?"

"I just wanted to touch base with you. Didn't want you to think that I'd forgotten you." His voice took on a sinister tone. "Didn't want you to forget me."

"Under the circumstances, that would be impossible."

"So what does Mick think about Elizabeth?"

"I don't know."

"Don't you? Hasn't he asked you about her?"

''He's asked everyone. No one knows a thing. No one suspects anything.''

''Keep it that way.''

''Or?''

He ignored her question. ''I'll be back over there as soon as everything is settled here. I'll say hello.''

''Don't bother,'' she muttered, but he'd already hung up.

She kept busy the rest of the afternoon and through the dinner rush. Sometimes she hated waiting tables, greeting the same people day after day, pretending interest in their lives and forcing friendliness into her manner. Sometimes she just wanted to walk away and never look back. Tonight, though, she was grateful for the distraction. She was glad to see every table filled, emptied and refilled. The Last Resort might not do much business as a motel, but thanks to Earlene and Sylvie, the restaurant had a reputation for the best home-cooked meals for miles around. People who would never spend a night in their rooms—both locals and tourists—were more than happy to eat in the restaurant, and some of them even left halfway-decent tips.

She was down to only one table of customers when Mick walked in. He wore jeans and a white T-shirt, his hair looked as if he'd combed it with his fingers, and he looked sleepy. He looked sexy. He chose a table near the windows, away from everyone else. When she took him a menu, he waved it off but accepted the iced tea she also carried. ''Just give me the special.''

Two days at the motel, and he'd already learned what all the locals knew: no matter what was on the menu, Earlene's special was the best. Tonight it was tender fried chicken, mashed potatoes and gravy, home-canned green beans and thick slices of early tomatoes from Earlene's garden.

Hannah wrote the order on her pad and started to walk away, but his hand on her arm stopped her. When she turned back, he looked uncomfortable. Embarrassed.

"If I said or did anything inappropriate this afternoon, I apologize."

"You didn't." He had only asked her to go to bed with him, offered her sex and passion and nothing else. No affection. No future. No nothing but lust.

"I was so…" Tired. Worn-out. Overwhelmed. Instead of choosing, he simply shrugged.

She gripped the menu more tightly. "It's okay. I'll get your order in."

She escaped into the kitchen, where she waited while Sylvie dished up his meal, then handed the plate to her. "There are your desserts for table 3," her grandmother said with a nod.

Hannah balanced the tray filled with sundae dishes and pie, then delivered those before setting Mick's dinner in front of him.

"Can you sit with me?"

She shouldn't. There were a million things she should be doing to get ready for closing, but she wanted to sit. She wanted to forget work and obligations and enjoy a quiet moment with a handsome man. Without hesitation she pulled out the chair across from him and sat down.

"Have you eaten?"

"I usually eat around five, before we get too busy."

"You know, if you could increase your occupancy rate, you could hire a waitress to handle dinner and you could end your workday at a reasonable hour."

"Oh, gee, such a simple solution. Why didn't I think of that?"

Her sarcasm made him grin. He looked younger, handsomer, much less worried.

"I can't increase the occupancy rate, I can't hire a waitress, and I can't quit at a reasonable hour. I'm stuck."

His grin faded, and he paid his food inordinate attention. "Maybe you're not."

"What do you mean?"

"Maybe you could just walk away. If you could, it would leave Brad one less weapon to use against you. Taking the motel from you isn't much of a threat if you're willing to turn your back on it and leave."

"But I can't. My mother…"

"Likes it here. She's comfortable here. It's familiar, and it's the last place, probably the only place, she lived with your father. But that doesn't mean she can't adjust. Have you ever tried to take her away?"

"After Daddy died, she spent some time in Vinita. She couldn't bear it. She can't bear being any farther away than Yates, and even then only for an hour or two. She gets nervous." *So* nervous—pacing, crying, wringing her hands, fretting obsessively. Even taking her to see Dr. Denton, who was also familiar and comfortable, was a chore that left Hannah as frazzled and fatigued as Merrilee. "Even if she could leave, the debts would go with us. And where would we go? How would I support the three of us? I told you, I have no skills."

"Maybe I could help you," he suggested quietly.

"And what would you want in return for your help?" Her voice was heavy with accusation and wariness, while inside a chilly emptiness spread. Sex was the obvious answer, and it made her feel dirty. It also shamed her because, if Merrilee's well-being weren't so closely tied to the motel, she would give his offer serious consideration. She hoped she would turn him down in the end, but who knew? It seemed that ten years of stress and struggle had weakened her moral fabric. After all, she hadn't turned Brad down.

"What would I want?" he echoed. "Sex. That's what you expect me to say, isn't it?"

She didn't answer.

"Well, darlin', as desirable as you are—"

"Ma'am? We'd like to check out now."

Her gaze followed the voice to the family at table 3. Rising quickly, she tore their check from the order pad, then met them at the cash register. She smiled, made change and small talk and pretended not to notice the three kids leaving fingerprints all over the newly cleaned windows.

"Generous tip," Mick remarked after she'd cleaned their table and returned to his with a handful of bills.

"Some parents tip based on how messy the kids were." These three had been particularly so. She'd been on her knees cleaning food and trash from the floor, had had to wipe not only the tabletop but also the underside and the chairs.

"I can be very generous, too." His dark gaze locked with hers. "But I don't pay for sex. If I help you, Sylvie and Merrilee, it will be because I want to, because I like you, because I have the money and it's the right thing to do. And if we ever make love again, it'll be because we both want it. It won't have anything to do with money, blackmail, paying old debts, feeling guilty or anything else. Do you understand?"

She understood and appreciated his honesty. Still, she argued with him. "You don't know enough about me to be able to like me."

"I know that your family means everything to you. I know that you've devoted yourself to this place, even though it's the last place on earth you want to be, because of Merrilee and Sylvie. You've sacrificed your dreams and your future for them, and you've done it without resentment or bitterness. You work hard without complaining. You've struggled without giving in."

"I've also helped frame an innocent man for murder," she reminded him, bitter now. "I've sold myself—body, honor and dignity—to hold on to this place, and I couldn't even do it right. I got suckered on the payment."

The last bit of resentment Mick held against her for Saturday night seeped away. He still wished she had come to him of her own free will, because she wanted him, because she felt the same connection he had. But nothing he could say or do could make her feel as bad about her deal with Brad as she made herself feel. His anger or scorn couldn't match her own.

And that just proved she was a better person than she gave herself credit for.

"I'm going out to the site this evening to look around Brad's office. Want to go?"

She looked as if she wanted to refuse the invitation, but when she responded, it was with a shrug. "I guess."

"Don't sound too enthusiastic, sweetheart," he teased, but he couldn't charm a change in her somber expression. Finishing his tea, he got to his feet and picked up his dishes before she could reach for them. "Come on. I'll help you clean up."

"I can't leave until Ruby gets here."

"No, but you can sit down and relax until then. Come on."

Earlene was already gone for the night. Sylvie sat at the kitchen table with a glass of milk and a pensive look on her lined face. When they walked through the door, she gave them a long look that slowly became a smile. "We had a pretty good dinner crowd."

Hannah responded with a murmur as she loaded Mick's dishes in the dishwasher.

"What did you think of Earlene's chicken, Mick?"

"It was good. Just the way my granny fixes it."

"And where does she fix it?"

"Monroe, Texas. A wide spot in the road out in the western part of the state."

"I never did take too kindly to Texans. They're an arrogant bunch. You ever plan on going back?"

"Only for visits. I like Oklahoma." His gaze followed Hannah as she filled a mop bucket with hot water and soapy disinfectant that smelled unpleasantly of pine. She moved quickly, waited patiently, gave no sign she was nearing the end of a long hard day that was only one more in an endless line of such days.

"Really." There was no question in Sylvie's response. "And what is it you like so much about our fair state?"

"It's a long list." He didn't think it would surprise the old woman to know that her granddaughter ranked high on it.

As Hannah started to lift the heavy bucket from the sink, he took it from her, then set its wheels on the floor. "What do you want me to do?"

"Sit down. Have a piece of pie with Sylvie."

"She's none too good at accepting help. She thinks she can do everything all by herself." Sylvie's tone was confidential, her voice loud enough for Hannah to hear. She gave the old woman a dry look, then, using the mop as a handle, rolled the bucket into the dining room. "If you really want to help, the counter needs to be wiped down—since we stack the chairs on the tables, we clean them in the morning—and the ketchup, salt, pepper and sugar need refilling, and so do the napkin dispensers. All that needs doing in here is sweeping and mopping. I'd do it myself, but frankly I'm tired. I'm not as young as I used to be." A gleam came into her sharp eyes. "I'll make you a deal, son. You help her finish up, and I'll take over the desk until Ruby gets here so you two can do something."

"You have any suggestions besides 'something'?"

"Go for a drive. Head over to Yates and get an ice-cream cone. Go skinny-dipping in the lake. Heavens, I don't know. I'm an old woman. You young people should have a million ideas."

"Are those the things you used to do with Hannah's grandfather? An evening drive, ice cream, skinny-dipping?"

Her smile was distant and gentle. She didn't answer, though. She didn't need to.

"It's a deal." He picked up the spray bottle of disinfectant cleaner and a clean rag from the stack beside it. "But, Sylvie, a trade wasn't necessary. I planned to help her, anyway."

"I know. That's why I offered the deal."

He was grinning when he went into the dining room. The radio behind the counter was tuned to a country-music station, and Hannah was humming softly as she turned the last of the chairs upside down on the tables. He would bet she had a sweet voice, throaty and full of heartache, perfect for songs about missed chances, cheating hearts and crying-in-your-beer hard luck. He wished she would prove him right by singing along, but she didn't. He wished he felt free to take her in his arms and move with her, slow and easy, like lovers, around the floor, but he didn't.

She'd gathered all the salt and pepper shakers, napkin dispensers, ketchup and hot-sauce bottles and sugar and sweetener containers on the counter. He found the napkins on a shelf underneath the counter, alongside commercial-size containers of condiments, and set to work.

"You don't have to do that."

"Yes, I do."

"I don't need your help. I do this every day."

"I'm not doing this for you. It's for Sylvie."

She began sweeping in the farthest corner, working with quick, efficient strokes. "How do you figure that?"

"If I help you clean up, I get to take you out while she watches the desk."

"I think you got the short end of the stick. We were already planning to go out to the resort when Ruby gets here, anyway."

"That's business."

"And this is...?"

He watched her for a moment, wearing a pair of damnably baggy shorts that fitted snugly at her waist and no-where else, a T-shirt too big even for him and a pair of plain white canvas sneakers, with her hair pulled back in a no-nonsense ponytail and any makeup she might have put on this morning long since gone. "Pleasure," he said softly. "Pure pleasure."

A flush warmed her face, and she turned back to the sweeping with vigor.

Once cleanup was finished, she tried to renege on his and Sylvie's deal, but her grandmother all but pushed her out the door. As they walked toward his truck, he casually asked, "Do you have a swimsuit?"

"Somewhere."

"Why don't you put it on? Unless, of course, you'd rather take Sylvie's suggestion."

She gave him a distrustful look. "I try never to take Sylvie's suggestions."

"Liar."

She merely shrugged and let herself into her quarters. He went into his own room, traded his jeans for a pair of cotton trunks, took a couple of towels from the bathroom, then went to the truck to wait. Only a moment later, she joined him, still wearing the baggy shorts and baggier shirt. Peeking out from the neck of the shirt, though, were the narrow ties of a swimsuit top in bright coral, turquoise and purple.

He asked for directions to someplace where they could swim, and she gave them, sending him to an empty bank far from the nearest manmade light. The road led straight to the water for launching boats, and a weathered dock extended twenty-five feet from shore. He followed her to the end of the dock, sat down beside her and removed his shoes as she kicked hers off.

The air was uncomfortably close and heavy, but a slight breeze offered some small relief and helped keep insects at bay. It created ripples on the water and cooled the heat he'd lived with since moving into the Last Resort. Since meeting Hannah.

She blew her breath out in a loud sigh. "This is where my dad always came to fish. He was on his way here the day he was killed. The place belonged to a friend of his, and we had free run. I learned to swim here, to bait a hook, to handle a boat. We pitched a tent right back there and had cookouts under the trees.'' Another sigh. ''I haven't been here in years.''

''Because of your father?''

Her blond hair glinted with moonlight as she shook her head. ''No time. And Daddy's friend sold it a few years ago. Some construction company came in from out of town, wanting to build a resort, and made him an offer he couldn't refuse.''

''You mean this belongs to Blue Water?''

She nodded. ''The resort's about a half mile that way.''

If pressed, he acknowledged ruefully, he would have guessed they were at least ten miles from the site. He would never get used to these winding back roads—unless he lived the rest of his life here exploring them. The idea wasn't totally repugnant.

After a time she tilted her head back to study the sky. ''It's nice out here.''

It was a far cry from the barrenness of Monroe or the metropolitan feel of Oklahoma City, but he liked it. He liked it a lot.

''Want to go for a swim?'' she asked.

What he really wanted was to watch her get ready for one. To see her slide her shorts down her long legs. Peel her shirt over her head and cast it aside. Stand on the dock wearing nothing but a skimpy little suit, the moonlight gleaming on the pale gold of her body.

Then he would want to remove the suit, to touch her all over, kiss her, seduce her, even if she didn't want to be seduced.

''Go ahead,'' he said, his voice thick. ''I'll join you in a minute.'' When he was sure it was safe to move.

She got to her feet, stripped off her clothes as if it weren't the sexiest act he'd witnessed in a long time, then dove into the water, giving him only the briefest glimpse of bikini and soft skin. She swam until she was little more than a shadow in the water, then returned, treading water a dozen feet from the dock. "What was Sylvie's suggestion?"

"The one you didn't want to take?" He stood up, discarded his shirt and dove, surfacing mere inches in front of her. "Skinny-dipping."

Her gaze was level and disbelieving. "My grandmother suggested that you take her only granddaughter skinny-dipping? Right."

"She likes me. She thinks I'd be good for you and good for the motel." That last was just a guess, but when Hannah remained silent, he figured it was a safe bet that Sylvie had said as much to her. "She thinks you need to lighten up and have a little fun."

"And she considers skinny-dipping a little fun."

"She liked it when she did it with your grandfather."

She burst into laughter. "Enough already. I don't want to know any more than that. She's my *grandmother*."

"Who was once young, pretty and sexy. Just like you."

Her lingering smile wavered, then disappeared, and she swam away. He gave her a twenty-yard head start before he followed, easily closing the distance. The water was refreshing, and the company was pleasant, if skittish. All in all, he couldn't imagine a better way to spend the evening. Well, if murder and arson charges weren't hanging over his head. If their future and even their lives weren't in limbo. If she weren't skittish, running away from a simple compliment.

If, when this swim was over, he could pull her from the water, remove her swimsuit and his own and make love to her under the stars.

In spite of the cool water and the breeze that chilled him, his body reacted to that last thought, just as it reacted to damn near every thought of her.

Finally they returned to the dock. He climbed out first, then extended his hand to her. She looked at it with wide-eyed wariness, then moved a few feet to the side and lifted herself out. He chuckled in spite of his disappointment. "You're a smart woman, Hannah."

"Why do you say that?"

"Because if you'd taken my hand, I wouldn't have let go for less than a kiss."

She gave him a long bottom-to-top look that seemed even longer since he remained standing and she was sitting. "You would have been here all night waiting."

"Are you afraid to kiss me?"

She answered with more honesty than he expected. "Yes."

"Why?"

"Because it wouldn't stop there."

No, it wouldn't, he agreed. Not unless she was much stronger than he was. "And would that be so bad?"

Her only response was a shrug.

He'd been dead on his feet when he'd propositioned her in his room this afternoon, but he remembered her refusal clearly enough. He wasn't offering money, he'd told her. Just pleasure, passion, need. And that wasn't enough, she'd said in a sad, regretful voice.

What more did she want? An emotional bond. Affection. Respect. Caring. A commitment. The possibility of love. The same things he'd been looking for when he'd met Sandra, the same things he was looking for today. He didn't like being alone, wasn't cut out for celibacy, loneliness or meaningless affairs.

He liked Hannah. He respected her. He'd thought the instantaneous connection between them was as strong for her as it was for him. From the moment she'd sat down at his table that night, he had responded to her in a way he had never responded to another woman, not even Sandra.

But maybe the connection had been one way. Maybe it

had been more fragile than he'd realized. Maybe it couldn't compete with her shame.

He sat down, leaning back against a piling, and watched the pattern of moonlight on the water's surface change and shift with each ripple. Like his life. The changes had begun the day Brad had walked into his office to propose construction of Blue Water's first luxury resort, and they hadn't stopped yet. He wondered where he would be, how his life would be, when they did.

"I've never indulged in casual sex."

She'd drawn her knees to her chest and was resting her arms on them, her face hidden from view. At his announcement she turned to look at him. "What about Saturday night?"

"There was nothing casual about that, Hannah, and you know it. You can be brutally honest about everything else. Admit that, money aside, shame aside, that night meant something to you. Admit that the sex meant something to you."

Her tiny shrug was barely noticeable.

"I spent more evenings in that bar than I want to remember. Do you think you're the first woman who's ever come on to me?"

"Of course not."

"But you're the only one whose offer I accepted. If all I'd wanted was an affair, I've had more opportunities than I could count. Some of Sandra's best friends made offers. Women we worked for, women who worked for us and total strangers made offers. Yours was the only one that ever tempted me. It wasn't just the sex. It was you." His voice dropped to little more than an earnest whisper. "I wanted *you*."

When she looked at him, there was yearning in her expression and disbelief in her eyes. In whom, he wondered, was her faith lacking? Him? Or herself?

"What time is it?"

He checked his watch. "Almost nine." The sun had long since set, and dusk had given way to night. With a moon that disappeared behind fleeting clouds and distant stars, it was a good night for snooping. It was a better night for not snooping.

She stood, shook her clothes, then stepped into her shorts. When she started to pull her shirt on, he stopped her. "Torment me for a while. Leave the shirt off."

She looked at him, apparently debating the wisdom, then tugged the shirt on over her head, anyway. Before he could feel too disappointed, though, she slid her hands underneath the shirt and, with a little wriggling and maneuvering, brought out the skimpy little top of her bikini. With a smug smile, she dropped it in his hand, pushed her feet into her shoes and headed for the truck.

He looked at it—two small triangles that not quite adequately covered her breasts, the rest all narrow strings to tie here and there. It was enticing enough on. It was too enticing off, because now she was naked underneath that thin, worn shirt. Now, if he slid his hands beneath the shirt, it would be just his skin against hers. Rough and callused against unbelievably soft, with nothing to hide the swelling his touch would cause, nothing to conceal the tightening of her nipples, nothing...

Ah, hell, he didn't need her to torment him. He was doing a damn fine job of it himself.

After putting on his shoes and shirt, he joined her in the truck, where she was blotting her hair with one of his towels. He watched until she was done, then, without a word, he started the engine and drove back the way they'd come.

She directed him onto a narrow dirt road that ran into another, then finally onto the road to the resort. There he drove onto the grass behind the trailer that housed Blue Water's on-site offices, shut off the engine and retrieved the flashlight under the seat. "You can wait here if you want."

Hannah shook her head. While she had little desire to go snooping through Brad's office, she had none at all to wait alone in the truck, not in this spooky place.

And it *was* spooky. In broad daylight the burned-out hotel simply looked sad. In the pale moonlight, it looked eerie, a macabre jumble of shadows, plans gone wrong, betrayals and loss. A woman had died in those ruins—not a very nice woman, by all accounts, but even so, she hadn't deserved such a death. Before this was all over, it was possible that Mick's death could be traced back to the ruins, too, as well as her own. And Brad would live his life as he always had, unsuspected by the law, untouched by guilt, unfamiliar with remorse.

Damn his soul.

Mick unlocked the trailer door, then called for her to join him inside. With one last look at the hotel, she did so, pulling the door shut behind her.

The trailer wasn't overly large—maybe eight feet by thirty—and was divided into three areas. The middle, where she found herself, was a common area. It was into one of the offices on the end that Mick went, using the flashlight to show the way.

"Do me a favor. Stay at the window and let me know if you see or hear anything."

She did as he asked, adjusting the blinds to give her a clear view of the road as it came out of the woods and into the parking lot. Behind her, she could hear drawers opening and closing, papers being shuffled. "It would have been a beautiful place."

There was a pause in activity, then it resumed. "Yeah. Exactly the sort of place where I would never go for vacation."

She glanced at him over her shoulder, then directed her gaze outward again. "Today when you came back from the city, for the first time you looked like a successful businessman. Most of the time no one would ever know to look at you that you have money.''

''Having money was never my goal. I wanted to build houses and know that I'd done a good job. I wanted the responsibility, as well as the advantages, of owning my own company. I wanted my name to be associated with quality work and fair and honest business practices.'' He made a derisive sound. ''Jeez, I sound like a sap.''

''No, you don't,'' she said quietly. ''But you don't sound like a good partner for Brad. Making money is *all* he cares about.''

''Well, darlin', if I'd known back then everything I know about him now, I never would have become his partner. It would have been better for us all if I hadn't. Without all that money, my marriage to Sandra would have ended long ago, so she would still be alive, and you and I wouldn't be in such trouble.''

''So what will you do now?''

''If I don't go to prison?'' He was silent a long time. ''I don't know. Blue Water Construction is done for, no matter what happens. I guess I could bring back Reilly Homes. Or maybe I'll just start over with something new.''

She wondered how much interest he might have in something old, like the Last Resort. It would certainly be a challenge, and he wouldn't have to worry about making too much money.

She smiled tightly. She'd been listening too much to Sylvie. With the state her life was in right now, marriage, a future or even a relationship should be the last thing on her mind. She had nothing to offer any man with Brad's threats hanging over her, and nothing at all to offer Mick except the truth about that night. Even that, thanks to Brad, was worthless now.

''There's nothing here,'' Mick said, then dryly added, ''Of course. If there's any evidence anywhere that points to a frame, Brad's not going to leave it here for me to find.

It'll be at his house here or at home or at the office in Oklahoma City.''

"Want to go there?"

"It's too late tonight, but tomorrow, yeah. We can check my house, too—see if Sandra left anything connecting them lying around.'' He returned everything to the way he'd found it, did a quick search of his own office, then they left the trailer.

The stench of smoke that had hung heavy in the air yesterday was nothing more than a faint odor tonight, with the breeze. It gave little more than a hint of the tragedy that had occurred there—tragic for everyone but Brad of course, she thought bitterly.

They returned to the motel and Mick walked her to her room. After unlocking the door, she looked up to say goodnight, but he spoke first. "I'm sorry about all this, Hannah.''

"It's not your fault.''

"If Brad hadn't wanted me out of the way, he never would have forced you into this.''

"If I hadn't borrowed money from him, then defaulted on the loan, he never could have forced me. There's plenty of guilt to go around, but none of it's yours.'' It was hers, Brad's and maybe Sandra's, but not Mick's.

She started to go inside, then turned back. "My swimsuit top?''

He let it dangle by the strings. It looked so delicate and small compared to his hand. Just the sight stirred a tingle of desire deep in her belly. "Maybe I'll give it back next time we go swimming.''

"Maybe? There won't be a next time without it.''

"You could always go topless—or take Sylvie's suggestion.''

She thought about their too-brief time at the lake—the cool water, the sweet breeze, the lazy pleasure of being out at night with nothing special to do. If she'd discarded her swimsuit along with her clothes, Mick would have done the same, and they might not have even made it into the water. She remembered too well the sight of him naked, remembered too easily her body's response to him. They would *still* be back there in the moonlight.

Rather than pursue a conversation that threatened to become more intimate than she could bear, she shrugged. "We'll negotiate for it then. I'll see you tomorrow." She went inside and was about to close the door when he spoke.

"Hannah? I had a nice time."

Slowly she smiled. "So did I. Good night."

Chapter 6

It wasn't a long drive to Oklahoma City, a short distance to I-40, then straight down the interstate, but it seemed to take forever. Hannah stared out the window. After a lifetime of wishing she was anyplace but Sunshine, tonight that was exactly where she wanted to be—at home in her dreary little town in her drab little motel, worrying about how to pay for a new roof or running clean towels and extra blankets to guests.

Or maybe doing wicked things in bed with Mick.

She'd seen little of him today. After breakfast cleanup he'd disappeared with Sylvie and hadn't reappeared until after a trip to the hardware store in Yates. The rest of the day he'd kept busy doing minor repairs in the guest rooms. When she'd asked him at lunch not to, he had ignored her and gone right back to the job afterward. She hadn't wanted his help, but she'd been so damned grateful for it. It had given credence to Sylvie's assertion that running the motel was easier with a man to help. Mick never would have let the place get into its current state of disrepair. Where she would have had to spend a fortune on repairmen, he had the skills and the tools and needed only supplies.

But his stay here was temporary, and so was his help. Whatever the outcome of the sheriff's investigation, he would soon leave the Last Resort, Sunshine and her. She couldn't allow herself to start depending on him.

The offices of Blue Water Construction were nothing like she expected. Knowing Brad, she'd been looking for someplace stunning, expensive, elegant. Instead, it was merely a small suite in a strip of nondescript offices, with a dentist on one side and a tax service on the other.

Mick smiled knowingly at her expression. ''We don't often bring clients here. Usually we meet at their homes or mine or Brad's. Or, in some of our larger subdivisions, we use the model home for on-site office space.''

Dim lights burned in the secretary's office, along the narrow hallway and in the office he identified as Brad's. His own office, at the rear of the building, was dark, the door closed.

They went to Brad's office first, where the interior was much more what she had envisioned. At the doorway, a serviceable, commercial-type carpet gave way to a beautiful Berber. Instead of cheaply paneled walls, these walls were heavily textured and painted pale ivory. There was blond wood, rich leather, lots of metal and glass. It was all very elegant, all very expensive.

She would bet Mick's office had industrial carpet, a beaten-up desk, gray metal file cabinets and chairs that were strictly utilitarian. She'd once thought he wasn't her type, but he was definitely her style.

While he sorted through Brad's desk drawers, she circled the room, studying the art that adorned the walls. Four large paintings, all heavily and elaborately framed, and she would be hard-pressed to describe them as anything other than blobs of paint on canvas. Either she was seriously art-challenged, or Brad had been suckered out of a tidy sum of money.

"What do you think?" Mick asked from too close behind her.

"I think I regret Mom throwing out my rainy-day pictures when I was a kid."

"According to Brad, this guy's an artistic genius. Personally I like paintings where I can actually identify what I'm looking at. I'm not much into impressionism or postmodernism or whatever this is." He gave the room a sweeping gesture. "There's nothing here."

Of course not. They couldn't be so lucky. If there had been any incriminating evidence in the first place, Brad had either destroyed it or secured it someplace—like a safe in his house—where they couldn't get to it.

"Let me check my office, then we'll head on over to the house."

She followed Mick down the hall and into an office the same size as Brad's. That was the extent of the similarities, though. This room was plain, with little to distract its occupant from serious work. The best that could be said about the dark gray carpet was that it was durable. The desk and file cabinets were wood that had seen better days, and the padded chair behind the desk was tattered and worn, the leather repaired in one place with a strip of silver duct tape. There were rolled-up blueprints on every surface, and handscribbled notes covered the bulletin board that hung near the desk.

The only personal items in the room were two photographs, in simple black frames with plain white mats. The man in the center of both pictures was an older version of Mick, with gray streaking his dark hair, but still sinfully handsome. His mother was mostly gray, too, and plump, her face lined with creases from life, hard work and frequent smiles. The two elderly couples, she assumed, were his grandparents, married more than sixty years and still happy. And the younger couple...

"My sister Janey and my brother Tom. My folks, my dad's folks and my mom's. This is Janey's husband and their kids—" he gestured toward a group in the second picture "—and this is Tom's wife and their twins. This was taken at a family reunion a couple of years ago."

"You look like your father."

He smiled, pleased with the observation.

"Why weren't you and Sandra there?"

The smile faded, making her regret the question. "She didn't like being reminded that I come from a family of farmers. She refused to go anyplace that didn't have a luxury hotel. She never liked my family, and they'd given up trying to include her. She didn't want to be away from her twenty-two-year-old lover for more than a day or two. She hated me." He shrugged. "Take your pick."

"They look like nice people."

"They are. When they met Sandra just before the wedding, they weren't impressed. They had hoped I would marry someone like Tom's wife, someone like Janey. Like you." He murmured those last two words as if not meant for her to hear. Part of her wished she hadn't. Part of her was glad she had. "For my sake they tried to accept her, tried to welcome her into the family, but she refused to be welcomed. The only thing she wanted was for them to stay out of our lives. She had no interest in family reunions, family holidays or family, period. Not even in having one of our own."

A family of her own had long been one of Hannah's dreams, and one of Sylvie's dreams for her. How disappointed her grandmother would have been if Hannah had married a man who'd refused to fulfill that dream. How disappointed *she* would have been.

She turned away from the photographs. "Last night you

searched your office at the trailer, and tonight this one. Do you think Brad might have planted evidence against you?''

''I wouldn't put it past him. He murdered my wife to get me out of his way. He burned down the resort to get out from under the debt. What's planting a little evidence?''

Hannah waited in the hall while he shut off the lights, then preceded him to the front door. ''Is Blue Water really so valuable without you?''

''Brad used to say that he was the dreamer and I was the builder of dreams.'' He grimaced at the flowery language. ''Good builders aren't that hard to find. Dreamers, whose dreams can be made reality without breaking the bank, are. He'll hire somebody, not as a partner but at salary, and they'll continue business as usual. Brad will have all his profit and most of what used to be mine. Yeah, it's a valuable deal.''

She still couldn't quite grasp it. Killing one person and sacrificing two others, simply for money. She could never be that desperate, and she *knew* desperation.

Their next stop was the house Mick had shared, at least for a time, with Sandra. Located in one of the city's newer, more exclusive neighborhoods, it was exactly what she'd expected—big, beautiful, costly as hell. It was a grand house that declared, ''We have money,'' in every way she could think of—from the ornate electronic gate in the wrought-iron fence that circled the property to the elaborate landscaping to the imposing bulk of the house.

It was so far from the Last Resort that the two buildings didn't belong in the same universe. How could the man who'd built this showplace for himself spend even one night in her falling-down motel? How could she fantasize, even for an instant, that he could want to stay at her place?

They followed the broad drive to a side entrance protected by a porte cochere. He let them in through glass doors, then shut off the alarm and turned on the lights. They were in an entry with soaring ceilings, marble floors and gorgeous oak paneling. The hallway stretched to the opposite side of the house, where more glass doors led to another porte cochere. Bisecting the corridor in the center was another hall. Doors opened into elegant rooms, and straight ahead, the most beautiful and intricate staircase she'd ever seen curved gracefully to the next floor.

"What do you think?" Mick asked. "Does it take your breath away? Leave you speechless? Make you a little jealous?"

She was more than a little jealous, she acknowledged as she nodded. The money spent on this marble floor could remodel and refurbish the Last Resort with plenty left over. The wood paneling could keep it running into the next century, even with no guests. The chandelier that sparkled above them could give Sylvie a life of leisure. And any of it could stir a yearning in Hannah. After living the way she had her entire life, she couldn't even begin to imagine living with such beauty, such money-is-no-object luxury.

"This is probably the most beautiful house I've ever built," Mick said, rubbing the toe of his boot along the edge of the Persian rug, "and from the day I started it, I hated it."

She gave him a sharp look to see if he meant it. She wanted to believe he did, wanted to believe that he no more belonged in such opulence than she did. He looked as serious as she'd ever seen him.

"Want the grand tour?"

When she nodded, he led her through room after room, past fireplaces of serpentine marble and rough-hewn granite, over elaborate inlays of exotic wood, around furniture that looked every bit as expensive as it no doubt was. With each new display of luxury, she felt a little more out of place, a little shabbier, a little poorer.

At last they reached the master bedroom suite—Sandra's bedroom, Mick called it. It was a restful room in soft tones of peach and teal, not frilly but definitely feminine. The bed was kingsize and made up in fine cotton. The sofa and chairs were overstuffed, the breakfast table delicate in comparison. The bathroom was as big as Hannah's bedroom, and Sandra's closet was twice the size.

They were leaving the closet when Mick came to an abrupt stop. The corner he was staring at was filled with custom storage compartments, and most of the cubbies were filled with matching pieces of fancy luggage. The bottom compartments, though, were empty, and judging from the look on his face, they shouldn't have been.

"What's missing?"

He didn't glance at her. "Two suitcases."

"Maybe she loaned them to someone."

At that he did give her a look. "Sandra's friends don't borrow luggage. They all have their own matching twelve-piece sets."

"So she took them with her to the resort last weekend." Two large suitcases for an overnight trip was a lot, granted, but Sandra seemed like the sort of woman who didn't know the meaning of traveling light.

But Mick was shaking his head. "She drove down for the sole purpose of causing me trouble, and then she was coming back home. She had plans that night."

"What time did you argue with her at the resort?"

"Two-thirty, maybe three o'clock."

"And by midnight she was dead. Where did she go when she left Eagle's Haven?"

Mick shrugged. He hadn't given the question any consideration. She certainly hadn't gone to a motel in the area. His in Yates was the nicest available, and Sandra wouldn't have set foot in it. "To Brad's house, I guess." For once in their endless fights, Mick had walked out first, getting into his truck and taking a long drive before returning to his motel. Brad had probably told Sandra that she was too upset to drive, had offered her comfort, a sympathetic ear and refuge at his place. He had lured her there with the intention of killing her a few hours later.

Had she had any hint of his plans before it was too late? Had she been scared? Or had he kept up his game until the very end?

"Can you tell if anything else is missing?"

He gave the closet a long look. It was better stocked than many shops, with more clothing, shoes and handbags than one woman could possibly need. With such quantity and the fact that he'd lived elsewhere for the better part of eighteen months, it would be impossible to know whether anything that should be there wasn't. Except…

He checked a distant corner, then scowled. "Her black dress is gone."

Hannah gave a long rod of black dresses a skeptical look, and he impatiently shook his head. "This was her favorite black dress. It was an Armani or something. It cost a fortune, and she loved it. It hung over here with some other designer clothes. They're all gone."

"It looks as if some shoes are gone, too." She gestured toward the racks, where the neat rows of shoes showed a number of empty spaces.

The lingerie drawers were half-empty. A check of the bathroom showed an absence of makeup and toiletries. The diamonds, emeralds and rubies were gone from the jewelry cases.

"She didn't need luggage for a one-day trip to the resort," Hannah said quietly. "She certainly didn't need an Armani or precious gems. She had plans, all right, but they didn't include coming back here after fighting with you."

He leaned against the dressing table. "Let's assume she and Brad were having an affair. She would want marriage. Being married to someone with money was okay. Being married to someone with money, power and prestige would be better."

"But Brad wouldn't want to marry her," Hannah said,

"because he's a snob. When he marries, he'll choose some-one whose pedigree is as impressive as his own. I assume Sandra wouldn't take his refusal lightly."

Mick's smile was humorless. "That's putting it mildly."

"She would make threats—make problems. She would certainly refuse to give him whatever share she got of Blue Water Construction. Instead of having you for a partner, he would have you *and* Sandra, and I imagine she would make doing business impossible."

Mick nodded.

"So he made plans to get rid of both of you at once. He told her to go to the site, to fight with you, to goad you into making threats in front of the crew. Then he took her to his house, waited until he was sure you were set up with an unprovable alibi, and he took her to the site, where he killed her." Hannah gave an exasperated shake of her head. "And we don't have a shred of proof."

Worse, he wasn't convinced there *was* any proof. If Brad hadn't put together the perfect frame, he'd come damn close. Mick had been the sheriff's prime suspect from the beginning, and if Hannah's alibi didn't check out—and he felt relatively sure it wouldn't—it would be easy for Brad to move her into suspect status right alongside Mick. But no one suspected Brad of anything, except possibly poor judgment in choosing his partners, both business and sex-ual.

Wearily he rubbed his eyes, then let his hands drop. "After the first four or five affairs, Sandra stopped trying to hide them from me. Maybe she left something that connects her to Brad."

"Photographs of the two in bed would be nice," Hannah said skeptically.

"I wouldn't be surprised." He left the closet, glad to be free of its close spaces and the heavy fragrance of Sandra's perfume. The fragrance was in the bedroom, too, though, faint but unpleasantly familiar, fading as soon as he stepped into the hall.

Sandra had claimed the room at the end of the hall for her own as soon as she'd seen the blueprints. It was glass on three sides, specially treated to keep out the hot summer sun, and gave a sense of being suspended above the earth. He'd originally intended it to be a sort of family room, back when he'd still hoped that, protests to the contrary, there might be a family. When she'd made clear that there absolutely, positively wouldn't be, he'd lost interest in the room—hell, in the whole house.

Sandra had turned the space into an office, complete with a computer system that, to his knowledge, she'd never turned on, with a fax machine, a multilined phone system and a social calendar that filled two leather-bound daybooks. Basically, that was what the room had been used for—making sure that she was the most popular belle at all the balls.

Searching her desk took only minutes. Most of the drawers were empty, and the few that weren't held nothing of interest. There was a stack of faxes—invitations issued and accepted, lunches planned, trips discussed. She'd said nothing to anyone about going out of town last week, and her date for Saturday evening—an appearance at a charity ball—was penciled in on the calendar. So were her plans for the rest of the week.

So why had she taken suitcases, clothes and jewelry to the lake last Saturday? And where were those things now?

Across the room, seated in a chair of fine leather and primitive wood, Hannah stifled a yawn. She'd been up since six, and it was now approaching ten-thirty. If she got to bed before one tonight, she would be lucky. He felt guilty for bringing her along, but he was glad she was here. Somehow she made a difference.

"Are you ready to go home?"

She yawned again. "Take your time. I'm fine."

"There's nothing here. Let's go." He left everything on the desk exactly as it had been and pulled her to her feet. They walked silently through the house, their footsteps muffled on antique carpets, echoing on tile and stone.

They hadn't gone more than five miles in the truck before Hannah dozed off. A bump jerked her awake, and she straightened, but her head began drooping again immediately.

"Take off your seat belt and lie down."

In spite of her weariness, he could recognize the apprehension in her gaze. "I'm fine."

"I'm driving, Hannah. I'll keep both hands on the wheel. I won't do anything to you while going seventy-five down the interstate—though I'm flattered that you think I could."

Apprehension turned to disdain. "If I thought you were the kind of man who would cop a feel from a sleeping woman, I wouldn't be here in the first place."

"Then lie down. Get some rest so I don't feel guilty for keeping you out so late when you've worked a long day."

She still hesitated. There was something intimate—something vulnerable—about one of them sleeping while the other was awake. He'd felt it Saturday night when he'd awakened to find her watching him, all big eyes and shadows in the dimly lit room. He'd felt defenseless, exposed—and incredibly aroused. She had been aroused, too. He'd realized it the instant he'd raised his hand to her, unerringly cupping her breast, feeling the hard nub of her nipple, seeing the anticipation that quivered through her, hearing the soft catch of her breath. Just like that, with one look, one touch, they'd both been ready, and with no preliminaries beyond the necessary condom, he'd pulled her astride his hips and...

Feeling beads of sweat pop out across his forehead, he gritted his jaw on a groan, turned the air conditioner a notch higher and locked his gaze on the road ahead. "Suit yourself, darlin'," he said as if the matter were of no importance. At least that was how he wanted to sound, but the strain in his voice and the tension in his muscles made a liar of him.

Within a few miles she was asleep again. She dozed fitfully, awakening every few minutes to seek a new, more comfortable position. Finally, with a scowl, she yanked off the seat belt and stretched out sideways on the seat, drawing her knees close to her chest. Her head was bent at an awkward angle, the back of it pressed against his thigh.

"Come on, Hannah," he coaxed softly. "We've seen each other naked. I've lain underneath you, on top of you, inside you. I think it's all right for you to lay your head on my leg."

After a long moment of stillness she sighed and moved. The instant her head touched his leg, though, the very instant her cheek rubbed his thigh, he wanted to call the words back. It *wasn't* all right. It was too intimate, too tempting.

He managed the miles by concentrating on everything else in the world but the woman asleep in his lap. He stared at the road, gripped the steering wheel, controlled his breathing, thought only of getting home and going to bed. Alone. When he pulled into the Last Resort parking lot in front of room 17 and shut off the engine, he breathed a deep sigh of relief. They were home safe, and he had nothing more than the beginnings of an erection, not even enough for Hannah to notice.

Uncurling his fingers from the steering wheel, he sat back and gazed at her. She'd slept without moving for the last hundred miles. The sleep of the exhausted. He'd slept that way himself after the last time they'd made love Saturday night. It had been months, maybe years, since he'd felt so satisfied, so peaceful, and he'd slept like it. Even when he'd awakened alone and with no sign of his mystery woman, he had still felt incredibly good. He'd thought there just might be a happy ending, after all. They would manage

to sell the resort, he and Sandra would go ahead with their
divorce, and he would somehow find lovely, sexy Elizabeth
again.

Then he had gone back to his motel, and the sheriff's
deputies had come calling with the news of Sandra's murder.

Lightly he touched his fingertips to Hannah's cheek,
brushing across her jaw, tucking her hair behind her ear.
She was every bit as lovely and sexy as her red-haired alter
ego and a hell of a lot more real. Elizabeth was perfect for
an affair. Hannah was perfect for forever.

For a long time he simply sat there, stroking her face,
taking pleasure in simple touches that would have made
her shy away if she'd been awake and on her usual guard.
Finally, though, when the midnight heat became uncomfortable, he gave her shoulder a shake. "Hannah? Sweetheart, we're home."

She didn't want to wake up. He gave her another shake,
and slowly she stirred, tried to stretch but couldn't and
opened her eyes. She stared at him for a moment, dazed,
then looked around. "We're home?" Her voice was husky,
thick, erotic.

"We're home," he repeated, more comfortable with calling this place home than the house they'd left two hours
ago. Three guesses why that was—and any that didn't include Hannah didn't count. "Want me to carry you to
bed?"

She smiled sleepily, then pushed herself up. "I think I
can make it."

Even though he'd known her answer before he'd asked
the question, he felt a bit of regret as he climbed out. He
walked to her door with her, leaning against the jamb after
she'd stepped inside. "Want to invite me in? I'd be very
good."

There was that smile again, soft and drowsy. She'd worn

it Saturday night, it and nothing else, and he had been lost. He was feeling pretty damned lost right now.

"I know you would," she said quietly. "That's why you're not getting an invitation."

When she started to close the door, he blocked it with his arm. "Are you ever going to make love with me again?"

"I'm trying very hard not to."

"Why?"

For a long time she gazed into the distance before finally meeting his gaze. "I don't have a lot to lose, Mick. I need to hold on to what I've got." Too quickly she said good-night and closed the door in his face.

As he walked to his own room, he wondered about her words. What would a relationship with him cost her? There was the potential for hurt, for disappointment, for falling in love and not being loved in return. There was the hassle of location. His home was, for the time being, in Oklahoma City. Hers was here. Long-distance affairs often failed for just that reason. But he wasn't overly fond of the city or his house there, and his future with Blue Water Construction was nonexistent. He wouldn't mind relocating.

Provided he wasn't relocating to the state penitentiary.

There was Saturday night standing between them. Her shame. His initial anger. And, to some extent, tonight. She hadn't liked his house, hadn't liked the pretentious display of money. He'd seen the way she looked at all of Sandra's high-dollar extravagances, had watched her draw a little further into herself with each new excess. She had compared that place for which he was responsible with this one and found hers lacking.

But he didn't like the house, either. It hadn't been home for a long time. The minute he'd seen it through the gate this evening, he'd known it would never be home again. Other than the few personal things he still kept there, he wanted no part of it.

Suddenly tired, he went into his room, switched on the air conditioner and stripped for bed. He would work on changing Hannah's mind tomorrow. As long as the sheriff didn't haul him off to jail—thank God he didn't yet have sufficient evidence—he would have time.

And that was all he needed, all she needed. Time.

Hannah lay in bed Friday morning, tired but unable to sleep again, dry-eyed and staring at the ceiling. She had known from the beginning that Mick had money. He and Brad were equal partners in the business, and Brad had a ton of money, not just family money, so Mick had plenty, too. In an abstract way it was easy to accept.

But there was nothing abstract about his house. He had *money*, with lots of emphasis. Some might consider him wealthy. He certainly earned a hell of a lot more than she did—more, probably, in one month than she made in five years. He was no longer just Mick, who wore faded jeans and scuffed boots, who worked hard and lived in a shabby motel, whose only sign of prosperity was the truck he drove. He was Michael Reilly, successful businessman, part-owner of a remarkably prosperous company and a fabulously grand mansion. He socialized with the city's rich and powerful, lived in their midst, went to their parties.

He was, like Brad, a man who would find her good enough for a little fun, but not anything more. With Brad she'd been willing to settle for that.

With Mick she wasn't.

Feeling blue, she forced herself to focus on what was before her. The ceiling in her quarters hadn't been painted in longer than she could remember. Once it had been white, but now it was a grayish muddle with yellow water stains where the roof leaked. Her walls had been white, too, the same plain white as every other wall in the entire motel, worn now to the same dirty beige. There were cracks in the drywall, old nail holes that had never been filled in, gaps around the window and door frames where the caulk had shrunk long ago.

Maybe she couldn't afford new carpet, new furniture or a new roof. Maybe a few coats of paint couldn't disguise the fact that the motel was on its last leg. Maybe she was foolish to even make the effort. But there was a five-gallon can of Morning Blush in the storeroom and all the brushes, Spackle and mineral spirits she needed. There was no reason to let them go to waste.

And what would it matter? Would the fact that she had pretty walls for the first time in years make more guests stay at the Last Resort? Would it impress Brad enough to make him leave her in peace? Would it help Mick forget that he was living temporarily in a run-down threadbare motel? Would it make *her* look any less run-down or threadbare?

Wearily she left the bed, showered and dressed for the day. In the office Ruby was watching her predawn aerobics show, the knitting needles in her hands clicking in rhythm with the too-perky instructor's count. The smells of breakfast were drifting out from the kitchen, where Earlene and Sylvie were already hard at work, and across the dining room, Merrilee drifted from table to table, putting chairs on the floor, dreamily wiping a cloth across each top. Her hair was done, her makeup perfectly applied, her patent leather heels showing not a smudge. If only she'd remembered to trade her nightgown and robe for a dress, she would have looked lovely.

"Morning, Ruby. Good morning, Mom."

Merrilee came one table closer, and Hannah could hear her soft, tuneless humming. She moved the chairs, wiped the surface and never noticed that she wasn't alone.

Hannah waylaid her at the next table, setting the chairs on the floor before Merrilee could, taking the cloth from her and giving the top a quick scrub. "Mom, you need to get dressed. The first customers will be here soon." She searched her mother's face for some hint of acknowledgment, not even hoping for recognition. At first she found nothing. Then, abruptly, a delighted smile spread across Merrilee's face. Hannah's relief was short-lived, though, because the smile wasn't directed at her but behind her.

"There you are, dear. I was wondering when you'd stop by." Merrilee glided past Hannah to slip her arm through Mick's. "It's been such a long time since we've seen you. Now tell me, what have you been up to? No, no, not here. Let's go the apartment where we can talk undisturbed."

He looked at Hannah, brows raised, but Merrilee pulled him away, still chattering. "Have you had breakfast? How about coffee?" Speaking imperiously to no one in particular, Merrilee commanded, "Bring breakfast and coffee to my quarters. Something sweet—doughnuts or, oh, how about some sticky buns with pecans?"

Feeling frustrated, angry and helpless as hell, Hannah watched them go, then all but slammed the next chair to the floor.

"Honey, I know it's upsetting, but breaking those chairs isn't going to make everything better," Ruby said. "I know for a fact that you don't have any extras or the money to buy new ones."

She was right. No extras, no money, no choices. It was the story of her life.

"You want to be the serving girl or you want me to?"

"I'll get it." She finished with the rest of the tables, then went into the kitchen. A few minutes later, carrying a tray laden with food and coffee, she pushed through the swinging door and made her way into Merrilee and Sylvie's apartment.

Mick and her mother sat in the small living room. She was babbling about the cold weather this morning and the promise of snow in the air while he listened without even a hint that he'd been taken hostage by a crazy woman. He

was a better sport about it than most people. Everyone tried
to play along with Merrilee's flights from reality, but only
to the extent that it didn't inconvenience them. Mick didn't
seem to mind at all.

Hannah set the tray on the table, then walked out without
a word to either of them. She didn't want to hear one more
word of Merrilee's silly talk, didn't want to deal with one
more reason to like the man she had helped frame, the man
she already felt far too much for, the man who could break
her heart if she let him.

The breakfast shift passed in a sullen blur. Her regulars
recognized her mood and kept the chatter to a minimum,
and the few guests who'd spent the night were no more
talkative than she was.

She was rid of the last customer when Mick came out
of the apartment, carrying the tray with its leftovers. "Your
mother's resting." He spoke quietly, somberly, not with the
pity, mockery or scorn she had too often heard over the
years.

Still, his soft words annoyed her, and she ignored them,
ignored him.

"You're welcome."

"I didn't ask for your help. Don't expect my gratitude."
She said it with a scowl, because she hated being rude,
hated charity, hated feeling helpless and hopeless and
alone. She hated being mean to him when she'd needed his
help and he'd given it so freely, hated that he'd been there
when she'd needed him, that he might be there the next
time but not the tenth next time or the twentieth.

Most of all, she hated who she was, who she'd become
in the past ten years. She wanted to be someone else, someone whose life was far removed from Sunshine, the Last
Resort and a fragile mother.

"Pardon me for interfering," Mick said stiffly. "I
thought—" His voice changed, grew quieter, urgent.

"We'll talk about it later. We have bigger problems right now."

She looked up, then followed his gaze out the window. Sheriff Mills and one of his young deputies were getting out of their car out front. Shivering, she wiped her damp palms on her shorts, then picked up the tray of dishes just as the bell over the door rang. "Have a seat, Sheriff," she said with false cheer. "I'll be with you in a minute."

The sheriff stopped just inside the door, looked from her to Mick, then back again. "Why, this is cozy. I didn't know you were staying here, Reilly."

"I left word with your office."

"Michelle forgets to give me my messages sometimes. I'd probably fire her except she's my brother's wife's niece. Gotta keep the family happy. So, Hannah, I guess telling me he was a guest here just slipped your mind the other day. I asked if you knew him, and you said, 'We've met.' Seems logical that you would have gone on and said, 'Oh, by the way, Sheriff, he's a guest at the motel.'"

"I don't make a habit of telling anyone who our guests are."

"You don't make a habit of telling a number of things, do you? Such as where you were last weekend." Before she could respond, he added, "Where you *really* were."

A chill of fear swept over her and made her breath catch in her lungs. Grateful for the table nearby, she set the tray down before she dropped it, pushed her trembling hands into her pockets and faced the sheriff head-on, praying that her voice worked without a hitch. It didn't, but the quiver was such a slight hitch, maybe it went unnoticed. "I told you. I was in Tulsa."

"I know that's what you told me. I've been trying to figure out why you lied about it."

Over at the registration desk, Mick was watching her, his expression carefully guarded. The deputy was watching her, too, enjoying her discomfort. Sheriff Mills simply waited.

"I didn't exactly lie, Sheriff," she said, drawing out the words while searching frantically for an explanation. It came slowly. "I *was* in Tulsa last weekend. I drove over Saturday morning, and I stayed until Monday morning."

"Then why did Miz Rebecca Marsters tell me she'd never heard of you in her life? That was your 'friend's' name, wasn't it? The name you gave me as the woman you stayed with?" The sheriff walked around behind the counter and poured himself a cup of coffee, sweetening it liberally before fixing his gaze on her again. "It took me a while to get in touch with her. I left about a dozen messages on her machine, and she finally called me back this morning. She apologized for not getting back to me sooner, but she had a good excuse. You see, she's been out of the country for the past month and has the passport stamps to prove it. She just got back home around midnight last night."

He waited a long, tense moment, then said softly, "So, Hannah, let's start over. Where were you last weekend? Who did you stay with? And why did you lie about it?"

She stared at the three waiting men, all too afraid that her panic was easily read on her face. She knew without looking that she'd gone pale, that her eyes were probably rounded and filled with fear. If the sheriff possessed any deductive skills at all, he would walk over, slap the handcuffs on her and take her away.

But he didn't move. He waited behind the counter, sipping his coffee, and watched her.

Forcing air into her lungs, she walked toward him and climbed onto a nearby stool. She clasped her hands loosely together, fighting the urge to clench them into fists, and worked out a relatively calm response. "All right, Sheriff. I *was* in Tulsa, but you're right. I didn't stay with Rebecca Marsters. Truth is, I hardly know her. We met briefly years ago. When I needed a name to satisfy Sylvie's questions about the trip, Rebecca's just popped into my mind."

"So where were you?"

"I stayed at a motel."

"Why did you lie to your granny?"

She shrugged and hoped she looked at least a little embarrassed. "You know how things are around here, Sheriff. We don't have any money to waste on something as frivolous as a weekend away. But I thought I would go stark raving mad if I didn't get away for a while. I didn't want Sylvie to worry about the money or my safety or any of those things she always worries about, so I lied to her. I told her I was visiting an old friend from school. I wanted her to think that the trip wouldn't cost anything more than gas up there and back, that I'd be staying someplace safe, instead of a busy motel, that whatever running around I did would be with someone who knew her way around the city."

"All right. So that explains why you lied to Miz Clark. It doesn't explain why you lied to me."

"I don't normally lie to anyone, Sheriff." At last she'd told the truth. But even though it was the truth, it didn't feel like it. "I thought it best to stick to the story so I wouldn't get the details confused. I mean, after all, I *was* out of town. I never met the dead woman. I don't know any redheads named Elizabeth. I have nothing to contribute to your investigation. That's why I told you the same story I told Sylvie. Because it didn't matter."

Behind her the deputy snickered, and the sheriff gave him a warning look before shaking his head at Hannah. "Lying to the police, for any reason, always matters, Hannah. If you've got nothing to hide from anyone but your granny, you should have told me the truth. I wouldn't have said anything to her about it."

"I just didn't think... I'm not an experienced liar, Sheriff. If I were, I would have known better." She said a silent prayer for forgiveness. All her life she'd been taught both in church and at home that lying was a grave sin, but surely

God would understand the mess she'd gotten herself into. Surely He would make allowances because she was truly repentant. She just couldn't stop lying yet.

Because she wasn't out of trouble yet. "So what motel did you stay at?"

She went blank. She had seriously hoped he would accept her explanation and let the matter drop, but obviously that wasn't the case. Now she had only two options: she could either tell the truth, or she could buy herself a little time with another lie. Telling the truth wouldn't get her far. The sheriff would waste no time asking Brad if he'd given her use of the family cabin for the weekend, and Brad would say no. The sheriff would go out there to see for himself, and he would see exactly what she and Mick had seen: a cabin that looked as if it had been unoccupied since last fall's deer season.

The decision to buy time was an easy one. Unfortunately she wasn't terribly familiar with Tulsa, even though it was the nearest city of any size. In her short time in college, she and her roommates had often driven over to shop, but she remembered little about those trips, except... "I'm sorry, Sheriff. I don't remember the name. It was one of the major chains, and it was located off the main highway..."

"Skelly Bypass? I-44?"

"Yes. And it was at the exit for the street..." She wrinkled her forehead as if in thought. "There's a mall about a mile or so away."

"Yale," the deputy supplied. "The Promenade."

"Yes, that's it." If memory served, there were several motels in that area. Naturally the sheriff would check each of them and find that she had lied again, but hopefully it would give her time to come up with yet another story, this one more plausible.

And what was going to be plausible after two elaborate lies?

"You don't have a receipt or something with the name on it?" Mills asked. "You run a motel, Hannah. You give everybody receipts."

"I threw it away."

"You pay by credit card?"

She made a sound that was equal parts disdain and amusement. "I haven't had a credit card in more years than I can remember. I paid cash."

The sheriff subjected her to a long, unsettling look, then finally directed his gaze toward Mick. "I have a few questions to ask you, too. Do you mind giving us some privacy, Hannah?"

"Of course not. I have work to do." She slid to the floor, grabbed the tray of dishes and went into the kitchen. As the door swung shut behind her, she gave a sigh of relief, then immediately felt guilty for being grateful that it was Mick's turn to be grilled. She shouldn't, though. At least he was telling the truth.

She was the one with all the lies.

Chapter 7

The door slowed to a stop, leaving the dining room in silence. Mick slowly shifted his gaze from it to the sheriff. The man was patiently waiting for him to make some move. He chose not to.

"I got an interesting call yesterday afternoon from Mr. Daniels, who'd gotten an interesting call himself from American National Fidelity. You familiar with them?"

Mick shook his head.

"Funny. They're familiar with you. Seems they have a life-insurance policy taken out by one Michael Reilly on his wife, Sandra. That's you, isn't it?"

"I never carried insurance on Sandra."

"They have forms with your signature on them. They cashed a check a few months back from your company, again with your signature on it."

"I sign every check Blue Water pays out, but I didn't sign one for insurance on Sandra."

"A company as big as yours doesn't have somebody to pay the bills for it?"

"We have a bookkeeper who prepares the checks. I compare them to the invoices and sign them so she can mail them." It had always been that way—at least, since the inception of Blue Water Construction. Back when it was Reilly Homes and Sandra was his one and only office employee, she'd handled the books. She'd made out the checks, and after they were married, she had signed his name to them, too. They had sometimes joked that if he couldn't tell her version of his signature from the real thing, the bank certainly wouldn't notice.

His muscles tensed, and a thin line of sweat trickled down his spine. He had a really bad feeling about this.

"So how would you explain a check drawn on Blue Water's account apparently signed by you, only not really signed by you?"

"I would say it's a forgery."

"Hmm. Interesting. Do you think your partner would recognize your signature?"

"He's seen it often enough." Often enough to learn to forge it? Or had Brad somehow persuaded Sandra to forge it for him?

"The insurance company faxed him a copy of the policy. He seems to think it's your signature. The bank's getting a copy of the check. They should have it later today."

"I didn't take out a policy on Sandra," he repeated tensely. "A few months ago we were already separated, already seeing divorce lawyers. You think I would take out a life-insurance policy on her when we'd already filed for divorce, then *kill* her? Jeez, how stupid do you think I am?"

"I don't think you're stupid at all, Mr. Reilly. But you have to admit—it doesn't look very good."

No, it didn't, he acknowledged, feeling trapped and scared and damn near desperate. "Why did the insurance company contact Brad?"

"Because the beneficiary is Blue Water Construction."

Damn Brad Daniels to hell. Getting total control of the

company wasn't enough for him. Getting out from under the Eagle's Haven debt with the insurance settlement hadn't satisfied him. He'd wanted a nice chunk of cash, too. Mick was damned lucky that Brad hadn't decided to cash in on *his* life-insurance policy, too. If he'd felt confident about staging a murder/suicide, no doubt he would have.

"How much is the policy worth?"

"A million even."

A million dollars. For getting rid of a woman who'd meant nothing to him. Brad would really clean up on this deal. It would take time to settle the insurance claims, of course, since the loss of the resort was due to arson and Sandra's death was murder. The insurance companies would want to be sure the money wasn't paid to the guilty party, but Brad had convinced the authorities of his innocence, and they would convince the insurance companies. Once everything was settled, he would come out of the deal with his net worth about doubled.

And all he'd had to do was destroy half a dozen or so innocent lives. All in a day's work.

"Now, the insurance company tells me it's rather unusual for a man to take out a policy on his wife, pay for it with company funds and make the company the beneficiary unless she plays a role in the company. Did Mrs. Reilly have anything to do with the ownership or running of Blue Water Construction?"

"No." Though Sandra had learned the business while working for him, she'd hated it. She'd especially hated that he was a hands-on sort of owner. She would have been happier if he'd modeled himself after Brad—wearing expensive suits, having business lunches and dinners in fancy restaurants, conducting meetings in some of the most beautiful homes in the city. She hadn't liked that he'd worn jeans and work shirts, that he'd spent his days working side by side with the crews.

Brad had claimed to be the dreamer while Mick was the

builder. Sandra had thought Brad was the brains while Mick was the brawn. Brad provided the class. Mick provided the brute labor.

"What other reason do you suppose a man might have for setting up a policy like that?"

Grimly Mick turned to stare out the window. For a moment he focused on the heat waves rising from the pavement. Then a movement across the road caught his attention. There, in the same place where he'd settled in to watch for Elizabeth, was a man, slender, blond-haired. Brad. He was over there, watching them, watching the sheriff rake them over the coals.

"Mr. Reilly?"

He glanced over his shoulder at Mills, then looked back. Just like that Brad was gone. "I suppose to ensure that he got a portion of the money without all the scrutiny that being the sole beneficiary would bring."

"That's what I suppose, too." The sheriff came out from around the counter, pulled a chair from the nearest table and straddled it. "Is that what you did?"

"No, it's not." Mick turned to face him. "You know, Sheriff, I've tried to cooperate, but it seems you've already got your mind made up that I'm guilty. You don't listen to anything I say. You just try to twist it to suit your preconceived notions. For that reason, I believe it's in my best interests not to talk to you anymore. My attorney is Trey Landry. He's in the Tulsa phone book. If you have any further questions to ask, ask him."

For a long time the sheriff just looked at him. Then, getting to his feet with a grunt, he grinned. "We'll be in touch, Mr. Reilly." At the door he turned back. "Does Hannah have an attorney, too?"

Mick shrugged. "As far as I know, she has no need for one."

"We'll see. Thank you for your cooperation. We'll talk to you again soon."

Mick watched until they were out of sight, then left the lobby and started across the parking lot. At the road's edge he heard Hannah call his name, but he didn't slow or look back. Beside the old gas station, he pushed through the vines, crouched and looked around. Were the weeds bent a little there, as if someone had stood on them? Had those leaves been torn from the vine by a person or by something as harmless as the wind or a wild creature?

It was a certain bet that toothpick hadn't been broken in half by the wind or a raccoon. When Brad had given up smoking a few years ago, he'd taken up toothpicks—at least, out here in the uncultured lake communities. He *had* been here. It hadn't been his imagination.

"Mick, what are you doing?"

"Brad was watching us. He set the sheriff on us, then came over here to watch the fun." He stood up and ground the toothpick halves into the dirt under his boot.

"He was here?" Hannah looked as pale as when the sheriff had first confronted her with her lies. Mick had wanted to offer her some sort of support then, but he couldn't. He wanted to now, but he shouldn't. Not out in the open. Not if Brad was anywhere around.

"He's tying us up into a neat little package for the sheriff and the DA to deliver to the jury, and I don't know how to stop him." He dragged his fingers through his hair. "Do you know anyone in Tulsa who would lie for you?"

She shook her head. "Do you?"

He shook his head, too. His only acquaintance in the city was his lawyer, and it certainly wouldn't do much for his case to ask Landry's help in providing the elusive Elizabeth with an ironclad alibi. "What about anyone else? An old boyfriend? Someone you went to school with?"

She gave another negative response, and he accepted her answer as fact. She worked such long hours that she didn't have much time to spare for friends or boyfriends, and there were few prospects for either in Sunshine. Besides, it took a really good friend to lie for you to the cops. Neither he nor Hannah was that lucky.

Resting his hand on her shoulder, he steered her toward the motel. "You know Mills will be back as soon as he finds out you weren't registered at any of the motels in that area. We've got to have a story ready to tell him."

"I'll tell him the truth."

"He won't believe it."

She stopped at the front door and looked up at him. "Sort of the truth. I'll tell him I was with a man."

It was stupid, totally irrational, but he felt a stirring of jealousy. "What man?"

She thought for a moment, then said decisively, "David. David Martin."

"And when he finds no record of that name at the motels?"

"He didn't register under his own name. He's married. He was afraid of his wife somehow finding out, so he used a fake name and paid cash."

He wondered if the sheriff would buy version number three. Maybe—if she looked ashamed enough, guilty enough. After all, she was a beautiful, healthy, young woman with the same needs as any other woman. She was surrounded by elderly or sick women and had little opportunity for sexual relationships in her daily life. She wouldn't be the first woman to take a trip out of town for the sole purpose of sex. Hell, Sandra had done it plenty of times.

"Where did you meet this man?"

"At a bar."

"Which bar?"

"I'll get the phone book and find one."

Mick shook his head. "I think it's a little too coincidental that both your alibi and mine involve having sex at a motel with a stranger we met in a bar."

With a nod, she chose a different course. "We met here

last summer. He was spending the weekend at the lake, and we had a fling then. I hadn't seen him since, but when I got a note from him saying he would be in Tulsa for the weekend and asking me to meet him, I agreed.'' She shrugged. ''I liked him. He was fun, and I needed some fun.''

''Where is the note?''

''I threw it away. I didn't want Sylvie to see it.''

''Where does he live?''

''Kansas. I don't remember the town.''

''How did you get in touch with him to accept the invitation?''

''I didn't. The note said he would be there. If I was interested, I could meet him at a particular restaurant at noon.''

He nodded, reasonably hopeful. ''Be sure you look up the name and address of a restaurant. Pick a popular one, one that's guaranteed to be really busy for Saturday lunch, so the staff couldn't be expected to remember you.''

She started to go inside, but hesitated. ''Do you think he'll believe me?''

She wanted reassurance. He offered the best he could. ''I doubt it. But without a lie-detector test, it'll be virtually impossible for him to prove you wrong.''

''Unless Brad pays someone to come forward and say they saw you and me together Saturday afternoon or having breakfast together Sunday morning.''

He wished he could tease her about having a wild imagination, but what she suggested was entirely possible. For an additional nail or two in their coffins, Brad very well might provide witnesses to their long-standing affair.

Once again she started to go inside. Once again she stopped. ''About this morning...''

''It's all right,'' he said, even though it wasn't. He wanted answers, explanations, insights. He wanted to know everything about her, wanted to share her most private secrets and her darkest fears.

On the last two at least, he was pretty sure he did.

"Sometimes I just get…"

Overwhelmed. Frustrated. Tired of struggling, of being responsible not just for herself but for everyone around her, of giving herself 110 percent to a job she never wanted in a place she'd wanted to leave behind.

He brushed his fingers across her cheek. "It's all right, Hannah. Forget it."

For just a moment she seemed to lean into his touch. Then, with a tight smile, she went into the lobby. After one last look at the station across the road, he followed.

"What was the sheriff doing here?"

At first he didn't see Sylvie behind the counter. She was so short and standing so still. How long had she been there? Long enough to see him and Hannah checking out the weeds across the road? Long enough to watch the involved conversation in which they'd made up more lies?

Long enough to see him touch her granddaughter?

Hannah gave him a look over her shoulder before disappearing into the laundry room. She was a coward—not that he blamed her. He'd rather answer the sheriff's questions than Sylvie's anytime. Still, affecting a casual air, he went to sit in front of the old lady. "He wanted to ask me a few questions about an insurance policy." Briefly, without a hint of the renewed anger he felt showing, he covered the highlights of the conversation. Sometime in the middle of it Hannah left the lobby, pushing the big housekeeping cart in front of her.

When he was done, Sylvie fixed a sharp gaze on him. "Did you kill your wife?"

"No, ma'am."

"Do you have any theories about who did?"

"Yes, I do."

"And have you shared these theories with Sheriff Mills?"

"No. I don't intend to, until I have proof."

"Have you shared them with my granddaughter?"

He hesitated just an instant too long. If he lied, she would know it was a lie, and so he said nothing.

Sylvie's expression shifted from solemn to grim. "Don't put that girl in danger. She's all we've got."

He offered his hand, and she laid hers in it. It was so small, so thin. "I won't let anyone hurt her." He would do anything to keep her safe. But what could he do about Brad? How could he protect her from him?

After a moment Sylvie's fingers curled around his, and she gave his hand a good solid squeeze. When he would have pulled away, though, she held on. "What else have you shared with my granddaughter?"

"You put me in a difficult position, Miz Clark," he teased. "My mother taught me to respect my elders, which sort of rules out the proper answer to your question."

"I've been disrespected before, so answer."

He leaned closer. "What's between Hannah and me is none of your business."

"That wasn't so hard, was it?" She tugged her hand free and shook her finger in his face. "Don't you make her fall for you, then get yourself sent off to prison."

"Believe me, staying out of prison is my top priority. Besides, can you imagine anyone *making* Hannah do something?" Anyone besides Brad, of course, who had succeeded only because of her devotion to her family.

Sylvie's expression turned sad and distant. "We made her come back here after her daddy died. We needed her help. Merrilee was beside herself with grief, and I..."

She had grieved, too. Mothers weren't supposed to bury their children, no matter how old those children were. Losing her son must have broken her heart, but she hadn't had the luxury of falling apart, as Merrilee had. Someone had to be strong for the family, someone besides her teenage granddaughter.

"I just didn't see a way we could possibly run the place without Hannah's help. I hated bringing her back. She'd had such plans." Her smile was faded and regretful. "A fourth-rate motel in a one-horse town like Sunshine doesn't have much to offer a young woman. There's no excitement, no young people, no picture theaters, no shopping. Me, I didn't mind. I was born here. I met my husband here, raised my son here, and I intend, God willing, to die here. Merrilee didn't mind, either. Wherever Mark was, was fine with her. But Hannah... It's been a hard, disappointing life for her, and she won't be free of it until her mother, God bless her, is dead and buried."

Mick didn't know what to say. He couldn't try to make Sylvie feel better by telling her that Hannah wasn't nearly as regretful over the way her life had gone as Sylvie was, because it just wasn't true. He couldn't remind her that she hadn't had a choice in bringing Hannah back, because she was well aware of that. Not having a choice didn't make such a decision any easier.

"She doesn't hate it here," he said, not entirely sure he was right. "She just wants—"

"To be someplace else. To be some*one* else."

"Maybe if life was easier here..."

Sylvie answered him with a challenge. "You gonna make it easier?"

"I could." He could give Hannah the benefit of his construction skills, along with the use of his checkbook, and make this place the classiest motel in five states. He could advance her the money for major remodeling, one or two rooms at a time, or he could invest enough to hire some badly needed help.

"And what would you want in return?"

The moment's consideration he gave her question wasn't necessary. He knew what he wanted. "Her. Hannah."

"In what way? For how long?"

"Isn't this a conversation I should be having with her?"

"Yes, but you haven't, have you?"

No, with Hannah, he hadn't gone beyond reminding her how good the sex had been and wondering, asking, if they might ever try it again. She thought probably not. He wanted a definite yes.

Standing up, he leaned his elbows on the counter. "I'm not making any plans for the future until I'm sure I have one. Like you said, I don't want to go falling for Hannah, then get myself locked up in prison."

Even as he said it, though, he knew it might already be too late. He'd started falling the moment she'd stopped beside his table Saturday night, and he hadn't felt solid ground under his feet since. If he had a future, one that didn't involve prison...

Hannah just might be it.

It was the middle of the afternoon when Hannah approached Mick in the dining room. He was sitting in one chair, his feet propped on another, and contemplating the scene outside the plate-glass window with a distant, speculative look on his face. Pushing her hands into her hip pockets, she stepped into his line of vision and waited for him to notice her. He did so slowly, with a look that focused somewhere around her midriff, drifted lazily lower, then slowly up, slowly enough to heat her blood as it went, brushing over her breasts, up the length of her throat, finally reaching her face. Her flushed, pale and flustered face.

"Where did you learn to do that?" she asked.

"Do what?"

"That look. That..." She shrugged and felt the worn cotton of her shirt brush her sensitive nipples.

He feigned innocence. "I just looked at you. If you didn't want me to, you shouldn't have stepped in front of me."

"Yeah, you looked at me as if..." Again she ran out of words, but this time she didn't shrug. She didn't move at all.

A smile, dark, secretive and wicked, played about his mouth. "As if I know how you look under those clothes? As if I know intimately the body you work so hard at hiding? As if I've experienced the pleasures of your body and would like to do so again?"

She struggled against the urge to hug her arms across her chest, struggled even harder against the urge to offer what he wanted, what she wanted, even if it would be wrong.

And it would be wrong, wouldn't it? She was trying to protect herself from him, wasn't she? Hadn't she acknowledged just this morning that he was so far out of her league that they didn't even play the same games? He was rich. She wasn't. He'd grown accustomed to so much better. She hadn't. He had options in his life. She didn't.

He would leave here.

She couldn't.

But he wanted her, and she wanted him. And loss was loss, whether she kept him at arm's length or not.

She managed to give him a chastening look. "Does your offer still stand—"

"Yes." He didn't look at all chastened. In fact, he looked extraordinarily pleased with himself.

"—to teach me how to repair the cracks and holes in the walls so they can be painted?"

His smile softened and turned intimate, and she *knew*, damn him, that he was thinking about the paint. *Morning Blush. It's an exact match for your cheeks when you're naked and sweaty and you've just—*

"All my offers still stand. Including the use of my bed until the paint fumes clear."

"And where would you sleep?"

"Who'd sleep?" He let his feet hit the floor with a thud,

then stood up, so fluidly unfolding his body. The man was fully dressed, in jeans and a chambray shirt, and yet the movement was purely sexual. Of course, as he'd reminded her, she knew what he looked like underneath those clothes. She knew his skin was a dozen shades darker than her own, that it was soft in places, hair-roughened in others, that she could make his muscles bunch and tighten with one lazy caress, that the lightest brush of her fingertips across his belly made his skin ripple and quiver. She knew if she unzipped his jeans and slid her hand inside, he would suck in his breath, would turn pale under the dark bronze, would catch her hand, hold it closer, swell to fit it.

Biting back a groan, she turned away and headed for the storeroom. She gathered an armful of supplies, and Mick got the rest, then followed her outside.

Maybe this was a bad idea, she thought, catching a glimpse of his reflection in the big window. The last thing she needed was to be alone with him in her rooms, with locks on all the doors and her bed only a few yards away. She wasn't very good at resisting temptation. It was only shame and a fierce need to protect herself that had kept her away this long, and both could be overcome with a little seduction.

And he was pretty damn good at seduction.

The sun blazed overhead, blinding in a cloudless sky. The heat made her long for a lazy day at the lake, wearing only what clothing was necessary, wading barefoot in the water, listening to the insects hum, relaxing away one long minute after another. It reminded her of childhood days at the creek out back, lying on her stomach on the bank with a cane pole dangling over the water and the dappled shade of a grand elm offering a few degrees' coolness. It was a perfect day for renting a boat and finding an isolated cove on the lake, for stripping down for a cool dip, then baking dry on the deck. It was even more perfect for making love on the deck, naked and carefree, under the sky and the sun, daring and natural and—

Scowling, she opened her door with more force than necessary. Sunlight fell in a merciless wedge across the room, highlighting tired, worn carpet, tired, worn furniture. All the Morning Blush in the world wouldn't give this place any more character, any more class. But at least it would be just the tiniest bit prettier, and every look at the walls would remind her of Mick and what could have been.

What still could be, if God and fate looked favorably on her.

He closed the door, set his load down and looked around. Was he comparing this to his beautiful house in the city, finding cheap-motel construction lacking next to his own outstanding work, thinking of marble floors and leather couches while looking at stained twenty-year-old carpet and garage-sale finds?

"First we need to get everything off the walls and move the furniture toward the center of the room," he said, lifting the coffee table onto the sofa, then scooting both from the wall.

They worked quickly and in silence, at least until Mick reached her desk. He picked up a picture frame there and studied it much the way she had studied the photos on his office wall. She didn't join him, didn't offer to identify everyone. He already knew her, Merrilee and Sylvie, and it was obvious the other two were her father and grandfather. After a moment he laid it down, then moved the desk. "You were a cute kid."

She didn't respond.

"You still are."

"That's just what every twenty-nine-year-old woman wants to hear," she said dryly. "Thank you."

"Okay, let's see... What does a woman of your advanced age want to hear?" He turned to lean against the desk while pretending to think. "How about, 'You were a beautiful redhead, but I like you better like this'? Or maybe, 'Last night when we got back to the motel, before I woke you, I sat in the truck and touched you—just your face—and I thought about how lovely you are and how good it felt to touch you. And I wished we could start over, without Sandra, without Brad or Elizabeth, just you and me, meeting for the first time, with no lies, no threats, nothing between us, just you and me...'"

His voice trailed off to a whisper. In the silence that followed, she heard the irregular beat of her heart, the faint shallow rasp of her breath, and she knew that all she needed was a touch, a gesture, a look, and she would forget all her reservations, would trade them all for pleasure and passion. For him.

But he didn't touch her. He didn't give her that gesture or look. Instead, he abruptly straightened, as if startled back into normalcy. "How was that? You like it better?" His words were teasing. His voice wasn't. It quavered unnaturally.

"I don't know." Her voice shook, too. "Maybe we should stick with 'cute kid.'"

He kept his distance while giving her step-by-step directions for repairing the damaged walls. When she finished, a good deal of the surface of the dingy walls was covered with white patches. Taking the Spackle and tools with her, she joined him in the bedroom, where he'd gotten a head start on the preparatory work. Once he was finished, he sat on the dresser in the middle of the room and watched her work.

"Hannah?"

She slapped a putty knife full of Spackle over a ragged nail hole. "Hmm?"

"Have you ever considered selling half the motel?"

"I can't sell the place. What would I do with Mom? And who would be crazy enough to buy it?"

"Half, Hannah. Merrilee and Sylvie would continue to

live where they are. You would continue to run the place, at least for a while. Later, maybe you could finish school or move to Tulsa or Oklahoma City. You could go ahead and do all those things you'd wanted to do ten years ago.''

Slowly, with her knuckles whitening around the putty knife, she turned to face him. He hadn't answered her last question—or maybe he had. "Sell half of it. To you."

He nodded, looking as serious as she'd ever seen him.

Just as slowly she turned back to her work. Go to school. Move away. Have a life of her own that didn't include twenty-four hours a day of worrying, fretting and working. Meet men. Go out on dates. Make friends. Live a normal life. Those were her dreams and had been since she was fourteen years old. She'd thought they were forever out of reach, but Mick was offering them to her once again. All she had to do was sell half the motel to him.

She should be thrilled, excited, overjoyed, and she did feel a shiver of anticipation. But only a shiver. She couldn't leave. Merrilee and Sylvie needed her. This place needed her.

It also needed him, or someone like him. Someone with money and know-how, someone who didn't mind hard work, a crazy woman or an outspoken senior citizen.

"Why would you do that?" she asked warily.

"No matter what happens with the sheriff, I'm out of Blue Water Construction. I like this part of the state, and I like a challenge. I think this place could be something. It's got potential."

"It's got a ten-thousand-dollar debt to Brad, and it's not worth fifty cents. Any way you look at it, it's a lousy investment."

"Brad's never going to collect on that debt. You paid him."

"Like I can prove it. I can see myself now, standing in front of a jury and claiming that Brad offered to write off my ten-thousand-dollar loan in exchange for my spending one night in bed with his partner. Who's going to believe that?''

His answer came in a soft, husky voice. "Every man in the courtroom.''

She faced him again. "You're serious. You're willing to buy into this place, to fix it up, to help run it.''

He nodded.

She turned away once more. Her hand trembled as she applied a glob of Spackle to the wall. He was willing to live here, right here, to stay, to not leave. He didn't want to go back to the city, to the rich friends and that big, gorgeous, unwelcoming house. He wanted to stay here.

That was what she wanted, wasn't it? Living here wasn't so bad with him around. In fact, with him around, *here* was quite possibly the best place she could be. Her future with him here was rosier than she could have imagined—if either of them had a future. "What if you go to prison?''

"Then you'll have the best possible deal—a partner who provides money and stays out of your way. And if you go to prison, too, Sylvie and your mother will be taken care of. They'll be able to hire enough help to keep the place going.''

Using her toe, she pulled a footstool over, stepped up and stretched high to patch a crack near the ceiling. The best possible deal, he'd said, and he was right. No matter what happened, he was offering an arrangement better than any she could have dreamed—a partner to share the burdens of the motel and her mother, an infusion of cash to fix up the place, business sense to help increase the occupancy rate and the opportunity to fulfill her nearly forgotten dreams. Best of all, barring arrest and a prison sentence, he would stay. Probably not forever, maybe not more than a year or two, but for a time he would be here. Working with her, living with her—at least, next door to her.

Best of all... She dawdled over the next patch, her thoughts consumed with the brand-new future he'd offered.

College, a new job in a career of her choosing, a new home, a new city, new opportunities—those should be the *best of all*. A month ago, if anyone had made such an offer with the promise that he would care for Merrilee and Sylvie, she would have jumped at it. She would have put the Last Resort and Sunshine behind her so fast her head would have spun. She would have marveled at her incredible good fortune, thanked God and gone.

This afternoon the dreams still held their promise, but she wasn't convinced they were exactly what she wanted. She tried to imagine herself living in an apartment in Tahlequah or Tulsa, working a regular nine-to-five job, taking classes in the evening, grocery shopping for one, cooking, cleaning and doing laundry for only one. She couldn't quite focus the image.

"Well?"

She looked at Mick. "I could move away, finish school, live and work in Tulsa or Oklahoma City or anywhere I want, and you would stay here and run the place and take care of my family."

Though he nodded, he looked as if the idea didn't set well with him. Which part? Being responsible for someone else's family? Or maybe, just maybe, her moving away?

"I would have to talk to Sylvie."

"Do that, but do it before the sheriff decides to arrest me and I wind up spending all my money on a lawyer."

"If this is a burden…"

He shook his head. "That was a joke. Eagle's Haven was about to bankrupt the company, but I have some money put aside. Plus, I called a real-estate agent we worked with and put my house on the market. A couple of Sandra's friends were interested in it a while back. We'll see if they still are. Anyway, money's not a problem."

She dabbed over the last nail hole, then set the Spackle and putty knife down. "Do you know how lucky you are?" There had never been a single day in her adult life that money hadn't been a very big problem. She could barely imagine what it was like to have enough. She didn't have a clue how it would feel to always have more than enough.

He gave her a long look that generated more heat than her poor air conditioner could combat. "I'm very lucky," he said, and she knew beyond a doubt that he wasn't talking about money.

"Right," she agreed with a touch of mockery. "You married a bitch, you went into business with a blackmailer and a murderer, and the one and only time you were unfaithful to your wife, you picked a—"

"Beautiful woman who made it worth everything that's happened since."

She swallowed her self-insults and, for one brief moment, closed her eyes, willing him to reach for her, to touch her, to give her any excuse to surrender. When he didn't, she opened her eyes and forced a small, disappointed smile. "Now what do we do?"

She knew the answers she would like from him—*You can come over where I can touch you, feel you, smell you. You can let me kiss you, and when I do, you can rub your body against mine. You can take off my clothes and I'll take off yours, and we'll forget our troubles together.*

Naturally he didn't say any of those things. Grinning, he got to his feet. "Now you paint."

With nightfall the temperature dropped a scant ten degrees. Even though the air conditioner was doing a decent job of keeping his room cool, Mick had settled outside with a tall glass of iced lemonade from Earlene's kitchen. His shirt was unbuttoned, his shoes kicked off next to the bed, and he leaned back in the single piece of movable furniture in his room, a straight-backed desk chair.

It was a few minutes after nine. He'd finished the last bit of painting in Hannah's bedroom nearly an hour earlier, had cleaned the brushes and rollers, then showered. Paint-

ing was one of his least-favorite tasks on a job. He'd always
been happy to pay the painters and the crews who mudded
and taped the drywall whatever price they asked, because
the good ones were worth every penny. But he hadn't
minded it so much this time, maybe because it'd been such
a small job. Maybe because he'd worked all but the last
few hours alongside Hannah.

Maybe because he intended to spend whatever time she
would allow—whatever nights—in those Morning Blush
rooms. Just as soon as he persuaded her.

Down in the office, she was talking to Ruby. The clerk
was a widow, Hannah had told him this evening, whose
children had taken her grandchildren to distant homes. She
lived alone and was a perfect choice for the job, Hannah
had insisted, even though he hadn't argued. Ruby was a
night owl, so the hours were no problem. She liked people,
the job got her out of the house, and the small salary she
earned supplemented her social security.

She'd gone into Earlene's background, too, stressing her
finer points, minimizing her age. That was when he'd
known that she had decided to take him up on his offer.
Unless Sylvie objected, she was going to sell half the motel
to him.

He had assured her that he had no interest in taking over,
only in being a part of the group. Part of her life, was what
he'd wanted to say. Part of her family.

Hannah came out of the office and started his way, and
he rephrased that last desire. He wanted to be the most
important part of her family. He wanted to belong to her
in ways no one else could. He wanted the right to touch
her, not just the big touches, the seductive ones, but the
other kind—his hand on hers, his arm around her, the casual little intimacies. He wanted...

Sweet hell, yes, he *wanted*.

She stopped in front of him, and he swallowed hard as
she asked, "What are you doing out here?"

"Cooling off."

She smiled faintly. "Cooling off? It's probably a good twenty degrees cooler inside."

"I've been listening to the night. Watching you. Waiting."

She took his glass, took a deep drink, then returned it before sitting on the concrete curb that separated parking lot from sidewalk. "Waiting for what?"

He shrugged, and she didn't press.

After a moment she said, "I talked to Sylvie. She's tickled pink at the idea of having you for a partner. She doesn't take to most people very easily, so you should feel flattered."

"I do." He grinned. "You should trust your grandmother's judgment."

"I do."

"So, pending the numbers, we have a deal?" He offered his hand, and, after a time, she shook it.

"We do." She wiped her palm across her forehead, lifted her hair off her neck, then sighed. "You want to go for a swim?"

It was a perfect night for it—no breeze, a nearly full moon, a sky full of stars and a lazy, draining warmth that seeped into a person's bones. It beat sitting here, where the day's heat still radiated from concrete and cinder block. It sure as hell beat going into his room alone, while Hannah went to some other room alone. "All right," he said.

She was on her feet and halfway to her room before he stopped her. "Didn't you forget something?"

She looked back blankly.

"You said we would negotiate for your swimsuit top the next time we went to the lake."

The blankness was replaced with a slow, lazy smile. "Keep it. I don't need it." She disappeared into her room and the door closed.

Mick grinned. He wished he could interpret her statement

to mean that she was ready to take Sylvie's advice. Most likely, though, it just meant she had another swimsuit to wear. Still, the mere suggestion of Hannah naked in the moonlight was greatly appreciated by certain parts of his body.

He was changed and waiting in the truck by the time she came out. She wore shorts and a T-shirt, with a beach towel slung around her neck. There were no telltale ties peeking out from the shirt, which meant she probably wore something sleek, one-piece and modest. So much for ogling her nearly naked body, he thought with real regret.

She directed him back to the same spot. While he removed his shoes and shirt, she kicked off her thongs, stepped out of her shorts and dove into the water, still wearing her shirt. Biting down hard on a groan, he watched her surface, a pale glow of white and gold, and strike out toward the lake middle. Just what he needed—a quiet night, miles from his self-control and Hannah in a wet T-shirt. Torment me, he'd said the last time they were here, and tonight she'd taken him up on it. They hadn't been here five minutes, and already he was hot enough to make the water steam. Already he was hard enough to hurt.

He watched her for a while before diving in, but this time he kept his distance. He didn't catch up to her, didn't swim close enough to reach out and touch her. He stayed several lengths away, swam until he was tired, then returned to the dock, where he found a comfortable place to sit and watch.

After a while she joined him, rising up from the lake like some sort of midnight fantasy. Water slicked her hair back from her face and made her shirt heavy, pulling it taut over her naked breasts, her flat belly and the curve of her hips. It ran down her legs and dripped from her fingers to pool at his feet, cool and sensual.

The shirt was her oldest and thinnest. Wet, it was damn near transparent. In the moonlight he could make out the shadows that circled her erect nipples, the shallow indentation of her belly button, the curls that sheltered the most intimate part of her.

He had seen her naked, had teased her about swimming that way. He'd appreciated her in a bikini and had regretted that tonight she'd chosen something more concealing. But this...this was the sexiest, most sensual, most provocative of all. This concealed and revealed. It was as innocent as a summer day, as wicked as a steamy June night. If he could have only one memory of her, it would be like this—beautiful, sexual, full of promise.

After standing there long enough for his mouth to go dry, his skin to turn hot and his body to turn to stone, she picked up the beach towel. The shorts on top fell to the dock, and something fell out of the pocket, landing with the rustle of plastic. She scooped it up, hiding it in her hand as she wrapped the towel around her. "Sorry for the shirt," she said, though it was clear in her voice that she wasn't, "but someone made off with half my swimsuit. This was all I had to wear."

She was in the process of sitting when he grasped a handful of towel and yanked her toward him. She stumbled, tried to catch herself and landed on his lap—on his erection. The instant she felt it, she became still. He kept her that way with one arm around her shoulders while, with his free hand, he worked her fingers open to reveal the item she'd palmed. It was condoms, a string of four, each individually wrapped, the same brand she'd provided last weekend.

"What about last night?" His voice was gruff, strained.

Hers was breathless. "Wh-what about it?"

"You were trying very hard not to go to bed with me again. Remember?"

She nodded.

"Have you changed your mind? Or did you decide to try very hard to drive me out of mine?"

She opened her mouth to protest and deny, but no words

came out. Her expression shifted, softened, making her sigh before answering very quietly and properly, "I've changed my mind."

Why? That was the obvious next question. Why had she pushed him away last night only to draw him closer tonight? But the answer, he feared, was as obvious as the question: his offer to buy the motel, to pour his money into it, to take over the responsibility for her mother and her elderly staff and to let her go away and seek the life she'd always wanted. Maybe she wanted to ensure that he wouldn't change his mind. Maybe she wanted more generous terms than she suspected he would offer. Maybe she felt she had to repay him. Maybe she was just so damn grateful.

Any of the possibilities were reasonable. All of them were painful. Later he could deal with reason and pain. Right now he wanted only passion, and so he didn't ask.

With his eyes open, he touched his mouth to hers. As kisses went, it wasn't much—just the brush of mouth to mouth—but it made him feel arousal, desire, strange sweet pleasure. For eleven years he'd kissed no woman but Sandra, whose kisses had grown steadily less passionate, less loving, until they had stopped altogether. But this simple kiss shared with Hannah made him remember what it was like to be wanted.

It made him remember what it was like to love.

Her tongue touched his lips, slid between them and into his mouth, sending a jolt through his system. His muscles tightening, his breath catching, he welcomed her, but just as quickly she withdrew. She freed her mouth of his, freed her towel from his hand and moved to her knees, spreading the towel neatly over weathered boards.

Then she touched him.

Her fingers grazed his arm, brushed the back of his hand, then wrapped tightly around it, drawing him onto his knees, too. Her touch spread a heat through his body that no

Oklahoma summer could match. His blood was thick, his skin dry enough to sizzle when she brought her body into contact with his, when her wet shirt touched and cooled, then transferred his heat to her.

As they knelt there, her arms around his neck, her breasts against his chest, his erection straining against her belly, he gazed into her face, more beautiful than Elizabeth could ever be, and thought about the question he hadn't asked. *Why did you change your mind?* If he asked and she answered any of the possibilities he'd already considered, he would have to walk away. He wouldn't have her, bought and paid for, again. No matter how much he'd enjoyed their one night together, no matter that it was the best sex he'd ever experienced, the fact that she'd been in his bed only on promise of payment tarnished it, cheapened it.

But what if she gave an answer he hadn't already considered—a good answer, one he could live with? Then *she* would walk away, because she would know that he'd suspected her of prostituting herself again. Either way, he would lose, and he had too little in his life that he could afford to lose the most important part. It would be best that he not open his mouth.

Unless it was to give her kisses—sweet, steamy, gentle, hungry, demanding kisses. He explored her mouth as his hands explored her body, gliding over wet T-shirt and damp skin. He stroked her back, her breasts, the flat of her belly. She was cool and hot, exquisitely responsive to the slightest of his touches. She trembled, clung to him and repaid him with her own sweet touches, her fingers brushing here, kneading there, cupping so tenderly there, until he couldn't bear any more.

He removed his trunks, tossed them aside, then knotted his fingers in the hem of her shirt. She watched him, her blue gaze steady on his face. He watched her, his gaze locked on her body, as he began pulling the shirt away, revealing rounded hips, narrowed waist, damn near perfect breasts. He tugged the shirt over her head, then wrapped it round and round his hands, pulling the fabric tighter as tension, hunger and unbearable need streaked through him.

She took advantage of his self-created bonds to touch him intimately, her small fingers unrolling a condom over him, her delicate hands tormenting his flesh when she was finished. He caught his breath, jerked his hands free and threw the shirt away, then pressed her down on the towel. The splash an instant later barely registered because he was between her thighs, probing, seeking entry into her body, finding heat and an incredibly snug welcome.

He moved, and her muscles tensed. Moved again, and her body clenched hard around his. Her face was pale, etched with need. Her breasts were swollen, her nipples hard, her arousal as intense as his own. Just like Saturday night, he knew this first time wouldn't last long, knew their bodies would betray them with a hot, quick, breath-stealing release, knew it would be the sweetest betrayal either of them had ever experienced.

He could try to make it last, could grit his teeth and think about anything in the world but Hannah, but tonight there wasn't anything else in his world except Hannah, who was sliding her flesh along his, who doubled his need with every movement, who tripled the heat with every breath. Her sensual thrusts enticed him as her soft little whimpers pleaded with him. He tried to resist, tried to prolong the pleasure, but his body responded on its own, meeting her thrusts, filling her deeper, faster, harder. His lungs emptied of air, his mind of thought. There was nothing but him and Hannah, and this incredible, exquisite, painful, killing hunger, driving, building, growing until it became unbearable, then growing even more.

Release came quickly. One second he was fighting for it, and the next it was there, holding his body utterly rigid, then leaving him trembling and weak, unable to breathe, unable to move, unable to feel anything but the purest, sweetest and most fleeting satisfaction.

She felt it, too, because after one moment dragged into another, after their breathing settled into a low rumble, after his heartbeat slowed to a relatively normal pace, she opened her eyes, gave him the sweetest, shyest, most wicked smile and a husky invitation.

''Let's do that again.''

Chapter 8

Long minutes passed—maybe days, weeks—before Hannah found the energy to move even one small muscle. She would simply stay there in Mick's arms forever if not for the very real possibility that they would be discovered in a few short hours by some early-morning fishermen—most likely fishermen she'd known all her life. Not desiring to be any more of an exhibitionist than she'd already proved, she forced herself away from the arm that held her close and sat up, scanning the dock. "Where's my shirt?"

Mick yawned, stretched, turned onto his side to face her. "I think it fell in the lake."

"Fell in?" She leaned over the edge of the dock, peering into the dark water, then, realizing the picture she was presenting, sat down again. He was grinning like a man who hadn't just experienced two incredible orgasms. "You threw my shirt in the lake?"

"You made me. You wrapped your fingers around my—"

With a warning look she cut him off, then pulled his

shirt on. "This was nice," she said with a supremely satisfied sigh. Mick's words—"Yeah, it was"—agreed, but
his tone didn't. His expression, suddenly serious and more
than a little bleak, didn't. "What's wrong?"

"Nothing. We'd better go." He sat up and reached for
his trunks, but she grabbed hold, too.

"Mick, what's wrong?"

"It doesn't matter." He pulled the trunks from her and
stepped into them, then shoved his feet into his shoes before
extending his hand.

She let him pull her to her feet, then picked up her towel
and shorts, returning the remaining condoms to the pocket.
Holding both in a ball in front of her, she watched as he
started toward the truck, but she didn't follow.

A few feet past the end of the dock, he realized she
wasn't coming and turned around. He looked as if he was
struggling with himself, wanting to talk but at the same
time wanting to keep whatever it was to himself. Clutching
her towel tighter against the chill growing inside her, she
watched him and waited, and finally he blurted out his
question.

"What changed your mind about sleeping with me?"

"Our conversation this afternoon. Your offer to buy into
the motel. Your pl—"

Something in his face changed, turned darker, colder.
"You know, you could have sold this place a hundred times
over if you'd taken out an ad. 'Run-down motel for sale.
Requires hard work and lots of money. Includes restaurant
and great sex with the boss. Warning: she doesn't sell herself cheap.'"

For a long time she stared at him, stunned, hurt. Then,
giving herself a mental shake, she pulled on the shorts she'd
intended to carry home, feeling too vulnerable and exposed
without them. She wrapped the damp towel around her
shoulders, seeking some protection against his insult,

against her shame that, under the circumstances, he was entitled to think that about her.

When she drew even with him, she stopped and forced herself to meet his gaze. He looked miserable and ashamed. "If you had let me finish, Mick, I was also going to say because of your plans to stay here. I can't risk a relationship with someone who has a better life someplace else, because my life is *here*. This is all I have to offer, and it's certainly not enough to make someone leave a comfortable home and a good job to come and live the way I do. Hoping that it might be is the best way I know to get my heart broken. But this afternoon you said you were willing to move here, anyway, for business, and I thought—"

She broke off, shook her head. "I can't even blame you for thinking it. It's only reasonable, once you start selling your body, that people are going to be confused about when you're selling and when you're giving." In spite of her best efforts, her voice quavered at the end. Ducking her head, she started for his truck and was almost there when his arms wrapped around her from behind, drawing her up short and snug against his body.

"I'm sorry."

Squeezing her eyes shut on the tears, she shook her head. "It's not your fault. It's Brad's and mine, not yours."

"Not yours, either," he disagreed fiercely. "He gave you no choice."

"He gave me a choice. I just made the wrong one. I should have told him to go ahead and foreclose on the loan."

"Then I never would have met you, and that would have been one of my biggest losses." Even though she tried to resist, he slowly turned her to face him, then kissed a tear from the corner of her eye. "And just for the record, darlin', I like the motel. I like the idea of fixing it up and turning it into a profitable business, but that's not why I want to stay here. You are, Hannah. You're the only reason.''

He kissed her then, long and hard, and made her legs go weak and her muscles quivery. When he backed her against his truck and lifted her so his arousal rubbed exactly where she needed him, she regretted bothering with her shorts, regretted ever leaving his embrace on the dock. She moaned, but it made little sound, lost in his kiss. When she reached for him, sliding her hand boldly over his erection, he pushed her back, ended the kiss and dragged in a deep breath.

''Let's go home.'' His voice was thick, uncontrolled.

Home. It had such a nice sound to it.

She climbed into the truck, fastened her seat belt, then gazed at the dock as he backed up. She had a lot of sweet old memories of this place. Now she had one new memory, one that would always take her breath away.

They drove back to the motel in intimate silence. She didn't even make a pretense of going into her own room. Mick unlocked his door, looked at her in silent invitation, and she walked inside. The air was cold, the only light coming from a bulb above the sink. He turned the air conditioner down a notch, then switched on every light in the room. At her questioning look he grinned. ''I want to see you. You were careful to control how much I saw last weekend because you didn't want me to know that you were a natural blonde. Tonight I want to see you in more than just moonlight. Tonight I want to see everything.''

She wished for a shower, a brush and something pretty to wear. Then he began closing the distance between them, all the while giving her a dark-eyed look that made her burn, and suddenly all she wanted was him. All of him, all night long.

Kneeling, he undressed her slowly, loosening the button that secured her shorts, sliding the zipper down inch by inch, lifting one foot, guiding the shorts over, then the

other. Before he discarded them, he removed the condoms
from the pocket and laid them on the dresser beside her.
Her fingers closed automatically around them, crinkling the
packets, then knotted as he brushed a long, slow, wet kiss
over her hip. The next kiss landed low on her belly, accompanied by easy caresses that robbed her of strength and
reason and made her cling to his shoulders for support.

"Definitely a natural blonde," he murmured as he rose
easily to his feet and pulled his shirt over her head in one
fluid motion. Claiming her wrist, he pulled her the short
distance to the bed, where he lay down, then drew her
close.

She leaned over him, feathering her fingers across his
chest, tasting him here, there, making his muscles knot and
his skin ripple. She worked her way to his lean hips, then
sat back and opened a plastic packet. He shifted on the bed,
restless, edgy, but made no move to hurry her along. She
eased the coiled latex from the package and held it with
two fingers while lazily stroking him with her other hand.
The condom was so thin, a delicate piece of nothing to bear
such responsibility.

She wished they didn't have to bother with it at all,
wished his wife hadn't been unfaithful, wished he hadn't
even had a wife. She wished all the men and women in
their pasts had never existed, that it had always been, would
always be, just the two of them together. She wished their
futures weren't so uncertain, wished they were at a place
in their lives where they could be thinking about forever
and babies and not prison or worse.

"Darlin'?" Mick's voice was hoarse, taut with discomfort. "You're killing me...."

Drawing her attention back to the task at hand, she po-
sitioned the sheath and, deliberately clumsy, worked it into
place, making him stiffen even more, making him groan.
Then she took him into place, rising over him, settling

slowly, deeply, sinking, taking all she could. When he filled her, she closed her eyes and sighed softly.

"Want to run away with me?"

She smiled. "Sure. Could we go someplace with a moderate climate? No hot summer droughts, no winter ice storms?" Then she laughed. "No, let's go someplace where it's warm all the time, where we can go naked and not care. A deserted island somewhere in the South Pacific maybe."

"I'm serious."

She opened her eyes and saw that he was. With only that glimpse, she became serious, too. "I can't leave here, Mick. I'm not even sure I want to."

"Whatever happened to wanting another life, another job, the variety and excitement of the city?"

"I've wanted that so long it's become habit. I just assumed it was still my dream. But when you said this afternoon that I could leave here and you would take care of Mom and Sylvie...I tried to imagine myself in Tulsa, being independent and free, responsible for no one but myself, doing only what I wanted." She smiled faintly. "I used to see my dreams so easily that it was like watching television. 'Hannah Goes to the City.' 'Hannah at Work.' 'Hannah Has a Social Life.' But this afternoon I couldn't see anything except 'Hannah Gets Lonely.' My life is here. My family is here." She hesitated, debated finishing the thought, then did. "You're here. Why would I leave?"

He shifted, and she felt it deep in her body. His hands claimed hers, then settled on her thighs. "If the motel was taken care of, if there was someone here to make sure that Merrilee and Sylvie were all right, if I was going, too, would you go?"

"But why would you... You mean if the sheriff arrests us. You're talking about running away to avoid prison. That would break Sylvie's heart."

"Any more than seeing you in prison would?"

She held his gaze a long time, then looked away. "It would certainly be a different and exciting life."

"But you'd rather stay here and take your chances with the sheriff and Brad."

Slowly she nodded.

"Even if you could be naked on an island in the South Pacific with me?" he gently teased, then pulled her close. "Then I guess we just won't let things get that bad. Somehow we'll find proof against Brad. Then you can spend the next few years naked in this room with me. Right now you can…" He murmured the rest in her ear, wicked ideas that made her flush and shiver, intimate words that prompted her to move against him, to withdraw, then take him once again deep into her body. He paced her, encouraged her, coaxed her along, until she shattered. Only a moment later so did he.

One endless, mindless moment drifted into another before he drew her onto the bed beside him, fitting her body snugly against his, and gave her a sweet kiss. "How about a new show?" he murmured. "'Hannah Takes a Lover.' And does it very well."

The last breakfast table was cleared, the last dish washed and the sweeping and restocking done when Mick joined Hannah at the registration desk. "What do you have in mind for today?"

She held his gaze, refusing to let hers slip one inch below his jaw. If she did, she would smile, and he would get that look, and they would go off to his room, and nothing would get done all day. Such pleasures would have to be restricted to nighttime hours, or else the motel would fall down around their ears in a matter of days. "Do you want to inspect your new business venture? Get an idea of what kind of trouble you've gotten yourself into?"

He gave her that look, anyway, accompanied by a wicked grin. "Oh, darlin', I know. Believe me."

She tried with little success to ignore the hunger he'd stirred. "Want to inspect the roof?"

"It's too hot. If we walk up there in heat like this, we're liable to do more damage."

"The rooms?"

"Now there's an idea. They're all empty, aren't they? Eighteen rooms. With eighteen beds."

She laughed in spite of herself. "You are shameless."

In an instant he sobered. "Not always. Not last night at the lake."

She started to reach for his hand, started to plead with him not to apologize again, because she'd deserved his insult more than she deserved his apology, but her gaze slipped past him, and instead, she clenched her hands into fists and muttered, "Damn."

He turned to look as the sheriff parked out front. This time he was accompanied by two deputies, both very young and looking self-important with their badges and the pistols on their hips.

The three men swaggered into the lobby and immediately turned toward them. "Morning, Hannah. Mr. Reilly."

Mick turned toward the sheriff. "I was going to call you later today. I wanted to ask you about Sandra's car."

"Silver Lexus. Pretty car. We've got it over at the impound lot. What about it?"

"I noticed when I was at the house in Oklahoma City that some of her things were missing—two suitcases, some clothes, shoes, jewelry. Were they in the car?"

His question went ignored. "Isn't it normal for a woman going out of town to take suitcases with her?"

"Sandra drove over here Saturday morning. She told me she was going straight back. She had a date that evening."

"But she didn't go straight back, did she? And there weren't any suitcases in the car. Huh. Interesting. Maybe I ought to have a look around your room, Mr. Reilly."

Mick scowled. "Maybe. When you have a search warrant or my lawyer says it's all right. You remember my lawyer? The one I told you to call if you had any other questions?"

Mills smiled. "I do. But you were asking me, remember? About your wife's pretty car. And it's beside the point, anyway, because I've come to talk to Hannah. I would appreciate it if you stayed around, though."

Hannah shifted nervously. "What do you need?"

"Are your mama and Miz Clark around?"

"Mom's in her apartment. Sylvie's gone into Yates."

"Good. Let's have a seat over here. You, too, Mr. Reilly." As he walked to the nearest table, the sheriff grinned. "A slice of Miz Clark's banana cream pie would sure taste good about now, with a cup of coffee."

"I'll get it," Mick volunteered, detouring behind the counter.

"You look pretty comfortable back there for a guest," Mills commented.

"I've been here almost a week with nothing to do."

"Why is that?"

"Because you asked me to stay around until further notice. It's a little hard to work when your work's two hours away and you're not supposed to go there."

"So rather than sit around bored, you've started helping out. Making repairs, serving meals, running errands. Awfully generous for a stranger, isn't he, Hannah?"

Her face turned pink, and she was sure the sheriff noticed. "Yes, he is. Then again, some people just don't like being idle. Sylvie's one of them. She's always got to be doing something."

Mick served Mills, ignored the deputies and took a seat. She ignored them, too, and waited for their boss to get to the point of this visit—her lies. She wished she hadn't eaten breakfast this morning, because her stomach was queasy and unsettled, and if she got much more nervous, she just might lose it all.

"I'm telling you, Hannah, Miz Clark makes the best pies I've ever had. Is she teaching you so you can take over when she's gone?"

Hannah hated the careless way he talked about Sylvie's eventual death and answered stonily, "My crusts aren't as flaky."

He took another bite, washed it down with coffee, then fixed his stare on her. "You know why I'm here. I had my girl call every motel within two miles of where you said you stayed last weekend, and no one had any record of you being there."

Grateful for the tabletop that hid her hands, she squeezed them tightly, trying to force every bit of fear and guilt out of her face and into her fingers. "I didn't say I registered under my own name."

"You didn't say you registered under somebody else's name, either. What was it?"

"I don't know. Actually, Sheriff—" she glanced at Mick and each of the deputies and felt her face grow warmer "—I was with someone."

"A man." He sounded skeptical. "What would be this man's name?"

"David Martin."

"Kind of a common name, isn't it? There must be fifteen or twenty of 'em in the Tulsa phone book alone."

"He's not from Tulsa. He lives in some little town in Kansas." Without waiting to be asked, she launched into the rest of her story, sticking to the facts she had rehearsed with Mick yesterday, embellishing nothing.

When she was finished, the sheriff looked at her a long time before finally speaking. "Let me see if I got this straight. You met this man with a pretty common name last summer and had an affair with him. Now I'm betting he wasn't a guest here where his name and address would be a matter of record. That would be too easy—but that's beside the point. After not seeing or hearing from him for a year, he sends you a note saying, 'I'll be in Tulsa without my wife. I want to have sex with you again. If you're interested, meet me at the Red Lobster on 51st Street at noon Saturday.' You destroy the note to keep your seventy-some-year-old granny from suspecting that you're having an affair, and you go and have a wild weekend with him. Then he goes back home to his wife, and you come back here, still not knowing where he's from, what name he registered under, what motel you spent those three days at or even what room you were in." He paused, then quietly finished, "Uh-huh."

"Must've been a *real* wild weekend," one of the deputies said with a snort.

Now her face was blazing. "Pardon me for not paying more attention, Sheriff," she said stiffly. "If I'd known I would need an alibi when I got back, I would have been prepared."

Without responding, Mills turned his attention to Mick. "Let's look at *your* alibi for a minute. Elizabeth. That was her name, wasn't it? How old did you say she was?"

"Late twenties." Mick sounded as defensive as she had. Lord help them, they were so bad at misleading the authorities that they were going to be the sheriff's best help in convicting them.

"And she was a redhead. Natural?"

"How would I know?"

Again the deputy snorted, then hastily put on a straight face at the sheriff's frown.

"You saw her naked, didn't you?" Mills asked.

"The room was dark."

"Was that at her request or yours?"

"It wasn't anyone's request. We went to the room. It was dark. We didn't bother turning the lights on."

"How tall did you say Elizabeth was?"

"I don't remember."

The sheriff pulled a notebook from his pocket and flipped

it open. "I kinda figured you wouldn't, so I brought my notes. Let's see...only name she gave was Elizabeth, she was in her late twenties, five-seven, 120 pounds, long curly red hair and blue eyes." Leaning back in his chair, Mills gave Hannah a long look. "Stand up for a minute, would you, Hannah?"

Swallowing hard and hoping her legs could support her, she did so.

"What do you think, Billy? She's about five-seven, isn't she?"

"Yes, sir. About 120 pounds, too. Long hair. Definitely blue eyes."

"So, except for the curly and red part, she matches your description of Elizabeth to a T, doesn't she, Mr. Reilly? Of course, curly and red can be done and undone real easy these days. I went home one day, and my daughter's hair was purple. Next morning it was blond again." He looked expectantly from Mick to Hannah. "So...is there anything either of you would like to tell me?"

The silence in the room was a perfect example of deafening, Mick thought, though he was half-surprised his heartbeat wasn't as audible to everyone else as it was to him. Looking at the stunned expression Hannah wore, he was completely surprised he couldn't hear her heart thudding.

Anything they would like to tell him? Mick would love to tell him to go to hell. Of course, to a man like Mills, that would be akin to an admission of guilt.

Keeping his hands motionless and limp on the table, he tried desperately to think of another lie, but he could barely put a coherent thought together. He couldn't think of anything original or halfway believable. All he could think of was the truth and how bad it would sound at this late date.

"Well?"

He glanced at Hannah, who looked utterly shocked. In making up her story, they had never considered that the sheriff might guess the truth about Elizabeth. They hadn't given the man enough credit.

He didn't have a clue what to say.

"Will it affect your answer any to know that the night clerk over at the Lakeside Motel in Yates said you've had a pretty, young blond woman making regular all-night visits to your room for the past few months?"

At last he found his voice and flatly denied the sheriff's assertion. "That's not true. In the eighteen months I lived there, the only women who ever set foot in that room were my wife and the housekeeping staff."

"According to the clerk, a woman matching Hannah's description was over there three, four nights a week since sometime in April. Driving a little blue car. You drive a little blue car, don't you, Hannah?"

She sat stiffly, unable to answer. Mick spoke, instead. "The clerk is lying."

"And why would he do that?"

Because Brad paid him to. He'd threatened to make Hannah a suspect, and he'd started by yanking her alibi out from under her. Now he'd added another layer of suspicion. No doubt, when the sheriff questioned him next, he would heap on more with his manufactured tale of a relationship between her and Mick.

"I'm waiting, Mr. Reilly. Why would this clerk—an upstanding member of the community, a hardworking man with no connection whatsoever to this case and no desire other than to see justice done—make up a lie like that?"

"Maybe he's not so upstanding. Maybe you just haven't seen the connection."

"Maybe. And *maybe* he's got nothing to hide. Maybe you do." Mills's gaze flickered over Hannah. "Maybe you both do."

Mick stared at the table, not trusting himself to look at either Hannah or the sheriff.

Mills turned his attention to her. "Hannah, I've known

your family all my life, and I just can't believe you'd get tied up with something like murder. If you know something about this case, you need to tell us. Anything at all, Hannah."

"You're right, Sheriff." She drew a deep breath, and color slowly seeped back into her face. Mick kicked her under the table, tried to warn her, to catch her eye, but she was rigidly fixed on Mills. "I *am* Elizabeth. I'm—"

"Hannah!" Mick said sharply, catching her hand, making her look at him. She could take back her words, could say it was just a lie. *He* would say it was just a lie.

"Mick, he's setting us up." Her voice was taut, her eyes intense. "If we wait any longer to ask for help, it'll be too late."

"It already *is* too late. He's not going to believe us."

"We won't know that until we try, will we?" After a long still moment, she turned back to the sheriff. "I'm the woman who picked Mick up in the bar. I brought him back here. I was gone when he woke up the next morning. He was here all that night. He never went near the resort. He didn't have anything to do with Sandra's murder."

Mills looked more serious than ever. There wasn't a hint of the satisfaction Mick had expected to see. "How can you be so sure of that?"

"Because I was with him. And because I know who killed her. It was the same man who bribed your motel clerk to lie. The man who blackmailed me into keeping Mick occupied Saturday night, then leaving him without an alibi. The man who left *me* without an alibi. The man who's been pushing your investigation toward Mick from the very beginning. The man who stood to gain far more from Sandra's death than Mick did."

"And who is this mystery man?"

Hannah looked at Mick, giving him the opportunity to answer, and he did so heavily. "My partner. Brad Daniels."

Mills sat back, hanging one arm over the back of the chair, and studied first one, then the other. "Brad Daniels," he repeated. "Of the manufacturing, industry, high-finance, blue blood, Social Register Danielses. And what would be his motive for killing your wife?"

"Getting rid of me. Getting control of the company. Getting out from under the resort. Staying out of bankruptcy court. A million dollars." Mick shrugged. "Take your pick."

"A million doll— From your wife's life-insurance policy. It gets paid to the company, and if you're in prison for her murder and he's the sole owner of the company, then he's the sole beneficiary." Mills nodded thoughtfully. "Interesting. So, Hannah, if you spent Saturday night here, where were you the rest of the weekend?"

"At the Daniels cabin on the lake."

"And if we go there, we'll find…?"

"A place that looks as unused as room 17 did when you checked it out. But I *was* there. I swear I was."

"A few days ago you swore you were at a girlfriend's in Tulsa. Yesterday you swore you were alone at a motel. This morning you just said you were with a man, and now you're swearing you were fifteen miles from here. You see the problem I have with believing you, Hannah?"

Her expression was as dismal as Mick had ever seen. He tightened his fingers around hers and drew the sheriff's attention his way. "You're planning to talk to Brad about this claim of an affair, aren't you?" He took Mills's shrug as a yes. "I'll bet you Sandra's insurance money that he tells you—with great regret, of course—that yes, I was having an affair with Hannah, that he'd known all along but he'd kept quiet about it because he was afraid it would make things look worse for me. And if you tell him about Hannah's claim that she spent last weekend at his cabin, he'll deny it. He'll say the cabin hasn't been used in months, that the gas, electricity and water have been turned off. He'll invite you to see for yourself, even tell you that the key's under the doormat.''

"But you don't have proof of any of this, do you?'' Mills asked. "As for your bet, Brad Daniels is your partner and friend. Of course he wouldn't want to volunteer any information that would be so damning against you. And if Hannah here used his cabin without his knowing, of course he would tell me it hadn't been used in months. Your story works both ways, Mr. Reilly—with him setting you up and with you setting him up. Considering who he is and that the dead woman was *your* wife and that he's been most cooperative and that you were involved in a nasty divorce, I have to say that right now I'd tend to believe him.''

"What's your theory, Sheriff?'' he asked sarcastically. "Rich people don't kill? Wealthy businessmen don't commit crimes? How do you think a great many of them got wealthy in the first place?''

"Brad Daniels was born into his money.''

"And his greedy effort to get more cost him a fortune. He needed to get rid of the resort, and he wanted to get rid of me.''

"So why kill your wife? Why not just kill you and leave *your* body in the resort while it burned?''

"Stage a suicide? No one who knew me ever would have believed it. An accidental fire in an unoccupied building? Very difficult to pull off. But setting me up for a murder?'' His smile was cool. "Piece of cake. All he needed was the right beautiful woman. The rest was easy.''

Mills studied them awhile, his gaze dropping more than once to their clasped hands, then he slapped the table as he stood up. "Interesting theory. Kind of out there, but interesting. I'll look into it.''

Mick wouldn't hold his breath waiting.

The sheriff and his deputies were on their way out the door as Sylvie was coming in. They greeted her, and she turned to watch them leave before approaching the table where Mick and Hannah still sat, no longer touching. "What did they want?"

"To prove that I killed my wife and to send me away for a long, long time." He rubbed his neck to ease the tension there. "Mills just had a few more questions he wanted answers to."

"You've hired yourself a lawyer, haven't you? Let him answer their questions." Sylvie stood looking down at Hannah, who was still pale and staring off into the distance. "You okay?"

She blinked, breathed, then gave her grandmother a smile. "I'm fine. Did you get what you needed in town?"

"Get what I needed?" She patted her gray curls. "If you can't tell, I reckon what I need is a new hairstyle."

"Oh. Yes, I forgot. Your hair appointment."

Sylvie sat down and wrapped her fingers around Hannah's wrist. "I've had a hair appointment every Saturday morning for forty-five years, and you forgot? What's wrong, Hannah? Are you worried about him?"

Surprising Mick, Hannah reached for and squeezed his hand. "I have faith in the justice system."

"Well, I don't," Sylvie said. "If I were you, son, I'd clean out my bank account and be on my way. By the time Mills decided to arrest me, I'd be so far gone he would never, ever catch up."

"I can't run away."

"Sure, you can. You tell the sheriff you have business to take care of at home and you'll be gone overnight. Once you get there, you get all the cash you can, take anything worth selling and hit the road."

Ruefully he shook his head. Even when he'd suggested it to Hannah last night, he hadn't been half-serious, though he'd said he was. He had never run from trouble in his life. It had been a nice thought, living with Hannah someplace where trouble couldn't stalk them, but that was all. Just a thought.

Before Sylvie could continue, he changed the subject. ''We need to settle the terms of our business arrangement so the lawyer can draw up the papers. What's the market value for a half interest in the Last Resort?''

''Figure it out for yourself,'' Sylvie replied. ''What you see is what you get. We have a lot of expenses. We're badly in need of major repairs. We have no assets. We operate on a wish and a prayer. Speaking as the original owner, chief pastry chef and bottle washer, I'd say the place is worth about fifty dollars. Wouldn't you agree, Hannah?''

''If you're feeling generous.''

Mick looked from one to the other, then shook his head. He named his own price, plus additional funds for repairs, and both women burst out laughing. It was a substantial amount of money—particularly for a business operating on a wish and a prayer—but it seemed a bargain to him. They would get the cash, and he would get them. A home. A place to belong. People to belong to.

''No cash,'' Hannah suggested. ''Just take care of the repairs.''

''You need operating capital.''

''You don't need to take on that kind of debt. You might have major expenses of your own before long.''

''No one sells half a business in exchange for repairs.''

''No one buys half a business that requires the kind of repairs this one needs.''

He looked at her for a long time, at the thin line of her mouth, the stubborn set of her jaw, the unyielding look in her blue eyes, and he grinned. ''You know, darlin', you could go away and let Sylvie and me take care of this.''

''Sylvie's not the owner. I am.''

''She's your business adviser.''

''That I am,'' Sylvie agreed. ''I've been teaching her about the motel business since she was just out of diapers. I imagine I'll be teaching you, too, and I hope to live long enough to teach my great-grandchildren. Keep that in mind, son, before you get yourself locked up in prison.''

Hannah's face flushed scarlet, and she stood up, gathering the sheriff's empty dishes. "I have work to do even if you two don't, so if you'll excuse me…''

Once she was gone, Sylvie sighed. "I wish you could take her away from here.''

"I offered. She doesn't want to go.''

"It's her mother and me, isn't it? We've kept her tied down so long that she doesn't know how to live without us.''

"It's that," he acknowledged. "And this place. You and Merrilee are family. This is home. Leaving your family and your home is tough. Believe me, I've done it.''

"Didn't you ever want to go back?''

"Sometimes. But I thought Sandra and I would have our own family, and she never would have moved to West Texas. Then that didn't work out, but I had the business.''

"And now that's gone, but you've got Hannah. Do you intend to marry her?''

He hadn't let himself plan much beyond selling the house he'd built for Sandra, buying into the motel and being with Hannah. His future was too uncertain. But in a perfect world, one without suspicion and doubts, without murder charges and prison sentences and Brad Daniels, would he marry Hannah?

In a heartbeat.

He looked at Sylvie, waiting expectantly, and answered, "If I don't go to prison, if she'll have me, yes, ma'am, I do.''

Sandra's house—Hannah couldn't bring herself to think of it as Mick's—sat brightly lit in the warm night. It was impressive, absolutely beautiful, but she still didn't like it. She would still rather not set foot inside the door, though she doubted Mick would agree to let her wait in the truck while he spent an hour or two inside looking for something to connect Sandra to Brad.

He parked near the side door, picked up the mail he'd taken from the box outside the gate, then pulled her out of the truck after him. Inside the house, after switching on more lights, he led her to a room at the back. Uncurtained French doors topped with arched windows opened onto a brick patio, where steps led to a pool, then to a broad green lawn that stretched into darkness. The pool was long, rectangular, a pretty shimmery blue that invited a late-night swim.

She preferred a moonlit lake.

Turning from the windows, she took a look around. This office was more like Brad's—elegant, beautifully appointed, lots of leather and gorgeous dark paneling. She felt as if she was in the domain of a high-powered attorney—one she couldn't afford. "Nice office."

"Sandra's interior designer did it. She refused to have anything held together with duct tape in the house." He sat down in a plush chair of brown leather, the kind that looked softer than a cloud and twice as puffy. There was a matching sofa against one wall and an armchair against another.

"You'll miss all this."

He looked up from the mail he was sorting. "I built this house to satisfy Sandra's need to flaunt our recent good fortune. I never wanted anything this ostentatious. I promise you, darlin', I won't miss any of it. I haven't even lived here for a year and a half. I never felt at home here."

"And you can feel at home at the motel."

"I can. I do. But..." He held his hand out. When she took it, he drew her around the desk and onto his lap. "Someday I'd like to build you a house somewhere nearby."

"Nothing like this."

"No. It would be two stories, white, with dark green shutters and a black door, and it would look as if it had been there a hundred years. It would have a deep porch that goes all the way across the front and wraps around both sides, and a porch swing and big brick fireplaces in the living room and your bedroom. The floors would be heart of pine, and the dining room would be big enough to seat all the children you'll have someday and all their children. There would be a bay window in the living room, where you would put the Christmas tree every year. There would be a room for Merrilee, if she ever wanted it, and one for Sylvie, if she ever needed it, and lots of room for babies.''

''Sounds perfect,'' she murmured, and it did. ''But where are these babies and grandbabies going to come from if I live there alone?''

''Not alone.'' He brushed her hair back and left a lazy, sweet kiss beneath her ear. ''With me. If I—''

He didn't finish. He didn't need to. Cupping his face between her palms, she kissed his mouth, then wriggled out of his arms and to her feet. ''Then we'd better find *something* to get ourselves out of trouble, because I always did have a dream about a pretty white house with a porch and babies.'' She circled to the other side of the desk for safety and sat down. ''What are you looking for?''

''Phone bills, credit-card bills, anything that might somehow connect Sandra to Brad. Even after I moved out, I always paid the bills and kept all the records in this desk.''

''Could you talk to her friends? Was there someone she would have confided in?''

''Not if Brad told her not to. He had more to lose with an affair becoming public knowledge than she did. Besides, her friends were *her* friends. They didn't like me, and they wouldn't talk to me, especially now, believing I killed her.''

He handed Hannah a stack of file folders, and she flipped through them to find neatly organized stacks of credit-card statements, one card per folder, each statement in chronological order. "No doubt about it. You're handling the paperwork at the motel."

Flipping through his own folder, he grinned. "You like my filing system?"

"It's amazing." She returned the grin. "You'll hate mine. It involves two-foot-high stacks on the bookcase." Falling silent, she turned her attention to the statements. The credit limit on this particular card was higher than her income for the past two years, and the itemized list of charges for the past month filled more than four pages. Restaurants, department stores, jewelry stores, car rentals, gift shops— "You have a pen and paper?"

He did. She made a few notes, moved to the previous statement and added a few more. After going back six months on that particular card, she moved to the next folder. Across the desk Mick was making notes, too, and wearing a frown. He had phone records and apparently wasn't too pleased with what he was finding.

Finally he sat back in the chair with a brooding look and waited until she closed the last file. "Well?"

She read through the list of items that had interested her—airline tickets, car rentals and shopping sprees in Dallas two months ago, in Houston a few weeks later, in Kansas City only three weeks ago. Interestingly hotel charges were missing.

Tapping his pen on the desk pad, he said flatly, "Brad was in Dallas on business two months ago—talking to a potential buyer for the resort. He met another one in Houston after that, and he went to Kansas City on family business early this month." He dropped the pen and picked up a stack of bills. "I have phone-card calls from Dallas, Houston, Kansas City and Brad's house at the lake. Sandra could never go anywhere for more than a few hours without checking her messages," he said dryly. "The bills for her cellular phone show three to four calls a week to Brad's house at the lake and his cellular. This latest bill covers up to a few days before she died. In the two weeks before she died, she started calling him three to four times a *day*. There are also a number of calls to his pager, followed every time by an incoming call that usually lasted awhile.''

''Almost as if...''

''As if what?''

''They were planning something.''

The thought had already occurred to him. She could see the evidence in his grim expression. Did that make it worse, she wondered, to suspect that not only had his partner been willing to frame him for murder, but his wife had helped? It must. Not loving him and betraying him with her affairs were one thing, but deliberately setting out to destroy his life... That was so much colder.

''Sandra's cooperation would explain my signature on the life-insurance policy. She used to sign my name to everything back when it was just the two of us. So...Sandra and Brad planned the setup together. She helped him get the life-insurance policy.''

''That would explain the check, too,'' she said, almost to herself. At Mick's quizzical look, she explained. ''When I first heard about Sandra's murder, I called Brad. I didn't realize he was behind it, and I told him I had to talk to the sheriff, to tell him the truth so you wouldn't be implicated. That was when Brad threatened to frame me, too. He said that if I made any effort to clear you, he would turn over to the sheriff a carbon from a check written the day before Sandra's death. It was on your account, to me from you, for ten thousand dollars, and the purpose, according to his theory, was to buy my testimony for your alibi.''

''So Sandra signed that for him, too.''

''And she showed up at the resort to provoke you into making a public threat.''

''But she damn well wouldn't have met him there that night to let him kill her.'' His voice turned sardonic, and his expression matched. "That would have been counter-productive."

"Right," Hannah agreed. "But she might have gone to help him start the fire. She might have believed the frame was for arson and only arson."

"Not if she forged my signature on a life-insurance policy on herself. She must have known that for the policy to pay, she had to be dead."

"Or they had to fake her death. They would set the fire, she would leave her car there, and then she would disappear. Brad would remain behind and convince the authorities that she had died in the fire."

"And how would he do that when there was no body?"

"Maybe he convinced her that the fire would burn so hot that a body would be destroyed. After all, they cremate people all the time."

"Yeah, in a crematorium, where the body is exposed to extremely high temperatures for an extended period of time. Even then, some bones survive. There's no way this fire would get that hot."

"Then maybe he told her he would acquire a body from someplace else—an unclaimed body from a morgue. Maybe she thought he intended to kill some homeless person in her place." She gestured impatiently. "He didn't have to have a perfect plan, Mick. He just had to fool Sandra. If she trusted him enough to get involved in his scam in the first place, she would have trusted him to handle the police and all the problems afterward. She would have believed that she would be waiting somewhere for him to join her with the insurance money and a wedding ring."

"Which would explain the suitcases, the clothes, the jewelry."

Hannah nodded.

"And all that is either at Brad's house, at the bottom of the lake or, most likely, destroyed in the fire."

"The suitcases and the clothes, probably. But being the

greedy bastard that he is, do you think it's possible he kept the jewelry?''

"I doubt it. There were some nice pieces, but nothing terrifically expensive. Certainly nothing worth risking getting caught. Besides, what would he do with them? Hock them? Give them to his next girlfriend? Save them for his future wife?"

The idea made her shiver with revulsion, but she wasn't convinced Brad was above such an act.

Mick left the desk, paced the room, then settled on the couch. He leaned his head back, his eyes closed, then swung his legs onto the cushions. "We're no better off than we were before. We know more, but we still can't prove anything."

Hannah joined him, sitting on the edge of the cushion, resting her arm across his middle. "We're getting there," she disagreed. "It's slow going, but we'll find the proof."

"Maybe Sylvie was right. Maybe I should get the hell out of Dodge while I'm still a free man."

"That wouldn't be the end of it. If Mills can't pin it on you, he'll make do with me. You'll lose, I'll lose, but Brad will be a richer, freer man." She rubbed her palm across his stomach, lazily back and forth, while contemplating her life alone if Mick went on the run. It was too bleak to consider, and so she didn't. She turned her attention to something much more interesting, much more satisfying. "When was the last time you had any fun in this house?"

His eyes still closed, he grinned. "The day I wired the chandelier in the entry."

She thought of the high ceiling and the marble floor below—far below. "And why were you thirty feet up in the air wiring the chandelier? Didn't you have electricians to do that?"

"I do a little bit of everything. It helps me to know that I'm getting quality work from my subcontractors. It also helps with the bidding process and earns me a little respect.''

''And what if you'd fallen?''

''The floor would've broken a fall.''

She toyed with the button that secured his jeans. ''The floor would have broken your neck, too, along with every other bone in your body.''

''And Sandra would have been a merry rich widow.''

Instead, she was dead, and Hannah was considering seducing her husband in her house. The thought sent shivers down her spine. Leaving the button alone, she curved her fingers around his side, tucking the tips between his ribs and the leather. ''How can we prove that Brad was having an affair with her?''

''Without the sheriff's help, I don't know that we can. I could tell him that Brad was in those cities the same time Sandra was, but he'd probably say it was just coincidence. We know she didn't charge a hotel bill, and she never paid cash for anything, but we can't prove that she stayed with him. We can't even prove that she talked to him in all those dozens of calls. About the only thing we can prove is that she's dead.''

After a long grim silence, he finally opened his eyes and grinned. ''Want to climb up here on top of me and make a little fun of our own before we leave?''

Though that had been her original intent when she'd sat down, she shook her head. ''Let's go home. It would be more fun there.''

He slid the records they'd combed through into a briefcase, then they left the way they'd come in. As the electronic gate closed behind them, she took one last long look at the house. Unless it was to help Mick pack, she would never come back here again. She was glad.

They were halfway home before she twisted in the seat to face him. ''What if I talk to Brad?''

''And get him to confess everything into a conveniently

hidden tape recorder?'' Mick sounded as if he would be amused if he wasn't so scornful of the idea. ''Darlin', you've seen too much television. He's in complete control. His plan is working perfectly. Why in hell would he confess anything now?''

''Because he likes to brag. He's already said things to me over the phone that implicate him. If I can get him to repeat them…''

Mick shook his head emphatically. ''He said those things because he thought you were scared senseless. Now that he knows you're with me, there's no way he's going to tell you anything.''

''But, Mick, this could be our best chance.''

''Best chance at what? Getting you killed?'' He took her hand, squeezing it tightly. ''Promise me you'll stay away from him, Hannah.''

She stared down, her lower lip caught between her teeth. ''Hannah?''

Still she said nothing.

He skidded to a stop on the shoulder, loosened her seat belt and pulled her across the seat to him. ''Damn it, Hannah, he'll kill you if he thinks you're a threat. Too many people depend on you—Ruby and Earlene, your mother, Sylvie…me. We can't lose you. *I* can't lose you. Promise me you'll stay away from Brad.''

She swallowed hard because she knew she was about to make a promise she might not keep, and she pressed her face against his throat to keep him from seeing it in her eyes. ''I promise.''

He exhaled heavily. Relieved? Temporarily satisfied? After a time he let her go, but not all the way across the seat. He fastened the center lap belt over her hips, then rested his hand possessively on her thigh. They drove the rest of the way home like that.

There were a half-dozen cars parked at the other end of the lot. It was a good night for the Last Resort. With Mick's help and his money, they would soon have plenty of good nights. With his presence, she acknowledged, all her nights would be good, whether there was even a single guest in the place.

"Are you tired?" she asked as they stepped onto the sidewalk.

"Not really."

"There's a place I'd like to show you. Just let me change shoes." She went into her room, traded sandals for loafers, grabbed a quilt, a flashlight and a few other necessities, then rejoined him outside. The moon was bright enough to make the flashlight unneeded until they moved into the heavy-growth woods fifty feet behind the motel. Even there the long-unused path was easy to follow as it made a straight run to the creek bank and the old bridge her father had built.

On the other side the trees were sparse and had been planted in the neat rows of an orchard. She walked between two tall spreading apple trees, turned in a slow circle, then faced Mick. "When I was a little girl, I used to dream about having a house here, where I could walk out in the front yard and pick an apple, a pear or a peach—" she gestured to each type of tree "—or go a few feet farther and wade, swim or fish. This was my favorite place to play, to read, to dream. This was where I came after my grandfather's funeral, after my father's funeral, after I realized that, like it or not, I was home to stay. This is a special place."

"Then this is where we'll build our house."

Not *your* house, but ours. She couldn't imagine anything she wanted more than a future with him, with Sylvie and Merrilee and babies filling their house and their hearts.

Well, just one thing.

With his help, she spread the quilt over the tall grass and stepped out of her shoes. She removed the condoms from her pocket—the few necessary items she'd picked up—and tossed them on the quilt, then undressed, dropping her shorts here, panties there, shirt on top. The whole time, Mick watched her from the opposite end of the quilt with a half smile and evidence of serious arousal.

Naked, she walked to him, kissed his jaw, his throat, removed his shirt. She helped him with his shoes, his jeans, the condom, then followed him onto the quilt.

This had always been a special place, she thought as she took him deep inside her body.

Now it was even more so.

Chapter 9

Sunday afternoon the sky opened up, swallowing the motel in a deluge of gray rain and grayer skies. Mick helped Hannah check the rooms for leaks, putting out buckets where necessary—and too many places it was necessary. After changing into dry clothes, he returned to the dining room with a legal pad and pen, made himself comfortable and began making notes.

The motel was in bad shape. He'd known that from the first time he'd seen it. But it wasn't beyond saving. With a new roof, cooling and heating systems, carpet, furniture, bathroom and light fixtures, dining room and kitchen—and parking lot, he added as rain turned the gravel lot into a pond—the place could be as good as new. And with all those repairs or replacements, it might be cheaper to build new.

But cheaper wasn't the point. He'd done his fair share of million-dollar remodels on homes built around the turn of the century. No one had ever suggested tearing those houses down and starting again from scratch. Of course, those houses had been quality construction to start with. The Last Resort was a cinder-block motel, nothing more, nothing less. And it was Hannah's heritage. It would be his children's heritage.

"Want some coffee or tea?" Hannah stopped behind him, resting her hands on his shoulders, automatically giving them a squeeze or two.

"No, thanks."

"What are you doing?"

"Making lists." He fanned through the pages of the tablet, where he'd listed subcontractors, repairs, remodels, supplies, priorities. After this rain the roof was number one.

"You're really serious about fixing this place up."

Catching her hand, he pulled her into his lap. "I am. I'm really serious about you, too."

She snuggled closer and curled her fingers around a fistful of his shirt, but didn't say anything in response. He wished she would. Just a simple "Me, too," would satisfy him.

Like hell it would. But it would be enough for now.

Since she didn't say anything at all, he turned back to business. "What do you think about restoring the motel to look like exactly what it once was—a fifties-era motel and diner?"

"It'd be like stepping into a time warp."

"People like time warps—especially when they have all the conveniences of today. They consider the fifties the good old days, when life was safer, happier, more idyllic."

"Sounds interesting." She sighed at the sound of her name from her mother's quarters. Merrilee's voice was weak—though strong enough to be heard out here—and quavery. "I'd better go. You're welcome to join us if you want."

He shook his head. She'd been baby-sitting Merrilee, who was having a bad day, since breakfast, coming out only briefly to help with the after-church dinner crowd.

Sylvie had taken off after cleanup, going to Yates to visit friends, and Mick had settled here. He didn't mind Merrilee when she was having one of those days, but he felt the need to get moving on the repairs and remodels as quickly as possible. He didn't want to find himself in prison at all, but it would be worse if the work he'd promised Hannah remained undone.

She kissed him, then slid to her feet and headed for the laundry room, the shortcut into Merrilee's rooms. At the doorway she looked back. "How serious?"

He knew immediately what she meant and grinned. "Serious enough to stay here forever."

After a moment she nodded, turned away and closed the door quietly behind her.

He continued to look at the spot she'd been for a long time, then quietly murmured, "Serious enough to fall in love with you."

It was crazy. He'd just taken the hard way out of a bad marriage. His present was uncertain, and he had no future, not until he was cleared in Sandra's death. The last thing he needed was to fall in love.

Or maybe it was the first thing he needed.

Either way, he wasn't about to question his luck. Whatever happened, he would get through it with Hannah. For Hannah.

And for all those babies they were going to have. They were going to make Sylvie a happy great-grandmother, and himself a happy man.

He'd just looked back at his lists when headlights flashed across the dining room and drew his attention outside. The car, a Grand Am that had seen better days, parked across three spaces right in front of the door, and Trey Landry climbed out. Mick laid his pen aside as the lawyer came inside, wiped his feet on the rug, then started across the dining room.

"Great day for a drive," Mick remarked as Landry

pulled off his damp jacket and wiped away the rain that dripped from his hair.

Landry muttered something that might have been a greeting, then asked, "How's it going?"

"Well, let's see. The sheriff's turned up a life-insurance policy on Sandra with my name forged on the application and the check. He's also found a witness, a clerk at the motel where I stayed the past year and a half, who claims that, for the last few months, I was having an affair with a woman matching Hannah's description. He discovered that Hannah's alibi for last weekend doesn't hold water, and in a misguided effort to turn his attention in the right direction, she confessed that she's Elizabeth. Now he considers her a suspect, too. And how was your week?"

"Hannah? The blonde you were flirting with when I was here before? She's Elizabeth?"

Mick nodded.

"And you knew that then? Of course you did. You spent the entire night having sex with her. More than likely you would recognize her even with her clothes on. Why didn't you tell me then?"

"She was being blackmailed. Telling the truth then would have hurt her, and it wouldn't have helped me."

"Blackmailed by whom?"

With his foot Mick pushed out the chair across from him. "Have a seat. We've got a lot to talk about."

Landry sat down, and Mick started talking. He told the lawyer everything they knew, everything they suspected, every theory they'd considered. When he was finished, Landry sat quietly for a long time. Finally he met Mick's gaze. "Are you willing to swear on your life that you had nothing to do with Sandra's death?"

"Yes."

"Are you convinced that Hannah can swear the same?"

"Yes. So...what do you think?"

"I think you two are in a world of trouble. I think you'd

better stop cooperating with the sheriff. And I think Hannah needs a lawyer.''

''Can you represent her?''

''It wouldn't be a good idea.''

''Can you recommend someone?''

''Yeah, I'll find someone first thing in the morning.'' Landry leaned back in his chair. ''Do you have the money for a private investigator?''

Mick nodded. ''Do you think a PI can help?''

''The one I use is good. She's resourceful, and she's not bound by the same rules of evidence—or ethics—that lawyers and cops are. If anyone can find proof of an affair between your wife and your partner, she can. Get me the phone and credit-card statements, and I'll turn them over to her tomorrow.''

While Landry waited, Mick retrieved the statements from his room. When he got back to the lobby, the lawyer was waiting just inside the door, watching as the rain slacked off. He accepted the files, stashed in a plastic bag to keep them dry, with one question. ''Is there anything else?''

''Just one thing. Can you draw up a partnership agreement?''

''Between you and...?''

''Hannah. I'm buying half the motel.''

''Why?''

Mick grinned. ''Because I like challenges. And if you can keep me out of prison, I intend to spend the rest of my life here.''

''With a woman you just met a week ago when she helped frame you on a murder charge,'' Landry said flatly. ''What was it? Lust at first sight, love at second?''

''You sound like a man who doesn't have much faith in the concept of love.''

''I don't necessarily see it as a good thing. People do crazy things for an emotion that comes and goes on a whim.'' He returned to the subject. ''You know, going into partnership with the woman you claim as your alibi for the time of the murder might not be such a great idea.''

"Why not? Are you planning to call her to testify?''

Landry considered it a moment. "I would've been happy to call Elizabeth—a stranger who has nothing to gain and presumably a lot to lose by testifying—but Hannah?'' He shook his head. "If I put her on the stand, the first thing the DA will do is impugn her testimony. He'll call all the people she's lied to about that night, and they'll convince the jury that you and she planned and carried out the murder together. She would do you both more harm than good.''

"So what does it matter if I've become part owner of the Last Resort?''

Landry shrugged. "It's your life. What are the terms of the purchase?''

Mick pulled a piece of paper from his pocket, placed there earlier for just this reason, and gave it to him. Just as Hannah and Sylvie had reacted strongly to the price he'd put on the place, so did Landry, but he didn't say a word. He just slid the paper into the bag with the statements. "If the sheriff comes around, don't talk to him. Tell Hannah not to talk to him, either. Give him my number and I'll set up a time when I can be present. And don't let him search your room or your truck for any reason. I'll be in touch with you tomorrow.''

Mick watched him leave, then continued to gaze out. Sunshine wasn't much of a town—a few blocks of nothing places like the motel. It couldn't even measure up to the minimal standards of the hometown he'd been so eager to leave behind seventeen years ago. Of course, he admitted with a grin, seventeen years ago, he'd been a kid, eager to get out and experience the world, looking for something better than what he'd always known. After all those long years of searching, he'd finally found it here, in a town smaller and drearier than the one he'd left behind.

Now if he could just manage to keep it.

Hannah was in the kitchen, looking for something to munch on, when Sylvie blew into the lobby, bellowing her name with more force than Hannah had thought her grandmother capable of. Backing away from the refrigerator, she closed the door and reluctantly, fearfully, pushed the swinging door open wide.

Sylvie stood beside Mick's table, untying the laces of a bright pink rain bonnet while her matching vinyl coat dripped water in a circle at her feet. Her face was pale, with two bright splotches of red centered high on her cheeks, and her hands were trembling. In fact, her entire body shook. Hannah had never seen her so angry, which seemed the best reason in the world to quietly slip back into the kitchen and out the back door. Who cared if it was still raining? She'd been wet before. Playing in the summer rain had been one of her favorite pastimes as a kid.

Before she could take even one small step back, though, Sylvie's sharp blue eyes zeroed in on her, pinning her in place. "Don't you even think about the back door, young lady. You get over here and sit down *now*."

Now in that quiet, commanding voice was the equivalent of anyone else's most furious shout. Hannah had heard it only a few times in her life, and never directed at her. She very quickly obeyed it.

Sylvie closed her eyes, breathed deeply a few times and finally managed to loosen the strings on her bonnet. She draped it over a nearby chair, hung the slicker over another, then rested her fists on her hips and gave Hannah another of those looks. "I've been to the ladies' auxiliary luncheon," she announced. "I don't get to go every time, you know, so when I do make it, I expect to fully enjoy the companionship of my friends and acquaintances. Only there wasn't much companionship today. Every time I turned around, someone was whispering behind her hand. Some of them didn't even bother to whisper. They just talked right out loud, knowing I was right there to hear them. And do you know what they were talking about?''

Hannah wanted to take the cowardly way out and simply shake her head, but playing dumb never worked with Sylvie. ''I imagine they were talking about Mick and me.''

''About Mick and you and the little tart Elizabeth.'' Sylvie slapped the back of one hand to her forehead as if suddenly remembering. ''That was redundant, wasn't it? You *are* the little tart, aren't you?''

Tart. It was a silly word, as hopelessly old-fashioned as her grandmother. Hannah had called herself worse, and so had Mick, but what should have been a laughable insult hurt worse than the others, because of its source.

''Some of them at the luncheon said that you changed the color of your hair and fixed it different, that you met him at a bar and brought him here to spend the night. Some of them said there never was an Elizabeth, that she was just a story you two concocted to cover up where you really were that night. They said you were with him, all right, but not here. They said you went to the resort with him, helped him bash in his wife's skull, then burned the place down around her. What do you say, Hannah?''

Mick looked more serious than he ever had facing the sheriff. Hannah felt more serious. After all, all the sheriff could do was arrest them. Sylvie could break Hannah's heart.

Lacing her fingers together, Hannah fixed her gaze on the napkin dispenser. Her voice came out low and unsteady. ''I used one of those temporary rinses and Mom's curling iron. I chose the name Elizabeth because I'd never known anyone by that name. I knew Mick would be in the bar, and I brought him here. I left early the next morning before he woke up. Before you were up.''

All the anger seemed to rush out of Sylvie, leaving her looking tinier, older, frailer. Mick pulled out a chair and guided her into it before returning to his own chair. "He was a *stranger*," Sylvie said, her voice heavy with revulsion, flat with disillusionment. "You spent the night with a stranger, and you lied to everyone about it. You let the sheriff suspect him of murder when you *knew* he was innocent. You lied to the sheriff. You lied to me."

"She didn't have much choice, Sylvie," Mick said, earning a scornful look for his efforts.

"You stay out of this. You're not a part of this family yet. I don't know why you would want to be, after what she's done. I don't know how you can even stand to look at her."

Hannah closed her eyes on the tears that welled. When Mick took her hand, wrapping his fingers tightly around hers, she blindly held on.

"I won't stay out of this," he said hotly, and Hannah opened her eyes to see the anger that turned his own face a deep bronze. "What happened that night between Hannah and me is nobody's business but ours. You don't have a clue why she did it, and until you do know, you're in no position to judge her. If you do, then you're no better than those spiteful old biddies you let tell lies about her."

"I didn't 'let' anyone tell lies," Sylvie said, her voice sharp with righteous indignation. "I almost poked Annabella Thompson in the nose. I would've, too, if Earlene hadn't gotten in the way."

"You didn't poke Earlene, did you?"

"No!" A chuckle escaped before Sylvie could stop it. She clamped her hand over her mouth, then, in control again, fixed her hard gaze on Hannah. "Why did you do it? I want to know everything."

Hannah looked at Mick, who nodded and held her hand more tightly. Drawing strength from him, she took a deep breath, then spoke in a rush, telling her grandmother everything. When she finished, the room remained silent for a long time, until Sylvie's deep sigh echoed.

"I knew Brad Daniels was no good. I *knew* he couldn't be trusted to treat you right." Sylvie stared off into the distance. "When he asked you to do this thing for him— to help this woman cheat her soon-to-be ex-husband, whom you didn't know from Adam—why didn't you come to me?"

"And what would you have told me?"

"Not to do it! Someone else's divorce is none of your business! You don't help somebody mess up somebody else's life just because you owe the first somebody some money!" Then her ire vanished, and she grudgingly offered a more realistic answer. "I'd've told you to get him so drunk that he'd pass out as soon as you got to the room and wouldn't wake up until the next day."

"I thought about that," Hannah admitted. "But he'd had a couple of drinks, and he wouldn't have any more."

"Just your luck. All the drunks in bars, and you get the one man who's not. Not a good thing in someone you're trying to frame. Not a bad thing in someone you're planning a future with." Sylvie patted Mick's hand affectionately. "You are still planning a future, aren't you? You don't hold this against her?"

"She did what Brad forced her to do. Believe me, I know how persuasive he is. Besides, it's not her fault I'm in this mess. If she had refused, Brad would have found someone else, and if I hadn't been as receptive to her as I was to Hannah, it wouldn't have mattered. At worst, I would have gone with her and would be in exactly the same situation. At best, I would have turned her down, gone back to my room and spent the night alone. I still wouldn't have an alibi."

"Would you have been as receptive to another woman as you were to Hannah?" Sylvie asked slyly.

He gave Hannah a look that warmed her from the inside out. "No. She wasn't the first woman who tried to pick me up. But she was the first who succeeded."

"You two need a plan."

"What we need is a confession from Brad," Mick said dryly.

"Well, you're not likely to get that—at least, not so it would matter. When everything's going exactly as he planned, why in the world would he confess? Not unless he planned to kill you as soon as he finished admitting to everything."

Hannah wasn't pleased that Sylvie agreed so readily with Mick on this. She knew Brad, knew how he liked to show off. She also knew how much he liked having her at his mercy. If she convinced him that she was desperate for a way out of this nightmare her life had become, if she persuaded him that she would do whatever she could to protect herself and her family—even become the state's best witness against Mick—he very well might talk to her. He might tell her all the little details that only the killer would know, so she could use them against Mick.

In fact, there was no *might* about it. He would tell her. She was convinced of it. After all, she wasn't the one he wanted most to get rid of. He'd made her a suspect only because she'd betrayed him. If it meant a guaranteed conviction for Mick, Brad would gladly change her from suspect to key witness.

But Mick had made her promise last night that she would stay away from Brad.

And she'd known when she'd made the promise that she might break it. If she succeeded, he would have to forgive her, wouldn't he?

And if he and Sylvie were right? If Brad talked only with the intention of killing her as soon as he was done?

Then she wouldn't have to worry about being forgiven.

Fear sent a shiver through her. Maybe she should forget the idea. Maybe she should just wait here with Mick for Brad to feed enough false evidence to the sheriff to result in their arrests. Yeah, maybe she should do nothing but wait while the DA used that fake evidence to railroad them to a conviction. Then she could spend the next twenty or thirty or forty years waiting in a cell at Mabel Bassett Correctional Center, regretting that she hadn't grabbed what looked like their one and only chance to prove their innocence.

She had a microcassette recorder in her room, a phone there that wasn't hooked into the switchboard here and Brad's numbers in her address book. All she needed was a reasonable excuse to go to her room alone and the luck to find Brad somewhere in the area. She would ask to meet him someplace that was public but at the same time offered some measure of privacy—a corner table in a restaurant. She would never be more than a scream away from help, never in any danger at all.

"I guess I'd better get changed and check on Merrilee," Sylvie said. "Earlene will be here before long to start supper." She stood up, hesitated, then clasped Hannah's free hand. "I'm sorry I lost my temper. You are the dearest thing in my life, and I can't bear the thought of you being in trouble that you don't feel you can trust me with. I am so sorry."

Hannah's eyes teared again, and she gave her grandmother a fierce hug. "I'm sorry, too," she whispered.

Sylvie held her a long moment, then, with a sniffle, walked away. She looked old and troubled, Hannah thought bleakly, and all because of Brad.

"Are you okay?"

She looked at Mick. "I'm a suspect in a murder case, I'm the subject of gossip among people I've known all my life, my own grandmother called me a tart, and I might spend the rest of my life in prison. Considering all that, yeah, I'm okay."

"You're not going to prison."

"You know that for a fact? Do you have a crystal ball you forgot to tell me about?"

"They can't connect you to Sandra or the resort in any way. All they have is a clerk claiming a blond woman made regular visits to my room and your own admission that you spent Saturday night with me. Blond women are a dime a dozen. I'll admit to other women, other blondes. That's my type, you know—blue-eyed blondes. I'll swear that I didn't know you until I moved in here, that I persuaded you to give me an alibi. I'll convince them that you lied about being with me. With all the other lies you've told and the partnership agreement my lawyer is drawing up tomorrow, Sheriff Mills won't have any problem believing you lied again."

She gave him a cool look. "Hell, why don't you just save yourself the hassle of a trial and confess to killing Sandra and setting the fire? Because what you're talking about will guarantee a conviction. Just go ahead and confess."

"I've thought about it." He said it quietly, grimly, sending a chill through her.

"To protect me?"

"There's no reason both of us should risk prison. I was Brad's original target. He only turned on you because I was trying to make you help me."

She stood up, braced her hands on the table and leaned nose to nose with him. "You will *not* do something stupid to protect me. You will not confess to crimes you didn't commit just because of me. I won't allow it. Either we're both cleared or we both go down, but I will not stand by and watch you sacrifice yourself for me."

He didn't flinch, didn't back away or blink. All he did was raise one very gentle hand to her face. "I'll do what's best for both of us."

"You don't get to make that decision on your own."

Smiling, he drew his fingers across her mouth, then pulled her an inch closer for a kiss. She broke free, fumbled his hand away and scowled at him. "Don't try to distract me."

"I think you're distracting me. I've already forgotten what we were talking about."

She knelt beside him, wrapping her arms around his middle, resting her head on his chest. "Promise me you won't do anything stupid."

"Doing whatever I can to protect you doesn't qualify as stupid."

"Please…"

"Darlin', I'm not planning to do anything right now. Those are my plans for a worst-case scenario. If we're both arrested, if Brad keeps buying witnesses to implicate you, then I intend to do whatever's necessary to keep you safe. But I won't do anything right now. I promise."

He held her for a long time, and she let him, putting off the lie she didn't want to tell, the call she didn't want to make, the chance she was terrified to take. She had so much at stake—their freedom, their futures, maybe her life. If she was wrong about Brad, she stood to lose so much.

But if she was right, she stood to gain more.

Finally Mick tilted her face up. "You want to go make love in the rain?"

She smiled faintly. She'd played in the rain countless times, but never that kind of play, never in the sort of summertime-warm light shower that was falling now. Though she was tempted, she shook her head. "I have a headache. I'm going to my room to get some aspirin."

"A headache. Such a sorry excuse," he teased. He touched his fingers to her forehead, her temple, her jaw, as if to erase the tension there, then pulled her to her feet. "Why don't you close the drapes, turn off the lights and lie down for a while? If Sylvie or Merrilee needs anything, I'll be here."

"For a while," she agreed, hating the guilt that filled her. Quickly, before it overwhelmed her or her courage fled, she left the office and went to her room. There she dialed Brad's house.

He answered on the third ring, sounding friendly, harmless. He wasn't, she reminded herself. He was the most dangerous man she'd ever known. As long as she kept that in mind, though, she should be safe.

He repeated his greeting before she managed to make her voice work. When she finally did, it was unsteady and weak. "Brad? This is Hannah. I'd like to talk to you. Can we meet someplace?"

Rain had given way to a light mist when Mick left the tablet full of notes, figures and calculations and walked out into the parking lot to face the motel. The dampness cooled his skin and collected in tiny drops on his shirt before soaking into the fabric. He ignored the mist as he stared at the motel, imagining it as it had looked brand-new, only better. It was easy to picture the neon sign above the asphalt parking lot, the big plate-glass windows that looked in on lots of chrome and an old-fashioned soda fountain. It was even easy to imagine cars filling the lot, instead of just the three that were there now—his, Sylvie's and Hannah's little blue—

He took a few steps toward his truck. Last night he had pulled into the lot and parked right next to Hannah's car. When he'd gone to the room to get the statements for Trey Landry this afternoon, her car had been right there. So where the hell was it now?

After another few steps he broke into a trot, then an all-out run. He let himself into his own room, then went through the connecting doors to Hannah's quarters. The lights were off, the air conditioner silent, the rooms empty. He knew it before he went into the bedroom, before he checked the bathroom. A bottle of aspirin sat on the counter, with a throwaway cup, still damp, beside it.

He returned to the living room and looked around again.

Two empty packages sat on the desk. One had held AA batteries, the other a blank microcassette. The address book on the desk was open to the D's. Brad's name was third on the list.

God help her, she had gone to meet Brad.

Fear building, he went back out. Footprints beside his truck were filled with water. Judging from the tire tracks, they led directly from the sidewalk to where her car had been parked.

Spinning around, he returned to the lobby only long enough to yell to her grandmother, "Sylvie, I'm going out!"

"Take Hannah with you. She could use…"

The old lady's words faded away as he shoved through the door and headed for his truck. Instinctively he turned out of the parking lot toward Yates. Maybe the town was her destination, or maybe someplace in between. Roads branching off the highway led to the resort, to the Daniels cabin, to Brad's rental house on the lake.

Dear God, she wouldn't go to Brad's house, would she? She couldn't possibly be so foolish, could she?

Of course she could. Sneaking off like this, meeting Brad anywhere, under any circumstances, thinking she could beat him at his own game… There was apparently nothing too foolish for Hannah to consider.

Driving with one hand, he punched Brad's home number into the cellular. The phone rang five times, then the answering machine picked up. He disconnected, then dialed again, this time Brad's cellular. On the second ring the bastard answered. Mick disconnected again.

Okay. Brad was in his car, which most likely meant he was meeting Hannah somewhere, but where? The resort? The turn was in sight ahead. If Mick wanted to check it out, he had to start slowing down soon. But what if he was wrong? What if he lost precious time driving that long curving road only to find the resort ruins empty?

At the last possible moment he swung the steering wheel sharply to the right, skidded to the opposite side of the resort road, then recovered. Maybe he was wrong. Surely Hannah wouldn't come here alone with Brad, not after what had happened to Sandra.

At least he hoped she wouldn't.

He prayed.

Hannah pulled into a parking space at Smoky Joe's Bar-B-Q, shut off the engine and looked around. She didn't see Brad's Mercedes anywhere. Good. She'd hurried to get here first, so she could choose the best vantage point inside. She'd wanted to be there waiting for him, calm and confident, when he arrived.

Patting her pocket to make sure the tape recorder was in place, she climbed out of the car and started toward the side door of the restaurant. She hadn't gone more than ten feet when a figure stepped out from behind a van and blocked her way. It was Brad.

He looked so normal, so handsome, with his blond hair, brown eyes, charming smile. Everything about him, from his clothes to his bearing to his self-indulgent attitude, spoke of wealth. Nothing hinted that he was a murderer.

"You're early," he said politely.

He'd given her an hour. She'd taken nearly forty-five minutes of it, finding new batteries, making certain the tape recorder worked, experimenting so she could turn it on blindly, building her courage.

That courage was fleeing now. Swallowing hard, she took an involuntary step back. They were alone in the parking lot, and the dining tables at the nearest windows were empty. The parking lot was behind the restaurant, out of sight of the street, with nothing on either side but the blank brick walls of the next-door businesses. So much for her careful plans. This was a lousy place to be with a killer.

"You know," he said, "I decided on the way in that I

wasn't in the mood for Smoky Joe's, after all. All the noise, all the smoke... Let's take a drive, instead.''

He came toward her, and she backed away until she had cleared the van. She gave the parking lot a quick scan. Her car was only twenty feet away, but even if she could reach it, the lock on the driver's door didn't work. The restaurant door was about forty feet in the opposite direction, but she would have to go around Brad to get there. Maybe she could run around the building, out of the lot and into the street, screaming all the way.

But he was too close. With a friendly smile he took hold of her arm just above the elbow, his fingers biting into her flesh, and steered her toward the back of the lot. There, on the far side of the Dumpster, was the Mercedes.

He unlocked the driver's door, shoved her inside and waited impatiently while she scrambled across to the passenger seat. Trying the passenger door was too great a temptation to resist, but it was locked, and by the time she'd located the button to unlock it, Brad was sitting only inches away.

"Better put your seat belt on, Hannah," he said as he fastened his own. "I'd hate for anything to happen to you on our drive."

"I don't want to go for a drive," she said as she fumbled the seat belt into place. "I just want to talk."

"When I'm ready." He backed out of the space, left the lot and turned toward Sunshine.

She'd made a terrible mistake. There were a hundred places off the highway where he could take her—isolated places, places anyone unfamiliar with the area would never find, places where a body would never be found. She didn't want to die. This was a really bad idea. Mick had been right.

Her heart contracted at the thought of him. She had almost told him this afternoon that she loved him. When he'd told her that he was serious enough to stay at the motel forever, she'd almost told him, but for some stupid reason she'd kept the words to herself. Maybe she'd wanted him to commit first. Maybe she'd wanted to wait until this cloud of suspicion was no longer over their heads. Maybe she'd just been a fool.

Now she might never get to tell him.

The Mercedes' wipers worked rhythmically, sweeping the windshield clean with each pass. Hannah focused on them, using their steady action and repetitive sound to keep her fear under control. After a few miles her gaze drifted past the wipers to the highway ahead. There was little on-coming traffic—a minivan, a bright yellow church bus, a couple of cars, a dark blue truck—

Catching her breath, she sat very still, allowing only her eyes to move. Mick's truck was exactly that model, exactly that color. Had he discovered that she was gone and come looking for her? She watched, waited, but just as the truck drew closer, Brad looked at her and spoke, distracting her, making her jump.

"Have you ever been to the resort, Hannah?"

"Yes." Her lips barely moved, and in her lap, her hands knotted into fists. Please, God, let it be Mick, she silently prayed while keeping her gaze locked with Brad's. *Let him see us, but don't let Brad see him.*

"Really? I suppose Mick must have given you the nickel tour." He grinned. "It used to be the fifty-cent tour, but fifty cents is a lot to pay for ashes and soot."

"The insurance company is going to pay a hell of a lot more than that."

"True, but most of that goes to the bank that financed the construction. I hate to admit it, but Mick was right. He was against the idea of the resort from the beginning. He said the place would eat us alive, and he was right. Damn his soul, he was right."

There'd been no sign of Hannah at the resort. Now Mick was headed toward Yates once again, indecisive as hell and hating it. Should he take the time to check Brad's house? Just because the machine had picked up Mick's call didn't mean Brad wasn't home. He might have been away from the phone or getting something from his car outside. But surely Hannah wouldn't go to his house. Surely even she would recognize the danger there.

But he couldn't count on her to be thinking clearly. The simple fact that she'd gone to meet Brad proved that she wasn't.

Gripping the steering wheel tightly, he cursed the traffic on the road. It was a rainy Sunday afternoon. Why weren't these people home where they belonged? Why wasn't Hannah home where she belonged? Damn it, if anything happened to her...

The thought turned him to ice inside. If anything happened to her, Brad was dead. It was that simple.

The oncoming car was only a few yards away before he glanced at it, was almost even with him before he recognized it as Brad's Mercedes. He whipped around in the seat, staring hard, and made out a figure in the passenger seat—slender, blond. Hannah! The fear in his gut told him it was. Thank God, she was alive.

Now he had to keep her that way.

The blare of a horn jerked his attention to the road again. He swerved back into his lane, hit the brakes and searched for a place to turn around. The tires bumped off the road, then back on, as he swung the steering wheel in a tight U. The Mercedes was almost out of sight, just a dark form ahead of the last car. As Mick debated what to do, the import's left-turn signal blinked. They were going to the resort.

He reached for the cellular and dialed 911. After a moment the call was connected to the Yates County Sheriff's Department. "Tell Sheriff Mills to get out to the Eagle's

Haven Resort.'' He thought of Hannah, of Brad and Sandra, and grimly, ominously added, ''Someone's going to die.''

Under the guise of turning to face Brad, Hannah looked at the road behind them. All she saw were headlights from approaching cars and taillights from those that had just passed. She couldn't identify the dark blue truck in the bunch.

As the Mercedes slowed, she looked ahead again. The turnoff to the resort was ahead on the left, broad and planted on either side with low-maintenance shrubs before it disappeared into the trees. She had thought it appealing the first time she'd seen it—a road that beckoned travelers to explore to its end. Now, for all the appeal she found, it might as well be a narrow dark lane cutting through a grotesque and menacing black forest.

''That was where the golf course would have gone,'' Brad said, gesturing out her window. ''One of the top designers in the field drew up the preliminary plans. This side was going to remain wooded, with a state-of-the-art jogging trail winding through. We had some hotshot horticulturist on tap to lay out the best woodland garden money could buy. This place was going to offer the best of everything.''

It had been his dream, Hannah remembered. But the dream had had a few fatal flaws. Now everyone else was paying for it. Barring a miracle, she would soon pay dearly.

He slowed for the last curve and came into the parking lot. On the left Lake Eufala was gray and choppy. On the right the ruins of the resort were forbidding. She looked that way, swallowed hard and couldn't look back again.

Brad pulled right up to the yellow police tape, then shut off the engine. ''Let's look around while we talk.''

Her muscles were so quivery that she wasn't sure her legs could support her, but when he unlocked the doors, she managed to climb out. She had changed into jeans before she'd left and pulled on a windbreaker. Now she adjusted the jacket over her right front pocket to offer the tape recorder protection from the drizzling rain.

Brad came around the car, took a firm grip on her arm again and pulled her underneath the yellow tape and onto a walkway that led toward the main entrance. "It would have been a beautiful place, Hannah. It would have brought in people from all over the country. It would have been one of the top resorts anywhere."

Surreptitiously she reached into her pocket and pushed the record button. "Then why did you burn it down?"

He gave her a look as they crossed the driveway, then climbed a set of blackened steps to the foundation. An unpleasant smoky smell lingered over the place as if it had seeped into the concrete, the stone, the steel. Even once the demolition was completed and all these tons of rubble had been disposed of elsewhere, that smell would remain in the soil, the trees and anything that dared to grow here. It was the smell of destruction. Of sickness. Of death.

"This was the lobby. There were the elevators. This was the bar. This was an atrium." He pulled her over and around sodden black lumps until finally they reached a place where the damage was minimal. Millions of shards of glass littered the tile floor. Soot smudged the stone walls. Ash and debris were scattered all over, but for the most part, the single-story room was in good shape. "This is the poolside restaurant."

This was where Sandra had died.

Hannah gave the room a more intense look. Had Sandra stood here beside the stone bar? Had she walked over to the glass wall, turning her back on Brad for one fatal moment? Was that a bloodstain there on the floor? Had she died there, less than five feet from where Hannah now stood? The thought made her shiver.

Brad strolled around the perimeter of the room, paying the rain no notice. Dressed in khakis and a bloodred polo shirt, with deck shoes and a tailored windbreaker, he looked ready for a sunny afternoon on an obscenely expensive sail-boat. He didn't look dressed to kill.

Circling around behind the bar, he rested his hands on the surface. The base was a solid slab of granite, rough cut, but the top was polished smooth and gleamed in the rain. "What is it you want to talk about?"

She faced him. All the time she'd been getting ready to meet him, she had rehearsed what she would say. The words came easily. She hoped they sounded convincing. "I want out."

"Out of what?"

"This whole mess. I can't go to trial, Brad. I can't go to prison. I haven't done anything wrong."

"What do you expect me to do?"

"You got me into this. You can get me out. Quit paying people like the desk clerk to lie about me. Quit pushing the sheriff to see me as a suspect. I'll do whatever you want. I'll tell the sheriff whatever you want. Just please don't set me up for this."

He looked skeptical. "And what about Mick? I've seen you two together. I know you're having an affair with him. I know you've told him everything. Do you really expect me to believe that now you're willing to be a witness against him? You spent last night in his bed, and today you're willing to testify against him?"

She knotted her fingers together. "I like Mick. I like sex with him. But that's all he can give me. You can give me freedom. You can keep me out of jail. All you have to do is fill in the missing details. I'll tell the sheriff how Sandra died, how the fire was set. I'll tell him that Mick told me. That will be all Mills needs to arrest him."

"Missing details. You talk as if you've already figured most of it out. Tell me your theory."

Hannah looked around for someplace to sit, but the only place was a low stone wall a dozen feet away. For the sake of the tape recorder, she remained where she was. "You

were having an affair with Sandra. You and she planned
this whole thing together. She forged Mick's name to the
life-insurance policy and to the check you threatened me
with last week. She came here last Saturday intending to
start a fight with Mick, to goad him into making threats
against her in front of witnesses. She brought suitcases with
her—clothes, jewels. She wasn't planning to go back to
Oklahoma City. She intended to go someplace, probably
under an assumed name, and wait for you to join her, with
the insurance money in hand and Mick in prison." She
looked again at the dark dried stain on the tile. "She never
knew she was helping plan her own murder, did she?"

Brad studied her for a long moment. "Quite a story. Did
you come up with that on your own, or did Mick help?"
He made a gesture as if an answer wasn't necessary. "Tell
me why I should trust you, Hannah. Convince me that
you're not playing me for a fool. Give me one reason why
I should believe you."

"I'll give you two. My mother and Sylvie. You know
me, Brad. There is *nothing* I wouldn't do for them. I've
taken money from you. Slept with a stranger. Lied to the
authorities. Lied to my grandmother. I've shamed and de-
graded myself. I've become no better than you. All I'm
offering is to tell more lies. All you have to do is keep me
out of trouble."

For another interminable moment he looked at her. Then,
as if reaching a decision, he shrugged. "Once Sandra got
her hooks into a man, she made him suffer. Mick can tell
you that. He was a fool for marrying her in the first place,
and he was a bigger fool for staying married to her. For a
time he thought things could be worked out, and then he
just quit caring. He didn't live with her, didn't sleep with
her or hardly even speak to her, but he remained faithful
to her. She was sleeping with anything that stood still, and
he was sleeping alone, because he was a married man."

He shook his head as if he couldn't understand such integrity.

He gave the ruins a sweeping look. "He hated this resort. He liked the challenge, liked doing top-quality work on such a grand scale, but he hated the debt, hated that one project could wipe us out. I convinced him that it wouldn't, but I was wrong. I didn't count on our buyers backing out, on bad weather or labor problems or cost increases—all the things Mick warned me about before we even started. He gave me the way out, you know. We'd be better off burning the place down, he said. The insurance would pay off the bank, we could cut our losses, and we could get back to our real business of building houses.

"I knew he was just talking. He would never do anything like that. He was just frustrated, angry. But it stuck in my mind. The more desperate the situation got, the more practical his suggestion sounded. Why not torch the place? The insurance would pay off the bank, and we would be out of trouble. We'd be out a lot of money. The resort had required so much of our time and trouble that we'd had to cut back on the houses that were our bread and butter. Our profits had dropped substantially. But we could bounce back from that."

"When did you decide to frame Mick for the arson?"

"Sandra was making sounds about getting married once the divorce went through. Mick and I hadn't been on the best of terms for the past six months. He blamed me for bad judgment, and I blamed him—" he smiled "—for being right. Then one day it just occurred to me that I could get rid of them both, have the company all to myself and make a nice bit of change on the side."

He gazed past her, his expression contemplative and not the least bit remorseful. He wasn't at all sorry that he'd killed his lover and framed his best friend. He wasn't at all bothered by the fact that he was soon going to kill her.

And he was. Hannah was convinced of it. He wouldn't

be talking so freely if he didn't feel supremely confident that what he was saying would go no further. She wished she'd listened to Mick and Sylvie and kept her distance. She wished she'd left a note for Mick, telling him she'd gone to meet Brad, so that when her body was found, the sheriff would look in the right direction. She wished she'd told Mick she loved him.

Most of all, she wished there was some way she could leave the tape recorder behind, hidden where the sheriff could find it, because she didn't doubt that Brad would search her before or after he killed her.

"You were right," Brad said. "Sandra never knew she was helping plan her own murder. I told her that I'd gotten a body from the morgue, a woman who had no family and would be buried in a pauper's grave. I convinced her that not enough of it would survive the flames to identify her conclusively, that the hick sheriff would see her car, know she'd disappeared and assume the body was hers. I told her it was in the ballroom at the opposite end of the hotel and asked if she wanted to see it, but she said no, it was too gruesome."

Hannah walked over to what had once been a glass wall and stared out at the empty swimming pool. There was so much rubble around, but no place where she could hide the tape recorder without crouching to do so. That would surely make Brad suspicious. "So she came here with you that night to set the fire, believing that by morning she would be settled someplace safe and far away. Instead, you crushed her skull."

"She never guessed she was one of the loose ends I had to tie up." His voice came from right behind her, making her jump, making her skin crawl. His hands gentle, he turned her to face him. "She wasn't as smart as you are. You know, don't you?"

"Yes." Her throat was tight with fear and unshed tears. It made her answer sound choked.

"I'm going to tell the sheriff that you called me, that you said Mick was forcing you to provide him with an alibi. I'll tell him that you were frightened, that you had proof of Mick's guilt, that you wanted to meet me at Smoky Joe's. I drove there and found your car in the parking lot, but there was no sign of you. I'll suggest that the sheriff check the resort. After all, criminals often return to the scene of the crime. He lured Sandra here to crush her skull, then set the place on fire. He might lure you here to crush your skull and set *you* on fire."

"He's probably out looking for me right now."

"Great. I hope he is. That means he'll have no alibi. He'll look that much guiltier."

She swallowed hard, swallowed her pride and begged. "Please don't do this, Brad."

"You leave me no choice. You think I want to? I told you to stay away from Mick. I told you not to cooperate with him in any way. But you did. Now you have to pay."

Tears filled her eyes, and her entire body began to tremble. "Please, Brad. *Please.*"

"Go over there."

His hands were still frighteningly gentle as he gave her a little push toward the bar. That was when she saw the gasoline can on the bar, right next to a three-foot length of two-by-four. She took a few stumbling steps, then with one last desperate surge of energy, she started to run. If she could make it to the parking lot, if she could just put some distance between them...

But he anticipated her move, caught her arm and swung her around hard, giving her a shove at the same time. Her feet slipped on the wet tile, and she went down, cracking her head against the floor. Lights exploded, then her vision went dark as waves of pain washed over her. She tried to speak but couldn't make her mouth work, tried to move but couldn't find the strength.

She was dimly aware of hands grabbing her jacket, lifting her, then of falling again, the side of her head slamming against the massive granite with excruciating pain. For one blessed moment she felt, saw, knew nothing. She wanted to stay like that, wanted to sink into unconsciousness, but she remembered Mick and struggled, fought her way back.

Rain splashed in her face and over her body, rain and something else, something pungent, cool... Oh, God, it was gasoline. Brad was pouring the contents of the gas can over her. She tried frantically to sit up, to move, but her body was a leaden weight. She wasn't able to lift more than one hand, and even that drained her of strength.

A shadow appeared above her. She worked to focus her gaze, saw three shapes that slowly merged into two, both of them Brad. He was looking down at her with sympathy, such heartless, soulless sympathy, and his mouth was moving. The sounds were slow to penetrate the roaring in her ears, the words slow to reach her brain.

"...sorry to do this, but you leave me no choice. If you hadn't tried to run, it would have been easier. I would have made sure you were unconscious first. You never would have felt the flames. But now..." His sigh was dramatic. "I'm so sorry, Hannah."

He moved, and a bright object, silver and gold, came into her narrow vision. In spite of the rain, the yellow flickered two inches above the silver, a pretty sight, welcoming in the bleak damp gray of the day. She stared at it, mesmerized as it came closer, then with a sudden terror, she realized what it was—a cigarette lighter, the flame burning high, coming closer, closer. Any instant now the gasoline would burst into fire, burning her alive, destroying her clothes, her body, her evidence to clear Mick...

"Nooo!"

The scream sounded with more power than Hannah thought she was capable of, but as a form raced across her field of vision, she realized that it wasn't her scream. Mick was here! Thank God, Mick had come to save her.

As his tackle brought Brad to the ground, the cigarette lighter was knocked loose. The flame went out immediately, and she breathed a sigh of relief as the lighter clattered, unlit, to the floor. She wished she could reach it, could throw it so far away it would never be found, but it had landed near the outside wall. Whatever strength she could summon had to be used for more important things.

Gritting her teeth, squeezing her eyes shut on the blurry vision that left her queasy, she lifted her arm, worked her fingers into the front pocket of her jeans, pulled out the tape recorder. From her lower vantage point, she could see a niche in the bar where the granite base didn't quite meet the polished top. To the background accompaniment of grunts, curses and fists against flesh, she turned onto her left side, dragged herself partway off the floor and worked the tape recorder into the recess. It probably wouldn't be found until the bar was removed during the demolition process, and Mick might already be in prison by then, but better late than never.

Exhausted, in pain and nauseated from a combination of the blows and the gasoline fumes, she sank down again and tried to focus on the two men. Brad landed a blow that knocked Mick off balance. He fell backward over a pile of rubble and tumbled to the floor. She heard a sickening crack as his head came in contact with the low stone wall, then for an instant his body was motionless.

"Mick?" In her head her voice was a scream. In her ears it had no sound at all.

Before she could try again, Brad turned to face her. He looked bruised and battered and was smiling the unholiest of smiles. The cigarette lighter burned brightly in his right hand. Ignoring Mick, who was shaking his head, trying to get to his feet, Brad stopped a half-dozen feet away. He was starting to bend when a shot echoed around them. His smile froze, then slowly faded, and he crumpled to the floor in a heap. His hand, still clutching the lighter tightly, landed in a pool of gasoline, and Hannah's world went up in flames.

Mick sat on the steps leading to the resort lobby, rested his bandaged hands on his knees and stared out at the parking lot. The local paramedics helped the flight crew load the stretcher onto the helicopter, then dashed away as the rotors picked up speed in preparation for takeoff. The medics who had worked to stabilize Brad until the helicopter arrived hadn't looked hopeful. Shot once in the chest and badly burned over most of his body, he was on his way to the burn center at Hillcrest in Tulsa.

Mick hoped he didn't survive the flight.

Sighing wearily, he tilted his head back and let the rain drizzle over his face. It had been a hell of an afternoon. After following Brad's Mercedes onto the resort road, he'd parked his truck a half mile back and set off through the woods. He'd been afraid to drive right up out front—afraid that Brad would panic and kill Hannah. He'd wanted surprise on his side, and so he had cut through the woods and sneaked up to the rear of the hotel.

He had almost been too late. When he'd seen Hannah lying there on the floor, when he'd smelled the gasoline and seen Brad holding the lighter, his heart had damn near stopped. He had moved on pure adrenaline, pure terror, and with the intention of killing his one-time friend and partner. Instead, it was Hannah who had almost died.

With any luck, Brad *would* die.

Footsteps approached across the driveway, stopping right in front of him. He stared at the muddy boots and dark trousers for a moment before wearily sitting back and raising his gaze to Sheriff Mills's face.

"How are you feeling?"

Mick shrugged. "Like I've been beaten and burned."

The sheriff's gaze flickered to his hands, treated and ban-

daged by the paramedics with orders that he see a doctor
right away. "You feel like talking?"

He didn't. He didn't feel like doing anything but going
home, stripping off his wet, singed and smoky clothes and
crawling into bed for a week or two. "What do you want
to know?"

"Not to me. To her." He gestured to the ambulance,
where Hannah stood with a blanket around her shoulders.

All he had to do was close his eyes, and he would hear
again her scream as the gasoline exploded into flames. It
had propelled him to his feet and across the room, had
allowed him to drag her away, to beat out the flames with
his bare hands without feeling the pain. She'd been unconscious by the time he'd carried her out of the ruins and into
the rain. He'd been terrified by her lack of responsive-
ness—and grateful, too, that she hadn't been awake to
know that her clothes had been on fire, that she hadn't seen
her shoes melting, that she hadn't felt the flames on her
skin.

The sheriff had insisted on taking her from him, on turning her over to the paramedics who had arrived moments
later. Mick had been surprised by their quick response, but
the sheriff had called them miles before he'd reached the
resort himself—which had been just in time to shoot Brad.

Moving awkwardly without the use of his hands, Mick
got to his feet and walked to the ambulance. Hannah's back
was to him, but before he'd covered half the distance, she
turned to watch him.

She stood barefoot in the rain. Her jeans legs had been
cut away so the paramedics could treat the burns on her
legs. Her jacket had been discarded, the synthetic fabric
partially melted by the flames and the heat. Her shirt was
sooty, her hair was singed, and ugly bruises were forming
down one side of her face.

She had never looked so beautiful.

He stopped a few feet in front of her and stared into her

face as if he'd never seen it before. As if he might never see it again. He had come so close to losing her today, so damn close that the fear still left him feeling weak.

Her smile was tentative. "Hi."

He scowled at her. "What the hell did you think you were doing?"

The smile disappeared. "Trying to help you. Trying to help myself."

"You almost got yourself killed."

"I know."

And she did. A deputy had retrieved her tape recorder, and the sheriff had played part of the tape for him. *She never guessed she was one of the loose ends I had to tie up,* Brad had said about Sandra. *She wasn't as smart as you are. You know, don't you?*

She had known she was about to die. She had pleaded with the bastard, had begged for her life. God forgive him, he hoped Brad suffered unbearably before he died. It was no more than he deserved.

She shifted uncomfortably. "I got the tape. I got his confession. You're cleared of Sandra's murder and the arson."

He raised his hand to comb through his hair, remembered the burns at the stab of pain and lowered it to his side again, settling, instead, on a deeper scowl. "Do you think I give a damn about being cleared if I have to lose you in the process? Damn it, Hannah, what the hell were you thinking?"

"That I helped get you into this mess," she murmured, looking chastened and hurt. "That I owed it to you to help get you out. That I..." She looked away, somewhere down around his feet, and her voice dropped, became softer. "That I love you."

He stared at her, feeling as if the ground had just tilted underneath him. He'd known that she loved him. After all, she'd talked about a future, about their house and babies.

Still, hearing her say the words made it official, made it real.

It turned a hellish afternoon into one of the best days of his life.

"I love you, Mick," she repeated, her voice, her look defiant. "I don't expect you to say it back. After everything that's happened, I wouldn't blame you if you walked away and—"

Clumsily he wrapped his arms around her, pulled her close and stopped her words with a fierce kiss. Just touching her made him hungry. Tasting her made him hot. She kissed him back, desperate and greedy, and clung to him when he finally ended it. He stared into her hazy blue eyes at close range. "Don't you know I love you?"

"I hoped."

"Don't you know I want to spend the rest of my life with you? I want to build that house for you and fill it with babies. I want to work with you, make love with you and grow old with you. Oh, Hannah…" He kissed her again, another quick, greedy, grateful kiss. "Will you marry me?"

She wasn't coy or the least bit indecisive. With the sweetest smile she offered the sweetest, simplest answer. "Yes."

And then, for a long time, neither of them said anything.

Epilogue

It was a warm September night when Hannah made her way across the wooden footbridge and into the field where the fruit trees grew. A bright sliver of moon shone overhead, making the flashlight in her hand unnecessary, showing the way to what had lately become her favorite spot.

Between two apple trees, she shook out the quilt she carried. Coming here on pretty nights had become a ritual for her and Mick. It was their special place, their place to relax, share their day and simply be together. He planned to join her here tonight, just as soon as he'd said goodnight to their guests. Wanting a few minutes alone, she had come ahead on her own.

It was nine-thirty on a Friday evening. Ruby was in charge of the desk, and out front the neon No Vacancy sign was lighting up the dark sky. Business was good at the Last Resort these days, though not entirely responsible for tonight's full house. Mick's family had come up from West Texas for the long Labor Day weekend—his parents, both sets of grandparents, his brother and sister and their families. Together they filled five rooms.

They were good people, she mused as she stretched out. They were kind to Merrilee and had welcomed her, Hannah and Sylvie into their family without the slightest hesitation. Remembering that they had remained cool to Sandra through eleven years of marriage, Hannah knew their welcome was significant. They had judged her deserving of their son, and she was relieved, because she surely did love him.

A light breeze blew through the trees, ruffling her hair, bringing with it the promise of autumn. Considering the summer they'd had, she was more than ready for the slower pace that came naturally with fall and winter. She was ready to nest in, hibernate and wait for spring.

It was amazing the changes a season could make. Three months ago she hadn't even known Mick's name. She'd been broke and darn near defeated, her future had looked bleak, and she had dreamed of walking away, leaving her worries behind and making a new life elsewhere.

These days she couldn't imagine living anyplace other than right here or with anyone other than Mick. Meeting him was the best thing that had ever happened to her. Marrying him was even better. Thanks to him, life was better all around. The motel was making a comeback. The remodeling process was slow going, only a few rooms at a time, but the results had been gratifying. On Tuesday they were breaking ground on the new house. Depending on the weather and the demands the motel placed on his time, Mick thought it would be ready to move into in about six months. Perfect timing.

Staring up at the sky, she sighed, thinking about everything else the summer had brought. The tape she'd risked her life for had been sufficient to clear both her and Mick and to pin responsibility for Sandra's murder and the fire on Brad. The sheriff's verdict on that hadn't mattered to

Brad, though. He'd died during surgery that rainy Sunday night.

Sandra's life-insurance policy had been decreed invalid because of the forged signatures. The company lawyer had argued for a lawsuit—based on the fact that Sandra had routinely signed Mick's name to documents throughout their marriage—but Mick had been happy to let the insurance company keep the money, and the company had been happy to comply. Blue Water's insurance company had paid off their construction loan after a thorough investigation of the arson, and Mick had immediately sold the company for a comfortable profit.

The burns on his hands had healed, leaving only a few small scars. Her injuries had been nothing—minor burns on her legs and arms and a concussion that had kept her in bed for a few days. Since he'd spent those days beside her, she hadn't minded.

Footsteps sounded on the bridge, then were muffled on the thick yellowing grass. She sat up and watched her husband approach. Dressed in jeans, a chambray shirt and boots, he looked as wickedly handsome as the first time she'd ever seen him—as every time she saw him. When she considered the threats that had brought them together, she was truly amazed at the love that kept them together. Triumph out of tragedy, Sylvie had proclaimed once she'd heard the whole story. Absolutely.

"Everyone's settled in their rooms," he said as he stretched out beside her. "Have you reached any decisions?"

"I love you."

"I know that. I love you, too. Have you decided about the house?"

Every night this week they'd come out here to choose the exact location for the foundation of the new house. Every night they'd gotten distracted by other things infinitely more interesting. This evening he'd told her to take advantage of the few minutes she would wait for him to make a decision, but even alone, she'd gotten distracted, anyway.

She smiled at the night sky. "You decide. Just don't let them do anything to this spot." This quilt-size patch of ground held too many sweet memories. They'd made love here under the sun and the moon, in scorching heat and cooling rain. They'd worked on the house plans here, had talked out problems with the motel here. She was convinced in her heart that they'd conceived their baby here.

As if he'd read her mind, Mick laid his hand over her belly. She was barely eight weeks along, according to the doctor. There was nothing to show, nothing to feel. Just an incredible sense of awe at what they'd created together from nothing but love.

"When are we going to tell them?" he asked, sliding his hand up to undo the top button of her dress.

"Tomorrow."

"Sylvie will be pleased."

"Thrilled," she agreed as another button slipped open.

"Our mothers will cry."

"And your father will be so proud." Now her dress was open to her waist. He left the buttons and, instead, turned his attention to her bare breasts. His gentle caresses made them swell, made heat pump with her blood and desire gather in her belly. His kisses made her moan and shift restlessly.

She wriggled out of her clothing. He stripped off his, moved above her and filled her with one long, sure stroke. There was no hesitation, no fumbling over a condom, not even the thinnest barrier between them. It was just him, just her, together.

"Mick?" She cradled his face in her hands, and he pressed a kiss to her palm. "Remember the better life I was always looking for?"

His dark gaze locked with hers, he nodded.

"This is it. This is what I always wanted, what I always needed. Life. With you. Forever."

Bending low, he brought his mouth to hers. "You and me. Sylvie and Merrilee. This baby and all the babies to follow. Together forever." Then he kissed her, swallowing the words she whispered with love.

Together forever.

* * * * *

You won't want to miss this wonderful author's next book. Look for Marilyn Pappano's exciting debut in Silhouette Special Edition this September!

DIANA PALMER
ANN MAJOR
SUSAN MALLERY

RETURN TO WHITEHORN

In **April 1998** get ready to catch the bouquet. Join in the excitement as these bestselling authors lead us down the aisle with three heartwarming tales of love and matrimony in Big Sky country.

A very engaged lady is having second thoughts about her intended; a pregnant librarian is wooed by the town bad boy; a cowgirl meets up with her first love. Which Maverick will be the next one to get hitched?

Available in **April 1998**.

Silhouette's beloved **MONTANA MAVERICKS** returns in Special Edition and Harlequin Historicals starting in February 1998, with brand-new stories from your favorite authors.

Round up these great new stories at your favorite retail outlet.

Take 4 bestselling love stories FREE

Plus get a FREE surprise gift!

Special Limited-time Offer

Mail to Silhouette Reader Service™

3010 Walden Avenue
P.O. Box 1867
Buffalo, N.Y. 14240-1867

YES! Please send me 4 free Silhouette Intimate Moments® novels and my free surprise gift. Then send me 6 brand-new novels every month, which I will receive months before they appear in bookstores. Bill me at the low price of $3.57 each plus 25¢ delivery and applicable sales tax, if any.* That's the complete price and a savings of over 10% off the cover prices—quite a bargain! I understand that accepting the books and gift places me under no obligation ever to buy any books. I can always return a shipment and cancel at any time. Even if I never buy another book from Silhouette, the 4 free books and the surprise gift are mine to keep forever.

245 SEN CF2V

Name	(PLEASE PRINT)	
Address	Apt. No.	
City	State	Zip

This offer is limited to one order per household and not valid to present Silhouette Intimate Moments® subscribers. *Terms and prices are subject to change without notice. Sales tax applicable in N.Y.

UMOM-696

©1990 Harlequin Enterprises Limited

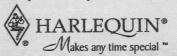

ALL THAT GLITTERS

by *New York Times* bestselling author

LINDA HOWARD

Greek billionaire Nikolas Constantinos was used to getting what he wanted—in business and in his personal life. Until he met Jessica Stanton. Love hadn't been part of his plan. But love was the one thing he couldn't control.

From *New York Times* bestselling author Linda Howard comes a sensual tale of business and pleasure—of a man who wants both and a woman who wants more.

BEVERLY BARTON

**Continues the
twelve-book series—
36 Hours—in April 1998
with Book Ten**

NINE MONTHS

Paige Summers couldn't have been more shocked when she learned that the man with whom she had spent one passionate, stormy night was none other than her arrogant new boss! And just because he was the father of her unborn baby didn't give him the right to claim her as his wife. Especially when he wasn't offering the one thing she wanted: his heart.

For Jared and Paige and *all* the residents of Grand Springs, Colorado, the storm-induced blackout was just the beginning of 36 Hours that changed *everything!* You won't want to miss a single book.

Available at your favorite retail outlet.

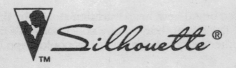